The
MYSTERY
of the
SCATTERED
CROSS

A JAKE JEZREEL ADVENTURE

DONALD CRAIG MILLER

WESTBOW
PRESS®
A DIVISION OF THOMAS NELSON
& ZONDERVAN

Copyright © 2024 Donald Craig Miller.

All rights reserved. No part of this book may be used or reproduced by any means, graphic, electronic, or mechanical, including photocopying, recording, taping or by any information storage retrieval system without the written permission of the author except in the case of brief quotations embodied in critical articles and reviews.

This is a work of fiction. All of the characters, names, incidents, organizations, and dialogue in this novel are either the products of the author's imagination or are used fictitiously.

WestBow Press books may be ordered through booksellers or by contacting:

WestBow Press
A Division of Thomas Nelson & Zondervan
1663 Liberty Drive
Bloomington, IN 47403
www.westbowpress.com
844-714-3454

Because of the dynamic nature of the Internet, any web addresses or links contained in this book may have changed since publication and may no longer be valid. The views expressed in this work are solely those of the author and do not necessarily reflect the views of the publisher, and the publisher hereby disclaims any responsibility for them.

Any people depicted in stock imagery provided by Getty Images are models, and such images are being used for illustrative purposes only. Certain stock imagery © Getty Images.

Some Scripture taken from the New King James Version
Copyright 1982 by Thomas Nelson, Inc.

Some Scripture quotes are paraphrased by Donald Craig Miller

ISBN: 979-8-3850-2675-3 (sc)
ISBN: 979-8-3850-2677-7 (hc)
ISBN: 979-8-3850-2676-0 (e)

Library of Congress Control Number: 2024911074

Print information available on the last page.

WestBow Press rev. date: 06/07/2024

Dedicated to
Ginny, my wife
and companion

And to
my mother
Eleanor Elizabeth Miller
for leading me gently
into the presence
of the Lord.
To her, I will forever be grateful

And to
my Navigator friends
who faithfully led me to the Lord
and set me on a straight path to follow Him,
instilling in me a love for the Word of God.

All my many pastors, Christian teachers,
and Christian leaders who have filled my heart
and life with Biblical truth and helped sustain
my daily desire to be surrendered to the Lord Jesus
and to live in a loving relationship with Him.

All of my Christian friends who have been an
ongoing source of strength and encouragement,
without whose help I may have lost my focus and
and slipped off the trail and fallen by the wayside.

All those giants of the faith during my lifetime,
Adrian Rogers, Charles Stanley, Billy Graham,
and many, many others,
whose steadfast preaching of the Word
helped solidify the doctrines of Jesus Christ
in Christians' lives and steer His church
in a godly path away from apostasy.

Contents

Chapter 1   The First Attack 1
Chapter 2   Speak No More in That Name 9
Chapter 3   Good Times – Brewing Storm 23
Chapter 4   Dangerous Mission 38
Chapter 5   Deadly Ground..52
Chapter 6   Sorry to Disappoint You, Sir....................................65
Chapter 7   The Case of The Government Client 69
Chapter 8   Grappling With a Snake 80
Chapter 9   The Hammer Falls..92
Chapter 10   Down Into the Slums 103
Chapter 11   Dungeon 108
Chapter 12   Death In The Camp 115
Chapter 13   Surprising New Beginning................................... 121
Chapter 14   Shifting Sands.. 129
Chapter 15   The Disgracing of Nicodemus 137
Chapter 16   Target: Damascus 142
Chapter 17   Something's Very Different.................................. 154
Chapter 18   Synagogue Gospel 164
Chapter 19   Midnight Escape... 173
Chapter 20   Hannah 181
Chapter 21   The Demise of Saul of Tarsus 187

Addendum 199
About the Author..201

Chapter 1

THE FIRST ATTACK

Hannah Haggai suddenly remembered! She quickly scooted her chair back from behind her desk where she worked as Detective Jake Jezreel's secretary. She needed to reminded her boss about an event that he had been too busy to attend lately. As she stood up, she could see her private detective boss sitting at his desk in his office. The door was open between her office and the detective's office. Jake was twisted around in his brown leather chair gazing out the second story window of his office. Hannah scooped up a stack of paperwork from her desk and breezed into Jake's office.

"I see you're at it again," Hannah laughed, as she walked up behind him. "You just can't keep your mind on your work, can you."

Jake Jezreel looked around at his pretty secretary and smiled. "No, ever since those joyful events of several months ago, the good feeling is still there. I hope I never come back down to earth. This is the happiest I've ever been in my whole life. And add to that the fact you and I are now engaged to be married, that makes this time all the more special. My head is still spinning in the clouds – and so is my heart."

"There you go again, thinking with your heart," she teased. "I thought a rough detective is supposed to think only with his head."

"It's tough to be a hard-boiled detective in these happy times."

Hannah smiled, her dimples denting her cheeks. Her soft brown eyes expressed love and happiness about their wonderful new situation. She laid the paperwork on Jake's desk and sat down in the wooden armchair next to the detective. Together they looked out from the elevated second story office window, gazing northward toward Galilee.

"You know, angel, when I spent all that time trailing Jesus up north, I didn't think it could get any better than that," he wistfully said, still gazing out the window. "Spending so much time with Jesus turned out to be the most fantastic days of my life, up 'til then."

"When you brought back all those stacks of research notes," Hannah recalled, "I got to know Jesus up close and personal through your notes. Each time I transcribed every one of those memos into your final report, I felt even closer to Jesus. We called that Case File: *"The Search for the Mysterious Second Adam"*. I wouldn't give a gazillion shekels for the reams of file memos you brought back from that investigation. In fact, those records are the most precious and valuable assets we have in this office."

"Hannah, you're right," Jake said, finally looking over at her. "Those notes really are the most precious possessions we have! You know, future generations, need to be able to read about Jesus and how wonderful He is. One day I think I'm gonna write a book about Jesus and I'll use my investigative notes to tell the story."

Hannah's face lit up. "Ooo, I like your idea, Jake!" she exclaimed, grabbing his arm in joyful expectation. "You can title the book *The Gospel According to Jezreel.* And when you write your book, you'll have to tell the whole story. You'll have to include the rest of your transcripts from your later investigation of Jesus' ministry."

"Right, it wouldn't be complete without the rest of the story," Jake stated. "Especially the part when Jesus came to Jerusalem the last week of His life. And when He was sentenced to death by the Sanhedrin. And when He was crucified on Golgotha ..."

"And when He rose from the dead!" she interrupted. "That is the absolute best part! You've got to include all that in your book! Every facet of Jesus' life! Wow! Now, I'm getting excited!"

"It would be a best seller! That would be quite a book, wouldn't it!" the detective exclaimed. "The full picture of Jesus' life! What a story!"

"What a story. Good times," Hannah said softly.

"Very good times ..." Jake's voice trailed off as he gazed back out the window.

They sat together quietly, reliving those wonderful days when they walked with Jesus.

"Remember when Jesus appeared to us in the upper room after His resurrection?" Hannah said, as she was caught up in her memory.

"I can never forget that. We saw the risen Christ! Alive from the dead! Nothing can ever take that fantastic experience away from us! It'll be etched forever in our minds."

They sat quietly for a moment. And then Hannah suddenly lurched from her comfortable seated position and jumped up.

"Oh, Jake! I forgot!" she exclaimed. "I'm sorry! I got so caught up remembering about Jesus, I forgot what I came in here to tell you. I came to remind you that it is almost time for afternoon prayers at the Temple. I remember you said that you wanted to go today,"

"Oh, yeah! Thanks, Hannah!" Jake yelped, jumping up out of his chair. "I completely lost track of time. Daydreaming too much. I guess I'd better get going. I have missed going to the Temple for prayers several times this week because of work. But I'm going to make it today! Thanks for your reminder. Gotta go! I love you."

Jake Jezreel found himself caught up in the emotional happiness of the crowds in the great city of Jerusalem. It had only been a few months since spectacular news had rocked the foundations of the capital city. That powerful, cascading newsflash declared the truth that Jesus Christ had risen from the dead! He was truly alive! He had instructed all of his disciples to carry on His work. And then in a final glorious gesture, Jesus ascended back into heaven to once again take up His rightful, preeminent position in heaven. That joyous news was still the buzz around the city.

And as Jake was swept up into the merriment of the time, he now found himself headed for the grand and glorious Temple complex for afternoon prayers. Jake had a good friend there at the Temple, one of

Jake's most reputable informants. His name was Elijah the Cripple. Elijah spent every day at the Temple begging for charitable gifts from the hundreds of passing parishioners who came to the Temple to worship. And the crippled man always stationed himself beside a gate known as The Beautiful Gate.

As Jake neared the Temple, he caught sight of two of Jesus' faithful disciples also headed for the Temple, the black-haired fisherman, Simon Peter and his fishing buddy John.

"Hello, Peter and John!" Jake called to the two disciples.

"Hello, Jake," they both said at once.

"It's a beautiful day. Can I join you?" Jake asked.

"Absolutely," said Peter, "we would love to have you worship and pray with us."

"Thanks," Jake stated. "These past few weeks have transformed my life. You fellas spent years with Jesus listening to Him teach. I feel it's a real privilege to be praying with you two men."

As the three men approached the Temple, they just happened to be entering at the Beautiful Gate. Jake realized he would be passing by his crippled friend, so he began to rustle around in his coin pouch for a few coins to give to Elijah. There was Elijah up ahead, sitting on his straw-colored, reed mat by The Beautiful Gate, tin cup in hand.

Elijah's full attention was aroused as the three men got closer to him. "Alms for the poor?" the crippled man asked.

Jake was about to say hello to his old friend when Peter spoke first. "Sir, look at us!"

Elijah perked up even more and a big smile crossed his face, as he expected to get a really good contribution.

Peter looked Elijah squarely in the eye and said, "I do not have any silver or gold to give you. But what I do possess I will give to you. In the name of Jesus Christ of Nazareth get up and walk!"

In shock, Jake watched as Peter reached out, took Elijah by the right hand, and lifted him up into a standing position. Instantly, Elijah's crippled feet and ankles gained strength and he stood up on his own, firm and steady. He stretched himself erect and straight in the exhilaration of the moment. Elijah looked at Jake with the glow of utter surprise and joy on his face.

"Jake! Look at me! Look at me! I'm standing up – on my own! Yahoo!" he shouted and began to leap straight up into the air. "I can't believe it! And look, Jake! I can walk, too!

Elijah couldn't contain his jubilation. "Thank you, so much, sir!" he said to Peter. "Thank God! Thank Jesus Christ of Nazareth!"

Jake teetered on his feet in shock. The intense, emotional power of the moment snatched his breath away. His good friend, Elijah, now was completely healed! Freed of his devastating paralysis! Jake couldn't contain himself. He burst out laughing. He had seen this phenomenon before when he had watched Jesus of Nazareth heal many hundreds of people in days gone by back in Galilee. Jake enthusiastically grabbed Elijah by both shoulders and they danced a happy little jig together in celebration! New legs were working just fine!

Peter and John continued on into the Temple. Jake, so overcome by the joy of seeing his friend healed, trailed behind them with Elijah. The former cripple cavorted in intense joy. He could not contain himself or stop leaping and shouting praises to God.

Such commotion erupting in the quiet house of worship, naturally drew a curious crowd to the uproar. Elijah continued to walk and leap and shout praises to God in the Temple. And the crowd all said, "Hey! Isn't that the very same crippled man who always sat at the Beautiful Gate begging for alms?"

Everyone in the crowd gathered in surprise and disbelief! "What could have happened to him?" they all cried out. "We don't understand!"

Elijah was so grateful that he began to cling to Peter and John in thankful gratitude. As Peter, John, and Elijah approached the section of the Temple complex known as Solomon's Porch the crowd of bewildered people closed in on them and swarmed around them. "What is happening? Please explain how this crippled man can now walk just the same as we can!"

Peter looked around at all the bewildered faces. He recognized his God given opportunity.

"Men, fellow Israelites, why are you so very amazed and puzzled at this event?" Peter announced. "Why are you gazing at us as if we had some kind of power to make this man walk. The God of Abraham, the God of our ancestors has brought glory upon His Son, Jesus Christ, who is responsible for this man's healing. This is the same Jesus whom you rejected in the trial before Pontius Pilate, who was resolute in declaring Him innocent and letting Him go free. But you rejected the Holy One. And then you put Him to death, the Prince of life, whom God has now raised back to life!

"And we are witnesses to Jesus Christ's resurrection. He is alive and filled with almighty power. And it is by Christ's power and faith in His name that has made this crippled man, whom you all see and can identify, well of his paralysis and given him strength. The faith which is given through Jesus, has bestowed upon this man his perfect fitness in the sight of you all!"

Jake scanned the faces of all the bewildered men in the crowd. Every one of them was stunned in surprise by Peter's point-blank response. None of them had expected such a shocking answer to their question.

Peter sensed the crowd's surprise. He preached on. "Men and brothers, I know you all acted in ignorance, not even knowing what you were doing at the time. Even your leaders acted in ignorance. They didn't understand what they were doing. But God was in control all the time. God fulfilled the words of the prophets and all scripture that Christ, the Messiah, must first suffer before He would be glorified.

"So, you must repent! Return to God. Turn back to God that your sins, for which Jesus has already paid for with His blood, may be forgiven and be purged clean! The very presence of God will then flood you with a wonderful, spiritual refreshing! And He will send to you the Christ, our Messiah!"

Peter looked into the eyes of his audience. Love came from his voice. "Moses even mentioned that everyone who rejected the

Prophet who would come after him, would be utterly destroyed. That Prophet is Jesus and anyone who will not listen to and obey Him will be eradicated from God's family. God sent His Servant, Jesus Christ, to you first and raised Him up to bless you when each of you turns from your wicked ways."

Jake was amazed. He had never heard such a powerful and concise description of the salvation Jesus can give! And some of the faces in the crowd seemed to be comprehending the depth of the power of the message of Christ's salvation.

Suddenly, out of nowhere, a raging group of priests, the commander of the military temple guard, and, a throng of Sadducees rushed in upon the scene! They were fighting mad! In their rage they shoved their way straight in between Peter and John and the rest of the crowd.

"What is the meaning of all this chaos! What do you think you are doing!" the priests shouted, right in the disciple's faces. "We are outraged that you would be spreading lies here in God's holy Temple! You are teaching the people false doctrine! You are proclaiming that Jesus of Nazareth has risen from the dead. That is a lie! All lies!"

"Sirs, it is all the truth – and you know it!" Peter stated firmly. "You know Jesus is alive!"

"Silence! That's enough!" the priests yelled. "No more lies! Commander of the guard! Arrest these two agitators, and throw them in prison! And while you're at it, arrest this fake cripple who is pretending to be miraculously healed! He can cool his heels in jail overnight along with his cohorts! Maybe he will think twice about faking being healed and causing an uproar just to get attention!"

Jake stepped forward, trying to protest the arrest but the commander shoved him away and grabbed the prisoners. Glaring back at Jake, the commander growled, "Stay right where you are. Otherwise, I'll arrest you, too!"

As the commander and the religious gang dragged their prisoners off to jail, Elijah yelled back to Jake, "Don't worry about me! I'm doin' great! This has been the best day of my life!"

As Jake stood there astonished, the people in the crowd began to barrage him with questions. "We don't care what happens to us. It might mean prison for us, too. But tell us what we must do to be saved!"

Jake suddenly realized he was the only man left to answer the burning questions of the crowd! The torch had been thrown into his hand. "I'm no preacher but all I can do is encourage all of you to follow the instructions that Peter just gave you. Repent and turn back to God so your sins may be forgiven and cleansed. Jesus will do that for you and give you eternal life. He did it for me. He will do it for you!"

Immediately many in the crowd who heard this Good News repented and believed on the Lord Jesus Christ, trusting in His Name. Jake stood in that crowd, stunned at the power of Jesus as that power swept through the lives of these people. Many surrendered to Jesus. The surge of salvation power flooded the crowd in the entire Temple compound. To Jake it seemed like hundreds of folks in the crowd had surrendered to Christ that day. Maybe even thousands!

Never in his life had a day jumped and dived and jumped back up again like a roller coaster. Great uplifting joy in the morning. A wonderful, inspiring miracle bestowed upon his good buddy, Elijah. Then the deflating depression of the sudden arrest and jailing of Peter, John and Elijah. And then the upsurge of hundreds coming to believe and trust in Jesus. As the detective slowly walked back to his office, he was having a hard time wrapping his mind around the whirlwind of events of the day.

Jake found Hannah still in the office just about to close up for the day.

"Well, there you are, boss," she smiled as he walked into the office. She rilted her head and stared at him. "You look like you've been to something much greater than a prayer meeting. You've got a very strange look on your face."

"Hannah, you won't believe this. But I'm going to tell you anyway. And then you can rejoice with me or you can just call me a lunatic."

Chapter 2

SPEAK NO MORE IN THAT NAME

The next morning, Jake stood in his office, staring out the window, reliving the extraordinary events of the day before. What had become of Peter and John overnight? What happened to Elijah? What about all those people who had surrendered their lives to Christ – what had become of them? He intensely wanted to get back out among the new converted Christians. And he had become antsy just sitting at his desk. But Jake couldn't leave the office. He was working on a case for … the Roman governor, Pontius Pilate! Yes, Pontius Pilate!

Jake pulled his thoughts back into present reality. As he sat down at his desk, he started arranging his notes from his current case he had been working on for the Roman governor. Pilate had become quite interested in Jake's detective work, due in part to Jake's famous dad, Jedidiah Jezreel. The senior detective had assisted Pilate on several occasions in tracking down the bad guys. Now the Roman governor had hired Jake to do some undercover surveillance of a rag-tag bunch of dissidents operating in Jerusalem.

It was easy enough for Jake to gain the confidence of the gang. He had wormed his way into the band of cut-throats by making them believe he was a hated enemy of Pilate. Once he got inside their mob, Jake was led right to the big man – the big boss – the ringleader. Everyone in the gang was convinced that Jake was in cahoots with them. And he poured on the act of being just one of the gang. They definitely weren't too bright! All Jake had to do was slip a simple papyrus message back to Pilate. Then the governor dispatched his Roman soldiers, who pounced on the gang's hideout and arrested the thugs! And – that was that!

Jake's thoughts were interrupted by a knock on the door to the outer office. Hannah opened the door slightly and poked her head in. Her beige tunic rippled as she stepped quickly inside Jake's office and finished closing the door behind her. Her soft brown eyes appeared quite serious.

Jake looked up at her. "Yes, angel? What's ya got?"

"Pharisee Nicodemus is here. He would like to speak to you," she said in a concerned tone. "He urgently needs to talk to you about that incident you were telling me about yesterday."

"Yes! Yes!" Jake said excitedly, standing up. "Please, shoo him in, Hannah. Maybe he brings news about the latest developments with Peter and John and Elijah."

Hannah quickly opened the door and spoke to the guest in the outer office. "Sir, please come in. Mr. Jezreel will be able to see you now."

The figure of the gracious gentleman, Pharisee Nicodemus, stepped through the open doorway from the outer office.

"Thank you, Miss Haggai," the finely dressed gentleman said to Hannah. "It is a pleasure to see you again."

"And I'm so very glad to see you," the girl smiled. "You always make my day more delightful."

Hannah closed the door and Nicodemus turned toward Jake.

Nicodemus was a tall man, about six feet two and quite distinguished looking. His dignified silver-gray hair and beard were meticulously trimmed. His aged face exhibited many years of sound, spiritual leadership for the nation of Israel. His long, flowing cream-colored robe edged in purple designated his status of honor among the people as a leader of renown.

"Hello, Jake," stated the elder statesman, as he made his way across the office. "It is good to see you." A sad expression replaced his normal kindly appearance.

"It has been a few weeks since we talked last," Jake stated with concern in his voice. As they shook hands, Jake noticed the sorrow in Nicodemus' face. "Sir, what is the matter? You look quite worried."

"You may have heard about the arrest which occurred yesterday evening."

"Yes, sir. I more than heard about it. I was there when it happened."

"Well, then you know that two of the main leaders of our Christian group here in Jerusalem were arrested yesterday in late afternoon, Peter and John. They were imprisoned overnight and are supposed to stand trial before the Supreme Court this morning,"

"So, the Sanhedrin is convening this morning? Is this a special meeting?"

"Yes, it is. The court thinks this matter of Peter and John preaching about Jesus in the Temple is so serious that it warrants an immediate special assembly," Nicodemus stated. "Many on the court call the incident in the Temple an 'uproar' or even worse. I'm supposed to be at that court trial today, even though many on the high court know of my devotion to Jesus Christ. The High Priest will be there, along with the seventy rulers of the Sanhedrin. Priests, rulers, elders, and scribes who teach the Law will all be there. This has turned into a momentous event. I have come to ask you if you would accompany me and listen to the proceedings."

"You want me to come with you? Are you sure?" Jake asked very puzzled. "I would not be allowed into the Sanhedrin courtroom proceedings, would I?"

"You would not be allowed into the main courtroom but there is a small anteroom off to the side where invited guests can observe the proceedings," Nicodemus stated. "You would be there as my guest. I'd really like for you to come and listen to what goes on in the court trial. With your knowledge of detection, you may be able to pick up on some of the attitudes that the members of the Supreme Court may have regarding Jesus Christ, Peter and John, and all of us Christians, in general."

"Sir, when you put it that way, how can I turn down such a

wonderful friend as you. Thank you for inviting me. When do we need to be at the court?"

"The trial is set to begin at ten AM this morning."

Jake was in his guest seat in the anteroom of the Sanhedrin's courtroom well before ten o'clock. He had left Hannah back at the office, to "hold down the fort" until he could get back from this urgent morning meeting.

As he sat in the anteroom, the detective could tell from the buzz in the building that these proceedings had a serious, even hostile quality about them. All of the most powerful men in Jerusalem were gathered in the courtroom. The place was packed. Jake could feel the political power gathered in this room. These men possessed commanding influence. They were the highest, most prestigious, most powerful men in all the nation of Israel!

Jake pulled out his papyrus note pad and began jotting down names. Many names he knew. Others he did not. But he did recognize the former high priest, Annas, dressed in his pompous white linen robes trimmed with gold embroidery. And there was Annas' son-in-law Caiaphas, who was the current High Priest. He too was clothed in his white priestly linen robes trimmed in gold. Jake knew that both Annas and Caiaphas were corrupt politicians. Annas was the person, many years before, who had established the Bazaars of the son of Annas, the crooked Passover money making scheme that Jesus had cleaned out of the Temple during the last Passover. Caiaphas was the unscrupulous politician who ordered the final directive to arrest Jesus and have Him crucified.

Jake had arrived with Nicodemus and watched as the gentleman took his seat next to his friend, Joseph of Arimathea. Jake also spotted Pharisee Obadiah and Pharisee Asa, whom he had had dealings with in former days. All four of these Pharisees were now committed and faithful Christians.

On his papyrus pad, the detective began to note the different political parties represented in the council chamber. Many Sadducees were in attendance. Quite a few of the Sanhedrin members were Sadducees. These men were the politically powerful, wealthy aristocracy. They controlled the Temple and had great influence in governmental affairs. But the one teaching of Peter that agitated and stirred up the Sadducees the most was Peter's preaching about Jesus' resurrection. The Sadducees vehemently denied that there is such a thing as a resurrection. They would not tolerate an ad hoc preacher, with no religious credentials or formal training, going around peddling what they considered false, phony resurrection theology. When the people began to get excited about Jesus' resurrection, the Sadducees naturally became alarmed and wanted to quickly shut up Peter and John before they continued to hawk this "travesty" among the population.

Jake also noted on his pad the presence of numerous Pharisees in the group. These men were equally powerful in government. When they had their verbal battles with Jesus of Nazareth, they clashed with Jesus over their narrow legalism and insistence on following all the additional rules of the "oral law". They hated Jesus and now they hated all of Jesus' followers. They had hoped to crush the "Jesus movement" when they crucified Jesus of Nazareth. Now, they were infuriated by Peter and John announcing to all the world that Jesus was resurrected and alive!

For some reason, many in Israel still considered Annas to be the high priest, even though he had been deposed. Jake could sense that Annas projected a charismatic presence in the courtroom. Annas certainly was a "glad hander" and blustery figure during the time that the men were coming into the court and gathering together. He skillfully played the crowd to the maximum. His overbearing alfa male demeanor and statesmanship put all the other men in the court chamber under his spell.

A hush fell on the courtroom as the prisoners were led into the center of this powerful assembly of politicians and religious leaders. The commander of the temple guard brought Peter, John, and Elijah into the courtroom and made them stand, directly facing Annas and Caiaphas and all of these powerful men in Israel! There they were, two simple fishermen, dressed in their tan-gray clothes, and a former crippled beggar, dressed in his tattered brown rags, standing before these educated, intimidating, influential men. The high court held the lives of these three men dangling in their hands.

Jake strained to see if he could get a glimpse of Elijah's face. Elijah was half turned away. The detective could only see his friend in profile. But what he saw sent happy shivers up his spine. Elijah stood with a big smile on his face that none of these pompous religious men could wipe off. Jake realized Elijah was at total peace in his spirit. He had been healed. He had found Jesus as his Savoir. What more could he ask for?

Peter and John also had smiles on their faces. Jake knew that they recognized the Holy Spirit was here, living in them and standing right here in the midst of these proceedings.

The interrogation began abruptly! No cordial preliminaries. Just straight bullying!

"We demand that you tell us by what power and authority you have caused this disruption in the temple!" several of the powerful leaders in the courtroom mockingly demanded. "We admit that some sort of healing occurred last evening. But we challenge you – you uneducated, ordinary, plain men – to tell us by what authority you performed this healing!" The contempt these powerful men had for the lowly, common scum standing before them dripped with scorn.

Peter stood before them like a gallant soldier standing his ground on the battlefield. Peter looked his accusers squarely in the eyes.

"Rulers and leaders of the people of Israel, members of the council," Peter began. "If we are being tried in this court for a beneficial deed done to help this weak, helpless crippled man and by what authority he has been made completely well, I will tell you. I am here to declare to all of you and all of Israel, as well, that by the name of Jesus the Christ of Nazareth, who was crucified by you and who God raised up from the dead, it is by Him and Him alone that the man standing here in our midst has been made totally whole. Jesus is the essential Stone which was rejected by you, who are supposed to be the builders of Judaism, but He has now become the chief Cornerstone.

"And there is salvation found in no other person. There is no other Name found under heaven given among mankind by which we can be saved!"

Every man in the assembly began to murmur among themselves, "Jesus of Nazareth healed this man? How is that possible? He is dead. And who are these men? These men are only common, uneducated buffoons. They are ignorant persons. And yet they speak with an authoritative boldness. They speak with the eloquence of well-trained and learned scholars."

Jake could hear their astonished whispers. Every leader seemed to be shocked by Peter and John's bold stand and articulate speech.

Nicodemus glanced over at Jake, sitting in the antechamber, smiled and nodded his approval of Peter and John's daring defense.

"It is quite apparent that these men have been spending much time with Jesus of Nazareth," many in the assembly began to say. "They talk like Jesus. They act like Jesus. And here before us stands the man who has been cured of his affliction. How can we dispute this fact that is staring us right in the face?"

Jake watched as the assembly of powerful leaders became befuddled and perplexed. They didn't want to discuss their confusion in front of Peter and John and Elijah, so they ordered the three prisoners to be removed from the council room. Once the prisoners were out of earshot, the heated debate in the assembly chamber began in earnest.

Jake watched in fascination. He continued to write on his notepad.

Annas spoke up. "This is a fine mess! What are we going to do with these three men?"

"The situation is getting out of control," stated one member of the Sanhedrin. "We all acknowledge that an astonishing miracle has occurred, performed by these men, and it is common knowledge to all the citizens of Jerusalem. We cannot deny that this miracle happened."

"But we can't have these men running around preaching that salvation comes from Jesus Christ," another Sanhedrin member brazenly stated. "Isn't that the very reason we had the Nazarene crucified in the first place. We wanted to stamp out the Nazarene's wicked influence and crush this movement of His followers. And did you notice these prisoners claimed that God is the One who raised the Nazarene from the dead! We've got to silence this type of inflammatory rhetoric! There is no place in Judaism for this kind of false religion!"

A Pharisee jumped up. "But you, sir, are a Sadducee. You Sadducees do not believe in the resurrection. But we Pharisees do!"

"But not this kind of resurrection!" the Sadducee fumed. "You Pharisees falsely teach resurrection at the end of time. Not now! Not today! Imagine if people believed that the Nazarene is really alive again and that he can actually save them from their sins!"

"Sir, you cannot shutdown the teaching of the resurrection!" the Pharisee argued. "The Scriptures teach it! The multitudes believe in it!"

"I don't care what the Scriptures teach …"

Annas leaped to his feet and yelled, "Stop! Stop! Enough infighting among yourselves! Stop this debate! We must decide what measures we will take against these prisoners!"

One of the priests stood up and raised his arms in surrender. "I don't see how we can get a conviction against these men. The people of the city witnessed the healing. They are extremely excited about this paralytic man being able to walk! He is more than forty years old and is well known throughout Jerusalem, since he has been begging for many years. The people saw the miracle happen and they are continuing to praise and glorify God for this miracle."

Annas, still standing in front of the group, raised his white robed arm, declaring his judgment. "Gentlemen, there is only one action we can take!" he vehemently shouted. "To prevent the further spread of these malicious lies among the people and throughout our nation, we must severely warn and threaten these prisoners! We will ban them from speaking anymore about this Name, this Nazarene Person! Are we all agreed?"

There was agreement by most in the room. Nicodemus looked over at Jake, sitting in the anteroom. He solemnly shook his head with a look of victory mixed with sadness on his face.

"Bring in the prisoners!" Annas demanded.

The commander of the guard ushered the prisoners back into the middle of the assembly and had them once again face the great leaders seated at the front.

"You troublers of Jerusalem and our nation," Annas gravely growled to the prisoners, sitting on his judgement seat. His aged face morphed into a reddish, fierce sneer. He snarled at them through clinched teeth. "We are going to let you go this time. But understand this – we forbid you to ever speak about Jesus Christ again! We are commanding you! You will not utter His name to anyone or teach anyone about Jesus Christ! Never again! Do I make myself clear!"

"We completely understand your requirements," Peter announced confidently. "But is it right in the sight of God to listen to your man-made-orders and obey them rather than to obey God? You will have to make that judgment. But we, as Christ's disciples, must tell the marvelous truths which we have seen and heard."

John agreed. "When you have seen the wonders and miracles of our Lord Jesus Christ, as we have, we are compelled to share with everyone what we have seen and heard," he proclaimed with great assurance.

In a fit of rage, Annas jumped up from his judgement seat. "You had better obey our warning to you!" thundered Annas, shaking his clinched fist at them. "You must obey! You *will* obey! You will be extremely sorry if you do not obey the command the Sanhedrin has pronounced upon you!"

Annas thrust his hand toward the door, pointing to the exit. "Now, get out of here!" he roared.

The commander of the guard escorted the now freed prisoners to the door of the Sanhedrin's meeting room and gave them one, last insolent shove, "Now, get out!" he ordered.

Jake looked over at Nicodemus and shrugged his shoulders. The elder statesman pointed to the main exit door, indicating they could talk there.

Outside in the fresh air, the detective found Nicodemus. Pharisee Obadiah and Joseph of Arimathea also rendezvoused with them outside.

"Praise God! That was powerful!" Nicodemus exclaimed. "The Lord and His Holy Spirit were definitely there in that room today."

"Peter and John were obviously filled with the Holy Spirit!" Jake stated. "They stood there in front of all those powerful men and let it be known that they could not be silenced from talking about Jesus!"

Obadiah frowned, "Their daring comments were brave but are *not* going to be received well with our Sanhedrin colleagues. All of us know that this debate is not over. It's only getting started."

"Well, at least for today we can see the Lord Jesus victorious over those who want to stop His plans," Jake encouraged.

"And this day has proven that the Word of God and the message of Jesus cannot be stopped!" Joseph declared. "Two of our main leaders were arrested and people were still being saved outside the courtroom!"

"This is all great news!" Jake exclaimed. "I've got to go tell my secretary, Hannah, the great news!"

"What do you mean, your secretary? You mean your sweetie!" Obadiah laughed.

"A correct translation of my words!" Jake grinned. "She will be so happy!"

As Jake ran back to his office building, he could see Hannah leaning out of the second story window, straining to catch a glimpse of the detective, as he brought word from the meeting. As he ran toward her, he called out her name. She caught sight of him and called back to him, "Jake, what is the news!"

"Peter and John and Elijah are free!" he shouted as he ran. "The assembly had to let them go!"

"Praise God!" Hannah shouted, waving both arms in the air. "God is good! He is so good!"

Jake ran up the stairs and burst into the office. "I wish you could have been there, angel!" he exclaimed, as he gave Hannah a big hug. "The Lord's power was all over that council room! It was an experience I'll never forget! Peter and John were so forceful in their defense. The religious leaders were utterly perplexed about

Elijah's healing, they couldn't convict our friends of anything! It was incredible!"

Hannah laughed in amazement. "I do wish I could have been there. That would have been soooo cool!"

"The only down side to all that happened is that the council demanded that Peter and John never speak about Jesus again or preach His Name in public," Jake stated.

Hannah's body flinched. "Oh, they'll never be able to obey an order like that," she said in shock, as she put her hands together in front of her mouth. "None of us can obey that order. Not after Jesus has commanded us to tell everyone we meet about the salvation that is found in believing in Him. Jesus is the Christ! How can we not tell people?"

"That is exactly what Obadiah was referring to when we came out of the meeting," Jake continued. "Obadiah said, 'this debate is not over, it's only getting started.' The religious leaders are not going to simply warn us Christians to stop speaking about Jesus. They sounded determined to silence all of us."

"Well, that is for tomorrow," the girl smiled. "But today we can rejoice!"

Just about that time, one of Jesus' disciples, opened the office door. It was Matthew. "Jake! Hannah! Come with me. We are celebrating the Lord's great victory in court today in our usual meeting place!"

"We're right behind you!" Jake exclaimed.

The detective and the girl arrived at the usual meeting place at about the time that Peter and John finished describing the powerful meeting with the Sanhedrin and the other religious leaders. The crowd of believers began praising God in one united voice.

"Sovereign Lord, You are responsible for creating everything," they prayed. "You predicted by the writings of our great king David, inspired by the Holy Spirit, that the kings of the earth rage against You. The kings of this earth assemble as one army to reject and stand against Your Anointed One, Jesus Christ, our Messiah. Even here in our city of Jerusalem, the rulers met and conspired collectively against Your holy Messiah, the Lord Jesus, whom You anointed and consecrated. Herod, Pontius Pilate, the Gentiles and the people of Israel carried out all of Your will and purpose to fulfill all that your Scriptures had predicted about the suffering of the Christ. Your will has been accomplished through these human instruments! You alone have done this!

"Now, dear Lord, hear and witness all of the Sanhedrin's threatenings. Please give to all of Your disciples the freedom to declare courageously Your Good News of Jesus' salvation. We pray that You will reach out Your hand to heal and perform signs and marvels through the authority and glorious power of the Name of Jesus!"

Suddenly, as their prayer ended the building in which the believers were assembled began to quake. Each believer held on to one another with the suddenness of the shaking. Hannah grabbed Jake's arm in instant reaction to the quaking. But it quickly became apparent to all who were assembled that this was not an earthquake. It was the Lord God moving in a powerful expression of His presence.

And just as suddenly, all of them in the assembly were filled with power of the Holy Spirit. They all found a new confidence within them to proclaim the saving power of Jesus Christ! And they did just that! Many quickly went out into the streets and began preaching the Word of God boldly.

Jake gazed at Hannah in disbelief. "Wow! What just happened?"

Hannah's face glowed. "The Lord revealed Himself to us today!" she exclaimed. "Just like Peter has told us again and again that the only way to really know God is by revelation of Himself to us! His presence actually was here!"

"Just like at Pentecost!" Jake exclaimed. "The Holy Spirit swept through this place! We've all been supercharged to go out and preach salvation through Jesus! Like Pentecost! What an awesome experience!"

And then Jake stared at Hannah with a strange expression.

"What's wrong, honey?" asked Hannah, mystified. "Why the sudden change? Aren't you happy?"

"Yeah, I'm happy," he said with a bewildered expression. "I'm all of a sudden in a quandary. I don't know if I'm supposed to continue as a private detective, anymore. Today has changed things. Maybe I should go out and become a street preacher. There are so many people who need to hear the Good News. I can't tell folks about Jesus if I'm snooping around in back alleys. I don't want to be wasting my time slumming around when I could be out preaching about Jesus."

Hannah smiled at her fiancée. "Think about it this way. You reach a lot of people through your work, right?"

"Yeah."

"You've got lots of connections to all sorts of people. High ranking people. People on the street. Think about all your snitches. Don't they all need Jesus?"

"Yeah."

"Maybe through your detective work you'll meet people who otherwise you could never talk to about Jesus. You know, the Lord could lead you uniquely to certain people who otherwise would never hear about Christ any other way."

"When you put it that way, I guess you're right," Jake laughed. "Being a detective will keep me sorta out there in the circulation of society, meeting new people all the time. I believe you might have the right idea, Hannah."

"You never know ... you never know," she coaxed. "God just might use your job of private detective to purposely direct you to important people in high places you would otherwise never be able to meet. Never in a million years! And He'd give you the rare opportunity to tell them about Jesus!"

"You're right, Hannah! I've got to keep my head on straight and be sure I'm following the Lord's lead – not my own."

With the glow of the Lord's presence still lingering, Jake thought hard about what he had just heard during the meeting with the disciples.

"Did you catch what our leaders prayed just now? It is hard for me to imagine that God fulfilled His plan through the crucifixion of Jesus. They recognized the Lord's sovereignty and total control in Jesus' suffering and crucifixion, even to the point of using Herod and Pilate and all the rulers to carry out His redemption plan. It's hard to imagine but it's true. Look at the result!"

"And I like it," the girl said softly. "God is great. And He is great all the time."

The couple left the building and headed back to the office, extremely happy in the Lord. Little did they realize that the events of this day and the prediction of Obadiah – "this debate is only getting started" – would quickly snowball far beyond a "debate."

Chapter 3

GOOD TIMES – BREWING STORM

It was the best of times.

The next few weeks was like heaven on earth.

One day, during these favorable times, Jake and Hannah stood at the second story window of his office and gazed out at the people below on Moriah Boulevard.

"Hannah, look down there," Jake observed. "Have you noticed there is an entirely different atmosphere here in Jerusalem lately? The city seems happier."

"There definitely is a peaceful feel these past few weeks," she smiled. "You know what I think it is? I think it has to do with all of us who are followers of Christ having realized we are a new family, a family of faith in Jesus."

"And you think that fact is effecting the rest of Jerusalem?"

"Sure. We believers have all got one common bond in our love and admiration of the Lord Jesus and for each other. The people of Jerusalem have watched us loving each other. They've noticed."

"Love for Jesus and each other," Jake repeated. "That's a good way to describe it. We love Jesus because He first loved us and sacrificed Himself for us. Jesus even taught us while He was here on earth to love each other exactly the same way He loved us."

Hannah's eyes perked up and she raised her finger to make a point. "Jesus made it abundantly clear when He taught us, 'By this love shall all men know that you are my disciples because you are showing love one for another.' Jesus' words are proving to be quite true. You see! We are showing the world that we are Jesus' disciples when we love each other! That's why I think there is a more pleasant atmosphere in Jerusalem. People in the city have taken notice of our love."

The girl's eyes then focused back on the people in the street below. "You see. Those people down there are seeing something they have never seen before … a group of people bound together by God's love. And those people want to find out more about that kind of love. The people who are not believers have taken notice that we Christians truly do love and care for each other. That kind of love has made Jesus attractive to the world around us. The popularity of Christ is spreading out into the Jewish community."

As the days went by, the church grew and strengthened. The disciples who had walked along with Jesus during His entire earthly ministry took the lead in teaching the doctrines of Christ to the many new believers. Jake and Hannah got caught up into this fabulous opportunity to learn as much as they could about the Savior that they loved.

Time passed. The Christian multitudes increased. Soon, the only area large enough for everyone to meet together at one time was in the temple complex, in Solomon's Porch. This was a risky plan seeing as the Sanhedrin had so forcefully demanded that the disciples never preach about Jesus again.

As the days went by, the unbelieving masses watched in admiration of the church and developed a great respect for them. And many of these skeptics became convinced that Jesus was the Christ and they repented of their sins, becoming Christians. An electric excitement enveloped the city. The exhilaration of salvation was everywhere!

But Jake had a detective's sense about human nature. He knew that the Sanhedrin had "laid down the law" and were very emphatic about their demand that the name of Jesus Christ would never again be preached in the capital city. It was painfully clear that the high court meant serious business. To Jake's analytical mind, it was only a matter of time before the lip blew off. And when things blew, the Sanhedrin would vigorously enforce their stated demand. But the problem facing the Jewish leaders was the overwhelming attraction of Jesus in the lives of His followers. The disciples were performing astonishing miracles in the name of Jesus and the crowds continued to be drawn to the message of Christ. Multitudes of the people, who saw the miracles and heard the preaching about Jesus, clamored to be saved. People even began to flow into Jerusalem from the outlying neighboring towns begging for physical healing of sicknesses and deliverance from evil spirits.

For the Sanhedrin, trying to enforce their "no preaching" ban was proving to be a sticky situation. They were afraid of the excited crowds, who were now supercharged in their enthusiastic adoration of Jesus' disciples. The religious leaders seemed stalled in their actions to enforce their demand. They feared starting a riot if they attempted to enforce their edict. Still, they were on the edge of their seats, watching, ready for the right moment. Nothing remains static. Jake knew that. The increasing friction along the two sides of the cataclysmic fault line continued to steadily build tectonic fracture pressure. Jake sensed the earthquake could erupt at any time.

One day the peace and tranquility suddenly did come to a crashing halt.

It was about 3:30 in the afternoon on Wednesday that Jake heard a commotion out on Moriah Boulevard below his second story window. He poked his head out the window. Several men were running down the street, shouting.

Jake yelled to one of them, "Hey, man! What's going on!"

"The high priest and his cronies have just arrested the twelve leaders of the Christians!" the man yelled back, as he continued to run.

Jake yanked his head back inside his office. "Hannah! Come in here, quick!"

Hannah burst into the office. "What's going on?"

"We've got to drop everything we're doing and get over to the council room of the Sanhedrin! It sounds like the High Priest's iron fist has struck again! I just heard that Caiaphas has arrested all the apostles!"

Hannah's eyes grew large and round. Her mouth formed an o shape but no sound came out.

"Come on, girl and get your notepad!" Jake ordered and grabbed Hannah by the hand.

Within a few moments the pair stood outside the Sanhedrin's high court building in the Temple grounds. A large crowd had already gathered around the exterior of the court structure. No one seemed to be going in or out of the main doorway. And then as Jake maneuvered around in the crowd, he could see why. No one was going in or out because two very large, burly Temple guards stood menacingly outside the door.

"Well, I guess we'll have to wait until someone comes out," Hannah sighed.

"Not necessarily," Jake said slowly as he looked past her and caught a glimpse of Nicodemus making his way through the tightly-packed crowd toward the court doorway. "Maybe Nicodemus can get me into the building." He started toward the advancing Pharisee but turned quickly around back to Hannah. "Will you be okay by yourself?"

"Jake, I am a big girl, now," she smiled. "I'll be just fine. Now, go! Catch Nicodemus before he gets inside the door! Go!"

Jake broke into a grin and patted the girl on her shoulder. "See you back at the office," he said and then spun around to plow his way through the mass of humanity to catch up with the Pharisee. As Nicodemus reached the court building entryway Jake stretched out his hand and touched the dignified gentleman's arm. Nicodemus glanced around. "Oh, hello, Jake. I'm glad you're here. Would you like to come with me?"

"I sure would. Very much so."

Nicodemus turned to the two brawny temple guards. "I am Pharisee Nicodemus. I have been summoned to attend this emergency court session." And pointing to Jake, "I am bringing my associate with me and desire that he be allowed to sit in the observation anteroom."

The pair of muscular guards halfway bowed to the honored gentleman, opened the entryway door and Nicodemus and Jake walked into the courtroom. The scene inside the high courtroom was total pandemonium. Angry men were everywhere. The cloud of rage and hatred in the room was thick and oppressive.

Caiaphas, the high priest, was ranting and raving, his red face glaring and his white priestly linen robes flailing.

"These preachers of *this* Name have deliberately defied our direct and clear order to cease preaching their false doctrine!" the high priest squalled as the other rulers were still gathering. "I am exceedingly outraged at the disrespect these common, ignorant riff-raff continue to display for our authority! They defy our final judgment we decreed the last time they were before us! They insidiously preach their deplorable lies all through Jerusalem and beyond!"

Standing in front of Caiaphas and the other assembled religious leaders were Peter and James and John and all of the other apostles whom Jesus had especially trained. Each of them was bound with ropes and forced to stand by the Temple guards humiliated like common criminals.

Caiaphas heaved an aggregated growl. "It is far too late in the day to begin a court proceeding this afternoon. It is impossible to start a trial this late in the day. Therefore, I am declaring an adjournment of these proceedings until tomorrow morning at ten o'clock. We will throw these insolent preachers into jail overnight. I am disgusted just looking at them! And I am too disgusted with these vermin to even deal with this matter this afternoon. Throw the prisoners in jail!"

Jake watched in dismay as the temple guards roughly dragged all twelve apostles out of the courtroom and off to the public prison. The poisonous cloud of anger and hatred lingered, hanging over the council chamber.

Nicodemus glanced over at Jake. "Well, I guess we will have to wait until the morning to see how God is going to defend His preachers," he stated with a sigh.

"Here we go again," Jake shook his head. "The apostles are again under the hammer of the Sanhedrin's heavy hand of judgment. More courtroom disputes. More hateful debate about Jesus."

"Pray hard between now and tomorrow that God will stand with His preachers and defend them," the gentleman advised.

"I certainly will do that. See you in the morning."

The next morning, Jake called Hannah into his office. "Angel, you know I've still got more investigating to do for Governor Pilate on this case of embezzlement of government funds over in the high-class district. But I really think I need to be in the Sanhedrin high court hearing for the twelve apostles this morning. Do you think you can follow up on this embezzlement investigation so I can go to the Sanhedrin hearing?"

Hannah tilted her head to one side and smirked. "Well, let's see, now," she said, tapping her forefinger on the side of her head. "How long have I been working for you? Three and a half years? I think I know your methods by now." She put her hands on her hips and pretended to be offended. "And I think I know the case about as good as you do, big boy. You can trust me. I'll get it done – just as if you were on the job. Maybe better." A sly smile crept across her lips.

Jake looked at her, shook his head, and cracked a smile. "Okay, I know you'll do a good job," the detective stated. "And, yeah, maybe better. Now, be sure you only interview the merchant whose government funds were stolen – Mister Thaddeus – and …"

"And get him to sign the affidavit. I know, I know how all this is done," Hannah retorted. "Boss, I know what to do. This isn't my first trip around the block! I promise I'll do all that needs to be done. You can count on me. Now will you go! Go on to the trial! You're of much more value to Jesus by being in that meeting!"

"Alright, already! I was just trying to be helpful."

"I know," the girl smiled with a glint in her eye. "But you need to be at that trial. Maybe you'll see or hear something there that will benefit the apostles later on."

"Got it. See ya later today."

Jake arrived at the high court building at around nine-thirty AM and waited for Nicodemus. In only a few minutes, the gentleman Pharisee walked up to Jake. "Are you ready to go in with me?" he asked the detective.

"Yes, I'm ready. I've been praying for the apostles all night. Praying for a miracle."

"Me, too. Let's go inside."

Inside the council chamber, the Sanhedrin was still being seated, as well as other prestigious rulers. There was a growing buzz of antagonism building among these powerful religious men. The primary accusers were the Sadducees who presided on the court, still objecting to the apostles teaching about the resurrection. And they continued to be annoyed that the apostles were using the Temple grounds to preach their message of salvation through Jesus Christ.

As the other influential priests and distinguished rulers were being seated, Caiaphas stood up and ordered the Temple guards to go to the prison and bring the prisoners to the courtroom. Five minutes passed. More influential and powerful men arrived. The courtroom was now packed to the rafters. Jake was squeezed into the tight space of the anteroom, along with the many other invited guests. He barely had enough room to pull out his note pad for note taking.

Ten minutes passed. Still no prisoners. The angry buzz in the courtroom intensified.

Twenty minute elapsed. Still no prisoners. The impatience of the rulers and religious leaders in the council chamber began to churn up more aggravation. Caiaphas was getting visibly annoyed. He stood up, his once placid face now morphing into a bright shade of fire engine red. He gazed angrily at the vacant doorway where the prisoners were supposed to be entering the courtroom.

Thirty minutes passed. Now Caiaphas was searing hot!

"It is ten o'clock!" Caiaphas shouted. "Where are the prisoners!" he raged. "Where are the guards!"

About that time, a guard (who must have drawn the short straw) sheepishly entered the courtroom. With shamefaced awkwardness he shuffled into the presence of the high court and stood, head bowed, and said, "Sirs, I regret to say ..."

Caiaphas yelled out, "You regret to say what?"

"Sirs, I regret to say that the prisoners have all escaped!"

"WHAT!" screamed Caiaphas. "What did you say!"

The cowering guard cringed into a standing semi-fetal position. "I beg for mercy Lord Caiaphas," he whined. "The prisoners have all escaped. But it wasn't my fault …"

The courtroom of powerful men exploded into enraged frenzy. Panic! Exasperation! Frustration! Distinguished leaders began yelling incoherently in fury.

"How can this happen!" many of them shouted in their frantic hysteria.

Jake glanced over at Nicodemus. The stately gentleman was looking directly at Jake nodding his understanding of the unexpected miracle God had accomplished

Very soon, the captain of the Temple guard, in his chocolate brown uniform, entered the courtroom, his entourage of Temple police in tow behind him. The captain sheepishly faced the high priest and the Sanhedrin. The tumult in the courtroom quieted down so everyone could hear.

The captain nervously cleared his throat. "Lord Caiaphas, dear members of the council. I must report to you a very bewildering event," the captain stated, his voice faltering. "I have just returned from the public prison. Last night we performed our standard lockdown procedures for securing the jail. All doors locked and secured according to standard regulations. More than adequate numbers of sentries were stationed outside the jail. We all were acutely aware of our solemn duty to guard these highly important prisoners. Each sentry faithfully manned his post throughout the night. They performed their duty.

"But sirs, when the order came to us this morning to bring the prisoners from the prison to the high court for trial, we opened the doors and – all the prisoners were gone! I am the Captain of the Temple Police and when I heard this fantastic news, I became frantic. I made a personal inspection of the prison confines, myself, and demanded that my men double check the prison cells, to be sure none of the convicts were hiding somehow under straw or their bedding. My trusted guards made the second sweep of the prison and found no prisoners. Sirs, I am at a total loss as to how these convicts escaped through locked and well-guarded prison doors."

The courtroom fell into a hush. Jake and Nicodemus glanced over at each other in wonder and disbelief.

Caiaphas stood up. "Gentlemen of the court, what are we to do? Our illustrious Temple police – or should I say incompetent Temple police – have been faithfully guarding vacant prison cells all night! How have these convicts vanished? Where have they disappeared to? What next? And what shall we do to these bungling prison guards to whom we have trusted to fulfill their duty of securing the prisoners and now they have failed us?"

As the tension in the assembly grew tauter and more strained, a servant of the High Priest ran breathlessly into the center of the meeting. "Sirs! Sirs!" the man gasped. "Please forgive my interruption! We have found the prisoners!"

Caiaphas threw his arms straight up in surprise. "You have found them!" he shouted in contempt. "Where are they?"

"They are preaching to the people in the Name of Jesus Christ in the Temple! They have been preaching since early this morning! And they have drawn a large crowd!"

"Preaching! Preaching! Again in the Temple!" Caiaphas raged. His eyes bulged and the veils on his neck stuck out. "Captain of the guard! Take your men and go and arrest those miserable scoundrels again and bring them right here to me! Right now! Immediately!"

The captain of the guard and his police force scrambled out of the courtroom, headed off to make the new arrest. The council chamber fell into a churning murmur of puzzled questions, awaiting the arrival of the prisoners and answers to the rulers' bewilderment. Jake busied himself writing as fast as he could, taking down every detail he had just heard. This was fascinating. God had worked a miracle in an unexpected, fantastic way. The detective glanced over at Nicodemus. The gentleman Pharisee was talking to Joseph of Arimathea in quite an animated manner. Now, all Jake could do was pray for God's wisdom and strength for the apostles as they soon would be arriving in the courtroom.

About twenty more minutes past before the captain of the Temple Guard finally brought back their newly arrested prisoners. But Jake noticed something very unusual about the way the group entered the courtroom. It appeared that the twelve apostles were leading the Temple guard into the assembly, rather than the other way around. The captain of the guard and his men trailed sheepishly along behind the apostles, giving every appearance of handling the situation very gently.

The captain spoke first to the Sanhedrin. "Sirs, these are the prisoners we found preaching in the Temple," he stated carefully. "They had gathered a large crowd of adoring listeners. We had to handle the situation very delicately. The adoring crowd was not at all pleased with our coming to take custody of these men. We feared a riot if we took the prisoners by force. By use of prudent maneuvers and rhetoric on our part, we were able to extract the prisoners from the temple grounds without a major incident."

"Yes, yes. Enough of your puny drivel," Caiaphas snapped, waving the back of his hand at them. "Stand aside, captain. I'm done with you."

Caiaphas stood up, rage aflame on his face. He pointed his bony finger at the twelve apostles.

"How dare you! How dare you scoundrels defy our last command to you!" he vented hotly. "Didn't we command you the last time you were before this assembly to never preach again about 'this Name'! You have deliberately defied our direct command to you! And now you have filled Jerusalem with your false teaching. And you deceivers are determined to blame us for this Man's death!"

Jake tensed up. "Lord, give them Your wisdom," he prayed under his breath.

Peter spoke up first. "Sirs, with all due respect," he began, "we must obey God first and foremost. We must obey the Lord God instead of men, if the command from men is contrary to God's command. The God of our forefathers raised Christ Jesus from the dead, whom you purposely killed by hanging Him on a cross. Then with His almighty power, God exalted Jesus to be seated at His right hand and made Christ the Prince and Savior, offering to the people of Israel repentance and forgiveness of their sins. We are witnesses to all these truths, as is the Holy Spirit, who is bestowed by God on all who obey Him."

Jake flinched at Peter's truthful accusation that the Sanhedrin had purposely murdered Jesus. Anger flashed across the eyes of all the council members. Peter had accused them all of breaking the Sixth Commandment, "Thou shalt not murder!"

The entire courtroom exploded into a rage! Peter's bold testimony infuriated the rulers in the courtroom. Yes, they had murdered Jesus! Yes, they wanted to stamp out His following and ministry by killing Him. Now Peter and the apostles publicly ripped open the ugly, raw wound. Peter publicly exposed the Sanhedrin's willful breaking of God's Law! The Sanhedrin's hypocrisy laid bare, in full public view.

"They know they're guilty," Jake said under his breath. "Don't any of them have a conscience?"

"We won't stand for your defiance!" Caiaphas screamed. In rage, he began pounding his fist on his High Priest's desk. "At Passover, I commanded that Jesus must die for the good of the nation of Israel! It had to be done! How dare you accuse us of sin! We were right in deciding to exterminate Jesus of Nazareth! We executed Jesus of Nazareth! We were justified in our actions! And, we will not hesitate to have all of you killed, as well! We would be justified in killing all of you, too!"

"Well said!" echoed angry voices across the courtroom. "Death to all the followers of Jesus of Nazareth!" more inflamed shouts cried out. "We must stop this false religion! Death to all the Nazarene's disciples!"

Vicious hatred flooded across the courtroom like a river of red-hot lava! Dignified, distinguished rulers jumped up and morphed into screaming madmen, shaking their fists violently in the direction of the twelve apostles. Some of them even started taking angry steps, advancing like a pack of vicious hyenas toward the disciples.

Nicodemus and Joseph stood up to try to stop the hellbent mob but they were shoved back into their seats. Jake instinctively yelled, "Somebody stop them! Stop them!" But others in the anteroom shoved him aside, as well, and began chanting, "Kill them! Kill the rebels!"

The courtroom blew up into chaos and white-hot violence!

Suddenly, one member of the Sanhedrin, stood and raised his arms in an attempt to stop the charging attack. Jake looked through the blur of churning humanity in front of him and realized the man standing up was the very well-respected Pharisee and teacher Gamaliel.

"Gentlemen! Gentlemen of Israel!" Gamaliel coolly addressed the fiery, out-of-control assembly. "Please listen to me! Please listen to me!"

When they all realized the man speaking was one of their most honored and trusted members, the wild courtroom began to simmer down. Pandemonium slowly subsided. Ravenous dogs went back to their seats. Order finally was restored to the courtroom.

Gamaliel lowered his outstretched, pleading arms. "We must never transact our important court business in a mob like fashion. Furthermore, we certainly must not conduct our legal deliberations in the presence of the accused persons. I order that these accused men be removed from the courtroom while we further discuss this matter to determine their ultimate fate."

Jake picked up his overturned chair that had been upended during the scuffle in the anteroom. He instinctively looked for Nicodemus and saw him readjusting his disheveled robe, which had been pulled catawampus during the may-lay. Nicodemus looked over at Jake. Jake halfway smiled and signaled his relief by wiping the back of his hand across his forehead. Nicodemus smiled back and nodded his understanding.

Once the apostles had exited the courtroom, Gamaliel addressed the smoldering assembly of religious leaders. "Men of Israel, be very careful what you are planning to do to these men who follow the Nazarene," he cautioned. "I want to remind you that there have been other upstart religious movements that have died out in their normal course. Not long ago a nobody named Theudas claimed great things about himself and gathered about four hundred men around him as his followers. He was killed and all of his followers were scattered, never to be heard of again.

"After him came another charlatan named Judas the Galilean. He started an uprising during the days of the census and convinced a large faction to follow him. He also died and all of his supporters scattered to the wind."

Gamaliel paused for dramatic effect. His eyes scanned the council chamber, making sure all eyes were on him. "Now in this present case before us, let me caution you. Back away from doing harm to these accused men. Leave them alone. If the doctrine these men are teaching is of their own origin, their religion will soon be defeated and come to nothing. However, if what they are preaching is from God, you will not be able to destroy these men. In fact, you may even be guilty of fighting against the Lord God Himself! So, step back away from these men and see what God will do with this Christian movement."

Gamaliel paused again. His eyes scanned the courtroom once more and said calmly, "Think about it, men. Think about it."

The whole assembly sat quietly in stunned silence. Gamaliel had effectively driven his point into their hearts. They all seemed convinced to listen to his advice. However, something still had to be done to pretend some sort of justice was being meted out against these prisoners.

Caiaphas sat quietly in his seat, thoughtfully looking down at the floor. He brought his right hand up to his chin and stroked his whiskers, trying to make a decision. His grim black eyes narrowed as an insolent expression crossed his face.

Caiaphas then looked up and ordered the prisoners be brought back into the courtroom. As the twelve apostles lined up in front of the Sanhedrin, the High Priest stood to pass judgment. He heaved an aggravated sigh, as he glared at the prisoners and paused for many moments. In disgust, he put his hands on his hips and decreed, "You prisoners are guilty of flagrantly defying our direct command to you to never preach in 'this Name' again. Because you have deliberately disobeyed our orders, I decree that each one of you be flogged and brought back before this court!"

Murmurs rippled throughout the courtroom. Some seemed to think Caiaphas' judgment was a good idea. Others thought Gamaliel's advice was the better one. But Caiaphas and his defiant anger held sway and the prisoner apostles were led out of the council room by the captain of the guard and his Temple police, to be whipped.

Jake's face transformed into a grave, ashen expression, as he helplessly watched the apostles being led outside to be beaten. He bit his lip. His mind swept back to that horrifying day when Jesus was scourged with a whip-of-nine-tails just before He was crucified. Jake remembered the sound of the whip's sickening hiss, as it sliced through the air and ripped into Jesus' back. Cold chills streaked through Jake's body, as he remembered. Gruesome memories twisted through his brain.

All the council members and rulers in the assembly hall remained, waiting impatiently for the beating of the apostles to be completed. All Jake could do was pray – pray for God's strength be given to the apostles, as they were beaten. In what seemed like agonizing hours of waiting, the captain of the Temple Guard finally brought the badly beaten and bloody apostles back into the high courtroom. He lined them all up to face the Sanhedrin. Caiaphas looked very pleased with himself.

"My, my. You men do look a mess," Caiaphas stated with great satisfaction in his defiant voice. "I hope this beating will teach you all a lesson. This beating will also be a reminder to all of you that we rulers are not to be defied. We are in charge. We mean serious business when we give you an order. We expect you to obey us. Now, I will again command you to never again preach or speak in the Name of the Nazarene. Let me remind you. You cannot escape our judgment if you ever disobey our command again." And then speaking to the captain of the guard, "Release these men. Get them out of my sight! This council meeting is adjourned."

The apostles were shuffled off through a side door and Jake was trapped in the crowded anteroom. It took several minutes to break free of the crush of people in the courtroom area and get outside the building. There he found Nicodemus. The stately gentleman had tears in his aged brown eyes.

"Jake, the hatred for Jesus is still very great," Nicodemus sadly said. "I can see how this whole situation is beginning to play out. The rulers and religious leaders hated Jesus and if anyone expresses a love for Jesus, they are automatically hated by the rulers, as well."

"It is obvious," Jake said. "Jesus made the statement something to the effect that since the evil world hated Him, the evil world would hate us."

"And I am very sad to say that the evil world has penetrated into our religious leaders," the statesman sighed. "What we observed today in that high courtroom is a despicable display of rampant evil in the guise of religious trappings and proceedings. The anger and hatred that flared up in there is a disgrace."

Jake gazed at the crestfallen gentleman. "I'm so very sorry."

"I love my nation," Nicodemus stated, tears welling up in his eyes. "I am very sad to see my nation standing against God."

"Then let's go out and tell everyone in the nation who will listen that Jesus is alive and that He can save them from their sins!"

The gentleman statesman smiled and wiped the tears away. "You're right, Jake. At least we can put up a fight until they arrest us, too! We can go down swinging!"

"That's the spirit! Now, let's go and find out where the apostles have gone."

"You go ahead," Nicodemus said thoughtfully. "I'm going to track down some of those Sanhedrin members who I think will listen to me. I'm going to try to convince them that the best course of action is to follow Gamaliel's advice. The leaders must make a decision to leave the Christians alone. I especially think I'll talk with one of Gamaliel's young protégées. I saw him in the courtroom today sitting next to Gamaliel. I've got a good feeling about him. I think he's on our side! His name is Saul of Tarsus."

Chapter 4

DANGEROUS MISSION

In spite of the vicious threats from the Sanhedrin, the apostles continued to preach the Good News of salvation through Jesus Christ to the multitudes in Jerusalem. This determined behavior continued to ramp up the tension within the city. The apostles fully understood that the persecution of the Christians was the same as the persecution of the Lord Jesus Himself. And they considered it a privilege to suffer for the sake of their Lord.

Nicodemus recognized this continuous escalating pressure against Christians. Several days after the trial of the apostles by the Sanhedrin, Nicodemus arrived in Jake's office.

"Jake, Nicodemus is out here, at my desk," Hannah stated as she cracked open the detective's office door and poked her head in. "I think he has come to ask you to do some work for him."

Jake seemed surprised. "I wonder what this could be about?" he said rubbing his chin with the back of his thumb. "Shoo him in, Angel. I'm anxious to hear what he wants."

Hannah swung the office door open. "Pharisee Nicodemus, please come on in. Detective Jezreel will gladly see you now," she gushed, being as overly polite as she knew how. A very happy smile crossed her pretty face, as she admired the stately gentleman.

"Thank you, so much, Ms. Haggai," Nicodemus equally gushed politeness toward her. "It is always a tremendous pleasure to see and speak to you," he said, placing his right hand up to his chest and slightly bowing to her.

"Sir, the pleasure is all mine," she beamed and she halfway bowed to Nicodemus.

They stood looking at each other for a moment longer and Jake shook his head at their sappy, syrupy politeness.

"Have you two been practicing being obnoxiously polite to each other," Jake laughed out loud. "You both really know how to pour it on in a generous plenty."

Nicodemus pretended to be offended. He tilted his head in an odd manner and said, "Sir, your secretary and I have the greatest respect for one another." And turning toward Hannah he asked, "Isn't that the absolute truth?"

"Why, yes, absolutely," she stated, feigning being offended by Jake. "Pharisee Nicodemus and I are good friends and our respect runs very deep. Did I ever tell you the story about the time when this wonderful gentleman helped me gather up my groceries when I dumped them out …"

"Yes, yes." Jake cut her off in mid-story. "I have heard that yarn far too many times." He stared at the girl curiously. "Hannah, don't you have something else to do? Like go file some files or tidy up your desk?"

"Yes, boss. I'll get outa your hair."

Hannah and Nicodemus smiled at each other one more time and then she closed the office door.

Nicodemus turned around toward Jake with a wonderful expression on his face. "I can see why you want to marry that beautiful woman. She is a fine person. One in a million. She is so rare a treasure, you should thank God that He has brought her into your life."

"I do thank God every day," Jake mused. "It was divine direction that brought her into my life."

"Oh? How so?" the gentleman asked.

"Her father was injured in a bad accident at his workshop. To help support the financial needs of her family while Hannah's father was laid up, she answered my advertisement in the want ads of *The Jerusalem Times*. She breezed into my office like a breath of fresh spring air and my life has never been the same since."

"So, when is the wedding?" Nicodemus asked as he sat down in the armchair next to the detective's desk.

Jake scrunched his face. He shook his head. "Well, it's not that easy. You see both of my parents are dead. Our customs instruct us that my father would be the one to secure a bride for me. Also, there is the matter of the dowry, the 'present', that our customs require to be given from my father to my bride and to her family. Since I have no living father, the presenting of the dowry to Hannah and her family is the problem that is holding up the marriage. And I don't have the money for an adequate dowry. So, things are sort of stalled out."

"Son, that should not be a problem too hard to solve," Nicodemus smiled. "Is Hannah's father agreeable to your marriage?"

"Yes, he is, very much so."

"Well, then, what is the problem?" Nicodemus clapped his hands in delight. "All you have to do is make an arrangement with Hannah's father to perform some sort of service that would compensate for the price of the dowry. You remember the Biblical story of Jacob working fourteen years so he could make Rachel his wife. His service to Rachel's brother took the place of the dowry. And also remember the story of Caleb offering his daughter, Achsah, to the man who conquered the people of Kiriath-sepher. It was Othniel who won the hand of Caleb's daughter by providing a service to her father. It shouldn't be too hard to figure out a similar method of providing a service to Hannah's father to compensate for the dowry."

Jake sat in his chair with a thoughtful expression on his face. "I hadn't even thought of it in that way," he stated. And then with a sly little grin he joked, "Of course, I don't think I want to do that fourteen-year thing, for Hannah to become my bride. And I don't know of any people Hannah's father needs to have conquered, but I can probably come up with something that he and I can agree on."

"I'm sure of it," laughed the gentleman Pharisee.

"Well, with that very pressing matter solved, what can I do for you, sir," Jake grinned.

The expression on Nicodemus' face slowly changed from jovial into much more severe. He looked Jake straight in the eye. "Mister Jezreel, I have come to you today about a serious …" He cleared his throat and rubbed his fingers across his mouth, as if to help his words come out. "I must get to the serious subject for which I have called upon you today. It is vitally important. No, it is imperative that I speak with you. I have come today to hire you to do some dangerous, clandestine work for me," the Pharisee gentleman said. His voice had a grave, ominous tone.

"Dangerous work? Why is it dangerous?"

"You already know the vile mood that the religious leaders are in, here in Jerusalem," Nicodemus stated in a matter-of-fact manner. "You know the threats they have made against any more preaching about Jesus. And you also know that in spite of their terrorizing threats, the apostles and the Christians have continued to preach and teach the multitudes about salvation through Jesus. This fact has not been lost on the religious leaders and the members of the Sanhedrin. They are watching. Watching in simmering anger as the Christians continue to defy their authority. Their anger is like a bubbling volcano. Sooner or later, it will explode. There can be no doubt about that fact."

Nicodemus stood up and gazed longingly out Jake's second story window. His despondent voice had a note of grief.

"It breaks my heart, but this fact is true," Nicodemus sadly said. "We are truly living in a time when the prophecy of the prophet Isaiah is coming true. Isaiah spoke for God when he prophesied, 'These people draw near with their mouths; they honor Me with their lips. But they have removed their hearts far from Me'. I remember a time when Jesus quoted this same verse from Isaiah 29:13 while He was preaching. Our leaders have become these very same men Isaiah prophesied about. Our leaders have become blind guides. Their hearts have become stone cold and far away from the Lord God. Now they are a bunch of paranoid, vindictive politicians ready to destroy anyone or any group they deem as being dangerous."

Nicodemus sat back down and shifted nervously in his armchair. "Someone needs to get down into the middle of all this rage and find out what evil plans the religious leaders are plotting. I am asking you to be that man who will descend down into the 'belly of the beast', so to speak, and find out their malicious plans. Maybe somehow you can work your way into the confidence of these same religious leaders. Then you might hear a tidbit of news that will provide a clue as to their impending plan of attack against the Christians here in the city."

Jake looked puzzled. "Since you move around in those political circles each day, what have you heard?" he asked.

"Nothing. And for good reason. I've been snubbed. Granted, I am around these religious leaders every day. But they won't talk to me. They know where I stand as a follower of Christ. They know already how I defended Jesus, last springtime, in front of the whole Sanhedrin before they arrested Him. They also know of my involvement in helping to bury Jesus after He was crucified. Because of this knowledge, the religious leaders will not speak to me. I am no longer included in their conversations. Therefore, I do not hear their secret plans. They always stop talking when I come into their conversations. They shut me out. I am sorry to say, I can be of no help to you in learning what is going on in their hateful plotting."

Jake sat quietly, taking in this whole explanation by the gentleman Pharisee. "Yes, this does sound dangerous. I would basically be a spy. And they wouldn't take too kindly to finding a spy in their midst."

Nicodemus gazed at Jake with a fearful stare. "No! No! It is too dangerous!" he exclaimed, bolting forward in his chair. "Far too dangerous! Mister Jezreel, I have no right to ask you to do this! Your life would be hanging by a thread every moment you would be down in the middle of that angry pit of hateful men."

"Now, wait just a minute, sir," the detective said, cocking his head to indicate a new determination that had just welled up inside him. "I'm already ready to dive into the 'belly of the beast'! You've piqued my interest to dig down deep into this bunch of 'leaders' and schmooze with them. A little chinwag here. A little chitchat there. Who knows what I might find out."

"But how would you ever be able to spy on them without getting caught?" Nicodemus was so distressed that he jumped up and began to pace back and forth. "It is just too dangerous. No, I can't ask you to do this! They would not hesitate to beat you or even …" The gentleman Pharisee couldn't get the words "kill you" out of his mouth.

"Listen, my friend," Jake soothed. "I've been in some pretty tight spots in this business. And I've never let a client down because I thought there might be a little risk involved. I get paid to take risks. I know the hazards. This is the business I'm in." Jake stood up behind his desk and walked around to put his hand on Nicodemus' shoulder. "Friend, I want to take this case. For the sake of my fellow believers. And for the sake of my Lord."

Nicodemus bowed his head. "I will be praying for you all the time, my friend. Our future safety as a church may hinge upon you and your investigation.'

As the gentleman Pharisee left the office, Jake called Hannah into his office so they could discuss the conversation he had had with Nicodemus.

"Hannah, sit down in the chair here by my desk. I need to make it very clear what Nicodemus has hired me to do."

"I already know," she said solemnly, as she sat down.

"You already know? How is that possible?"

"I listened at the door," she stated.

"You listened at the door?"

"Yes. I knew whatever Nicodemus had come to discuss with you had to be important, so I listened at the door."

"Oookaaay … do you do this very often? I mean, listening at the door."

"No, this was my first time. But I knew it had to be important, so I just decided that I would listen in and find out what was going on."

"Okay, so what do you think about Nicodemus' proposal?"

"Do you really want to know what I think?"

"Yeah, I do. I need your input and ideas."

"Well, I agree with Nicodemus. I think this case is too dangerous. It's lunacy. However, I know you and I know it doesn't make any difference to you if there is risk involved. And I know that once you agree to take a case, you're like a bulldog. You're locked in and latched on to the very end, no matter what. So, what can I say? It's insane. It's irrational. But what can I say?"

"Well, thanks for your honest assessment. Now … give me some input as to how I can pull off this investigation."

"You're actually asking me for suggestions on how to investigate this case?"

"Yep, I need my sweetie's very studious thoughts about how I should proceed. Many of the religious leaders already know who I am and what I look like. How could I ever get into their midst without being found out?"

Hannah paused for a moment. Then she thoughtfully said, "It's very elementary, my dear detective. You are very good at disguises. Come up with a great disguise and you can walk in anywhere undetected."

Jake scrunched his face. "I don't know. I certainly can't use my dirty beggar's outfit like I did the last time. They would never let me even get anywhere near the religious leaders."

"Yeah, you did look pretty silly in that getup, anyway."

"It was convincing enough at the time, I'll have you know. And I seem to recall that I scared the wits out of you with it."

"You didn't scare me. I just acted scared because I wanted to make you think you could fool everybody with your silly costume. You know, give you some confidence."

"Alright, we both agree that the beggar's disguise is out. So …" Jake began rolling his hands in front of him, as if to be pulling a fresh idea from Hannah.

"I don't know, Jake," she said shaking her head. "This is all happening too fast. Try to think of some of the other disguises you've used."

"Well, remember that time I used some of your dad's leathercrafting clothes to pretend I was a leather merchant," the detective recalled.

"Not good. Remember, you were trying to work your way into the leathercrafting union to expose the graft going on there," Hannah cautioned. "Somehow, I don't think that would work in this case."

"Okay, how about the time I dressed as a horse groomer, so I could investigate some of the shenanigans going on among the stable workers at the king's royal palace. I was working for King Herod's, family."

"Jake, remember you never got to actually meet with any of the royal family on that case," she reminded. "You helped the royal family find the corruption but you reported only to their representative. Never to the them. For this assignment you've got to get right up close and personal with the religious leaders."

"Well, you think of something."

The couple sat looking at each other for a long time, thinking.

"Nothing?" Jake asked.

Hannah shrugged her shoulders and gave a bewildered expression.

"Let's face it," Jake finally said. "I'm not an aristocrat. I'm not an honored man in society. And I look like average Joe worker guy. It would be hard to disguise a non-descript face like mine as a nobleman."

Hannah suddenly brought her hands up to her mouth in a surprised gesture. Astonishment flashed over her face.

Jake saw her expression and asked, "What? What? Have you thought of something?"

"Oh, Jake, you're not going to like this idea," the girl said, halfway looking away.

"Come on! You've got to tell me your idea. Spill it!"

Hannah hesitated. "No, you just wouldn't like this idea. It's an off-the-wall idea."

"You'd better say it! Come on!"

Hannah hesitated again. Then announced her plan.

"Could you dress like a religious leader?"

Jake sucked in air hard, as if the girl had stuck him with a pin. He glared at her. "What! Me a religious leader? Join the enemy? You have got to be kidding!"

"No, I'm not kidding. It would be a perfect disguise," she said in a whisper, her eyes gazing off toward the ceiling.

"No, no, no! Never in a million years. No! Me, a religious leader? No way!"

"Why not a religious leader?"

"Think of something else, Hannah," Jake firmly said. "Anything else!"

The girl sat quietly in the armchair. She looked down at the lap of her beige tunic and silently, thoughtfully smoothed out the non-existent wrinkles. She never looked up. Then she folded her hands in front of her. Not a word spoken.

Jake stared at her. "It's impossible," he finally said. "You realize that, don't you? I'm farther away from a religious leader than the man-in-the-moon. And that's pretty far. How would I ever be able to impersonate a Pharisee or a Sadducee?"

Hannah looked up at Jake. "You've always told me that your best disguise is to blend in with the people you're investigating. It is a relatively straightforward fact that if you want to blend in with people, you've got to look and act like them. Somehow, we've got to make you look like a religious man."

"Good luck with that," he smirked. "I'd have to learn how to be a hypocrite."

"Now, now, don't be like that. Come on. Work with me on this," she encouraged.

"Okay … give me some time to think about this. A religious leader. Hum. It sounds wacky. Idiotic. But it does sound logical. Yeah, but how would I pull it off. All the religious leaders in the city know all the other religious leaders. How could I ever expect to show up one day and be accepted by the religious elites of Jerusalem?"

"I didn't say it was a perfect idea," the girl giggled. "But we can fine tune it so it will work."

She hesitated once more as another idea popped into her head. "You said it yourself. You have a non-descript face."

"Okay, just because I've got a common Joe face, you don't have to rub it in."

"No, no. That's a good thing," she said excitedly. "Jake, there are thousands of religious leaders in this city. They each can't possibly know all the other religious leaders in Israel."

"I don't know. They're like a fraternity, a tight knit brotherhood. They actually do know one another," Jake stated.

Hannah sat quietly thinking. Another idea sprung into her thoughts.

"Okay, how about this angle," she announced. "There are also many more thousands of Levites throughout Israel. They live all over Israel. Didn't you tell me one time that you have a Levite heritage?"

"Well, yeah. But that's like I'm related as a cousin to some of the Levites four or five times removed," he laughed. "Not really a Levite. Just far, far related to them."

"Well, that qualifies you to say you're a Levite. You've got Levite blood running through your veins!"

"Ahh, that makes me shiver just to think about it!"

"Then don't think about that part of it. Think about this. Being a Levite could be the key to your disguise. There are thousands of Levites from all over Israel who serve in various shifts at the Temple. They are divided into many divisions and organized to only serve once a year for just a few weeks and then go back home. Then the next shift of Levites come in from who-knows-where in Israel to do their service time. There is such a large turnover of men that it would be nearly impossible for everybody to know everybody who is a Levite. Nobody could possibly know all the Levites! And because of that fact, it would probably be very easy for you to impersonate one of them."

Jake looked at Hannah in disbelief. "How do you know all of this stuff?"

"Oh, I keep up with these things. Does that surprise you? I keep my eyes and ears open. You're not the only detective in this office."

"I am impressed, girl. You sound very convincing, like you even know what you're talking about."

"I *do* know what I'm talking about." she stated, narrowing her eyes at him.

"But why a Levite?" the detective squirmed. "Why can't I just …" He stopped in mid-sentence when he saw the scowl on her face.

Hannah stared at Jake in disbelief. "Don't you get it? You'll look just like one of them. They'll think you're one of them. Isn't that what you've always taught me – blend in, blend in."

"Yeah, but …"

"Don't you see? These religious men will talk freely around you, if they think you're one of them." The girl stood up and put her hands on her hips. "It's pretty clear to me. How 'bout you, boss?"

"Yeah, I get it," he confessed. "But, what would be my cover? I just can't walk into the midst of the religious leaders and say, 'Hi, how ya doing. I'm a Levite.' I've got to have a cover, a title. A name to go by. And I can't lie. I don't want to dishonor Jesus while I'm doing His work."

Hannah thought for a second. "Dig back into your family heritage. You can use that."

"Okay. Well, my family originally came from the city of Jezreel in the tribal territory of Issachar. That's where our family got our surname Jezreel. The city is part of a plains area called the Plain of Jezreel or sometimes it's referred to as the Plain of Esdraelon." Jake paused thoughtfully. "Hey, that's it!" he exclaimed as the light bulb blinked on in his head. "I can introduce myself as Jacob of Esdraelon. And I would be fully telling the truth. My family did come from the Plain of Esdraelon!"

"You're smarter than the average detective!" Hannah laughed. "Good thinking! That sounds like a perfect cover. I think it will really work!"

"Yeah, it does sound that way, doesn't it. Now, the big question. Where can I get Levite robes to complete the effect?"

"Nicodemus," Hannah said without hesitation. "If anyone can get a Levite outfit for you, it would be him."

"Then I'll need to get in touch with Nicodemus. I'm sure he must have access to Levite robes and such. And with the Levite head gear, my appearance should change somewhat."

"With the Levitical linen turban on your head, you'll certainly look like a different person," Hannah smiled. "Even people who know you would likely not recognize you simply because they wouldn't be expecting you in that costume. Sweetheart, you're going to look like a new man!"

"I'd better be! I'm counting on it," the detective mused. "Jake Jezreel the detective must disappear when I become Jacob of Esdraelon and descend into the 'belly of the beast'."

And then Jake's expression changed to worry. "Hannah, I can't impersonate a Levite. I don't even know the first thing about what they do and the way they do their work."

"But you don't have to worry about that," Hannah said confidently. "You won't actually be doing any Levite duties, if you just mill around in the Court of Israel. Levites will be serving in the restricted Court of the Priests. But there is no need for you to go up there. You certainly would not be allowed in that highly restricted area."

Jake thought for a moment. "Yeah, that's true. In the Court of Israel, I can rub elbows with the high-class leaders. If they think I'm one of them, they'll just think I'm an off-duty Levite, hangin' out with the high mucky-mucks." Then with a sly look in his eye he said, "But that Court of the Priests sure does look tempting ..."

Hannah stopped him and pointed her finger at Jake. "Don't say anymore! That Court of Israel is as far as you go! The Court of Israel is the limit. Just because you're wearing a Levite outfit, don't start thinking that you're invincible! Don't you dare enter the Court of the Priests! They will kill you on the spot!"

"I promise. I promise I'll stay only in the Court of Israel. If I was caught with one foot in the Court of the Priest, I'd be a dead man! I don't think I'd like that very much."

"Okay, then. You show me exactly what your plan is, so I won't worry about you getting killed," Hannah stated, with one hand on her hip and the other on the desk top.

"Alright. Let me map out my plan of attack," the detective said, as he pulled out a clean sheet of papyrus from his desk drawer. He began to draw a sketch of the temple complex. "Now, right here is Solomon's Porch. I think the best way to pull this off is to enter through Solomon's Porch. That way I can just walk straight ahead through the Soreg barrier into the Sacred Enclosure." Jake sketched and labeled each position on his chart.

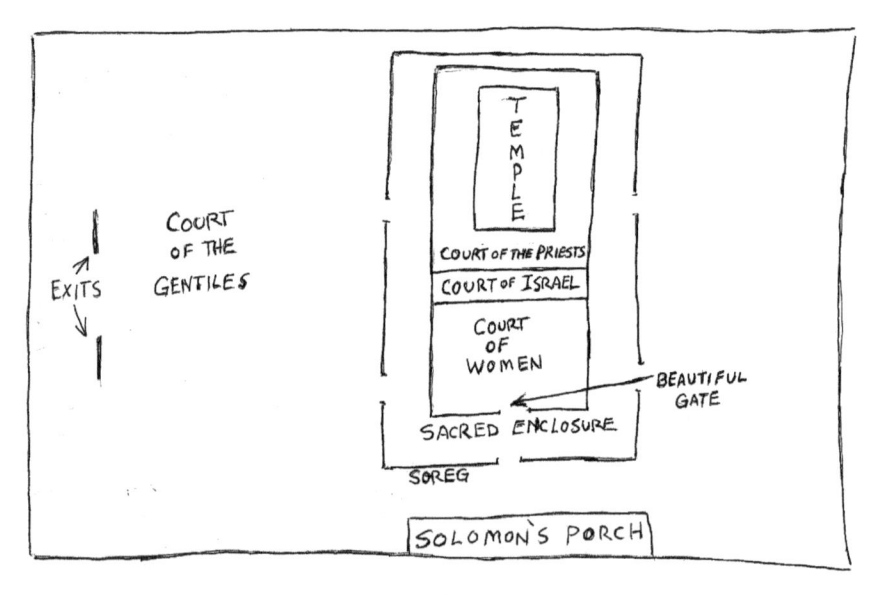

Jake's diagram of the temple complex.

"Next, I'll climb the steps up to the Beautiful Gate and on through into the Court of the Women.

"Then I'll be ready to climb that final set of steps up to the Court of Israel ... the Court of the Men. That's where I can get all the info I need. I'll just mill around in the Court of Israel and keep my ears wide open. I won't even look past there into the Court of the Priests."

"You'd better not!" Hannah stated, narrowing her eyes. "You don't even want to know what's going on up there in the Court of the Priests."

"I'll be a good boy. I promise. There's nothin' in there for me – nothin' but trouble. Besides, if I take one false step just pretending to be a Levite, I'll be in plenty of trouble, as it is."

As Jake sat leaning over the drawing, he drew two more lines on the lefthand side. "Those two lines are my escape plan. That's the two exits to the Double Gate. I've got to plan for all possibilities. So, I've got to pre-plan getting my little self outa there. When I think I've finally got all the info I need, I'll exit stage left, out the two exits of the Double Gate. That way I can get out of the Temple and out among people."

Hannah sat down beside Jake. "Please be extra careful, honey," she pleaded. "I love you so very much. Don't take any senseless chances."

Jake laughed. "Well, you know me. I know I'm really sticking my neck out on this one. But I've got to take risks. If I don't, well, I might as well close down my private eye business and become a butcher or a baker."

The girl stared at Jake for a long time. "I worry about you. I do trust you to think fast on your feet. You always do. But this is serious. Deadly serious."

She now began having second thoughts. "I'm really sorry I even suggested this insane trick."

"Please don't worry about me," Jake said. "Don't forget, I've got the Lord with me."

"I know," Hannah said as tears welled up in her eyes. "I'll be more at ease if you'll promise me to stick to your strict surveillance plan. Just go and observe. Nothing more. It will be risky enough just impersonating a Levite. And whatever you do …"

"Yeah, I know," Jake interrupted, "do not cross the boundary into the priests' area. Listen, I'll be alright," he said, trying to comfort her. "You know how well my disguises work. They have gotten me in and out of other dangerous situations. I think I can pull this one off just the same. I'll be extra careful."

"You'd better be," the girl stated in a more feisty tone, wiping her tears away. "I want you back in one piece."

Chapter 5

DEADLY GROUND

Uneasy apprehension stalked Jake's steps as he stepped into the Temple precincts. He now was Jacob of Esdraelon – Levite. As he left Hannah and headed for the Temple, the girl had encouraged him, "Now, this white linen Levite uniform really makes you look authentic – because it is. You look very convincing. But, please, don't overplay your hand."

"I promise I'll be as non-descript as I can be," Jake told her. "My life is gonna depend on the genuineness of my disguise."

The white linen Levitical tunic he wore, which Nicodemus had provided, made the detective appear very distinguished. And just like Hannah, Nicodemus had warned Jake not to wander into the Court of the Priests. "The Court of the Priests is a sanctified, sacred place in the Temple grounds. Levite clothes don't give you the right to venture where only priests and Levites can go. You know the penalty for anyone crossing over into that consecrated area. Death on the spot!" With that dire warning pinging around in his head, Jake pulled the white linen Levite turban down a little bit more to cover most of his forehead. Gotta hide his true identity.

As Jake walked closer to the main Temple in his Levite robes, he noticed people in the crowd acknowledged him and treated him with great respect. He was encouraged by this special behavior. Apparently, these people were showing reverence for his "office" as a Levite.

"So far so good," Jake muttered to himself. "This disguise is working. Now comes the real test." He took a deep breath and pressed on.

Jake crossed the expansive Court of the Gentiles full of worshippers. He stopped momentarily at Solomon's Porch to get a feel for the size of the crowd and nail down his escape route if things went wrong.

From there, the detective crossed a short stretch of pavement and climbed several steps up to the next level known as the Sacred Enclosure. A low wall, known as the Soreg, formed a boundary line around the Sacred Enclosure and the Court of the Gentiles. This wall cordoned off these exclusive precincts. Jake stepped through one of the openings in the Soreg and entered into the Sacred Enclosure. Jake read the warning placard attached to the Soreg, as he walk through the opening. No unbelieving gentile was allowed to enter the Sacred Enclosure, upon penalty of death.

Then up he went the several steps to the next level three feet higher, the Court of the Women. Jake entered this Court through the Beautiful Gate. The Court of the Women seemed to be extra busy today. The Temple treasury was located in this Court, over to the right of the courtyard along the wall. There, thirteen collection boxes lined up, their trumpet-like mouths yawning wide open, beckoning worshippers to disgorge their temple offerings. There were numerous worshippers clustered around the collection boxes depositing their money. Jake made a mental note that this crowd could be a hindrance in escaping if his undercover plan blew up. Also, he noted that both of the side entrances were jammed with people milling about. That left only one way out of the courtyard, the Beautiful Gate where he had just come in.

On through this large courtyard filled with worshippers and up more steps to the next level ten feet higher, the Court of Israel. Only the men of Israel could enter this area.

As he reached the top step of the Court of Israel, the detective paused. He'd never been in this elite space before. This was foreign territory to him. This area was reserved mainly for the upper crust, high-class aristocrats. But this court was his target ... the prime "simmering pot" of radical ideas against Christians.

Jake felt his heart pounding hard. He felt flushed. Right in front of him were the steps to the next level three feet higher, the Court of the Priests. That was the "dead line" for intruders. He knew the lethal chance he would be taking by ascending those steps. Hannah's warning blared in his ears. Nicodemus' threats of death pinged loudly around in his brain.

'I will just hang out here in the Court of Israel and listen to what some of the leaders are talking about,' Jake thought to himself. *'I'm sure there will be banter back and forth among them. Maybe I'll get a hint as to what sort of devious plot they may have heard about or may even be cooking up.'* As Jake strode in among the men in the Court, they began to acknowledge him, greeting him cordially. *'It's working,'* Jake thought. *'As a Levite, they are comfortable talking freely around me.'*

There were already some high-ranking dignitaries meeting other noblemen and engaging in conversation. Jake's plan was still pretty sketchy but here he stood trying to "wing it" as best as he could. He quietly assumed a prayerful-looking posture, hands folded reverently under his chin. He listened. And he listened. And he listened, silently snooping and eavesdropping on the conversations all around him. He tried to look pious, as a Levite should. *'Maybe they won't ask me any questions, if they think I'm praying,'* he thought.

But then, out of nowhere, Jake felt a tap on his shoulder. He stiffened, just knowing he had been discovered. The detective slowly turned around, only to find another Levite standing there.

"Aren't you going to serve today?" the real Levite asked.

"Serve?" Jake fumbled for words.

"Won't you be serving with the priests today?"

"Oh ... yes, I ... ah ... I just stopped here in the Court of Israel in preparation and for a time of prayer," Jake mumbled, swallowing very hard.

"Well, we need to go up into the Court. It is nearly time for the morning sacrifice."

"You go ahead," Jake muttered. "I'll be along in a minute."

"No, no," stated the real Levite. "We need to go, now. There is not a moment to lose."

With that statement, the Levite latched onto Jake's arm and started to briskly escort the detective toward the steps leading up to the Court of the Priests. Jake balked slightly.

"What's the matter?" the Levite asked. "You are hesitating. Are you a new Levite?"

"Very new."

"I thought so," the real Levite said. "I didn't think I recognized your face. Come on. I'll help you."

Before Jake could say anything else, the real Levite began to drag Jake up the steps into the Court of the Priests! Jake crossed the 'dead line'! Hannah's frightful warnings again screamed in his ears.

'Now you've really done it!' Jake thought in shock. *'The ascent of death! You've really bought it this time!'*

As the pair of Levites climbed closer to the top, Jake recoiled in his thoughts. *'All I can do, now, is make it up as I go along! I've got to wing it as best as I can. Father, please … help me!'*.

Jake took another deep breath. One of the temple guards scrutinized the pair of Levites only long enough to acknowledge their certified Levitical office and let them pass on into the Court of the Priests.

As Jake ascended the final step, at the top level, a whole new world stretched out before him.

There in front of the detective lay the Court of the Priests and the magnificent Golden Temple, up close and personal! The grandeur of the Temple took Jake's breath away! King Herod had renovated and embellished the old Temple which had been built by Zerubbabel many centuries before. King Herod's rebuilding project required enormous amounts of money, consumed many years and, in the process, had expanded the Temple complex exponentially. The Court of the Priests was exquisite with the gleaming golden façade of the towering temple building, the beautiful, huge bronze alter, with its ramp, and the other splendid furnishings. Jake stood in awe at the gorgeous site directly before him. The priests busied themselves in their duties. The Levites also bustled about performing their tasks.

Jake had to quickly get his amazement with the Temple under control and get down to business. The detective had a whole lot of spying to do – without getting caught! *'Lord, help me,'* he prayed silently.

Jake's new found Levite friend was helpful. "You watch me," he told Jake. The detective stopped long enough to watch what his new friend and the other real Levites were doing. He knew he had to imitate whatever they were doing. Some Levites were filling water basins. Some were stoking fires. Some were preparing the sacrifices. Others were simply preparing to clean up behind the priests.

Jake knew that the legitimate Levites would be assisting the priests in the morning offering. He said another quick prayer as he strode closer to the area where the Levites were gathering for their service. *'Keep your mouth shut,'* the detective thought to himself, *'and you won't say the wrong thing.'*

"We'll be carrying water today," the Levite friend told Jake. "Just do what I do."

Jake mimicked his new Levite friend carrying water to the basins used for cleansing by the priests.

"Thank you, Lord, for this friendly Levite," Jake prayed softly. "He is providing the good cover I need. I know you sent him my way."

As he walked among the other linen clad Levites, Jake simply smiled at each one and walked on. When he wasn't carrying water, he assumed a pious posture with his hands folded in front of him and head slightly bowed. Some of the Levites spoke a morning greeting and Jake simply returned the greeting. *'No problem, yet,'* he thought to himself.

The priests moved into their positions of service and began conversing with some of the more prominent Levite leaders. The next thing he knew, it was time to really get to work!

Jake's game plan continued to be pretty thin. He figured his best option was to act eager and mimic whatever the other Levites were doing. This approach seemed to be working at first. But then some of the Levites Jake was working with began performing skilled operations, something a Levite should already be proficient at doing. He fumbled through some of the procedures and noticed a few scowls on the faces of his fellow workers. He tried to think fast and sheepishly apologized, "I'm new at this. Please forgive me for being inept at this part of the ceremony. I'll try to follow your lead a little better."

Jake's new Levite friend vouched for him. "He's right. He's pretty new at this work. I'll help him."

This explanation seemed to satisfy the group of Levites. The scowls on the Levites faces turned to compassion. They now joined in, guiding Jake more carefully in their procedures. As the Levites performed their duties, interacting with the priests, Jake overheard some of their "shop talk". He could tell that their paranoia of Christians played on their minds. The priests especially seemed to be suspicious and fearful of the Christian movement.

"There is no place for this dubious new sect in Judaism," Jake heard one priest say to a Levite. "And they are multiplying. This new sect of Christians is dangerous to the unity of our religion and our nation."

"You are so right," another priest said as he worked. "If these Christians are allowed to continue to teach their dreadful doctrine, there may be riots in the streets. We've already seen the chaos these Christians have created in our city."

Another priest spoke up, "If there are riots in the city … the Romans will come crashing down hard on all of us. They don't care who started the riot, the Romans just want to crush the disturbance. Our nation could not stand that. Israel might become divided, fractured, maybe even become nonexistent.

The general mood of many of the priests seemed to be sullen, confused, and suspicious regarding this new Christian splinter group.

The morning sacrifices soon were completed and Jake breathed a little easier. He also was freer to mingle in the Levitical gathering. The priests were now freed up to go about their other routine activities. Jake kept his ears open to the surrounding conversations in the Court of the Priests. Any tidbit of information could give away what the religious leaders were plotting. But even though he ranged right in their midst, Jake still didn't hear any new info of a definite plot by the religious leaders.

However, Jake suddenly realized the Lord had positioned him with an unexpected advantage. From his elevated viewing position, three feet above the Court of Israel, Jake noticed he could overhear conversations below him with greater ease than before. In fact, he could stand almost on top of the various discussions below him and hear every word. To him, as a detective, he found it quite fascinating.

Jake recognized a few of the priests and Pharisees. He avoided them to ensure that they didn't recognize him. His Levitical robes provided a very flimsy barrier of protection from detection and Jake didn't want to press the issue.

Then Jake noticed a knot of very loud hotheads gathered just below him in the Court of Israel. The detective drifted closer to them and listened intently.

Some of these religious hotheads had been at the apostles' trial last week. They were engaged in a very heated, animated discussion. There was plenty of derogatory comments flying around in their debating. Nothing very specific. Just hot! And then as chance would have it, a young protégée of Gamaliel made an appearance in the Temple compound, with the obvious intention of meeting with these religious hotheads.

The protégée's name was Saul of Tarsus.

This piqued Jake's interest! This young protégée was the very same student of Gamaliel that Nicodemus wanted to talk to after Gamaliel's speech at the trial of the apostles. Jake figured that Gamaliel's student would be defending his prestigious teacher's opinion to stop harassing the Christians. So, the detective eased even closer to the discussion that just was beginning.

Jake's opinion of Saul very quickly changed.

"Are you men as angry as I am about this splinter group called Christians?" Saul of Tarsus asked the other hotheads.

"Yes, yes! We are! We are very angry at them," they all said together. "They dishonor our revered 'oral laws.' They defy the honored authorities of our nation and have little respect for them. They dishonor our nation by calling down condemnation on our great leaders …"

"That is my opinion exactly!" Saul interrupted. "Nothing has infuriated me more than this off-shoot religion. There is a good chance that this false religion will ruin Judaism and draw away many people to this devious creed. Masses of gullible people are already being deceived into believing these lies. It is a pity how easily people can be fooled. If the Christians are not stopped, they will mislead and destroy the religion of whole populations of Jews throughout Israel!"

"How can we stop them?" one of the agitators sniveled. "Our leaders know that the followers of Jesus are out among the people preaching their deceptive religion. But they do nothing about it!"

"I know and that disturbs me to no end," Saul stated. "Why won't our authorities arrest the leaders of this false religion and either lock them up for good or just execute them?"

"Do you think our religious leaders would ever do that?" one hothead asked.

"No, they are too afraid. But I would," Saul stated flatly. "I wouldn't beat around the bush. I'd go straight for the jugular. I'd arrest them all and throw away the key! Or better yet! Exterminate them! Exterminate them all if need be!"

"But that would be against Roman law," lamented one antagonist. "Only Governor Pilate can authorize executing people. You remember how the governor had to approve of the execution of Jesus of Nazareth."

"I remember," Saul said. "But maybe we still could get away with it. Maybe it would all depend on the circumstances of the execution and the way it is done. There are ways to get what you want."

One of the hotheads protested. "But Saul, what you are advocating goes against the teachings of your teacher, Gamaliel," the troublemaker remarked. "He recommended that we leave this band of rebels alone and let God squash their religion."

"My teacher is wrong," Saul growled. "Sometimes God needs a little help to do His work. We will help God squash the life out of these despicable deceivers. And we can do it quite expeditiously."

Right about that time, a Pharisee who knew Jake from a previous investigation walked up and began talking to the group of angry men. Jake saw him approach and quickly tried to look away but it was too late. The Pharisee looked straight up at him and made eye contact. Immediately a flash of recognition swept across the face of the Pharisee. He appeared to recognize the detective but then outwardly dismissed the notion. He started to talk to the gaggle of hotheads.

Jake slowly moved away with his back turned to the Pharisee. He knew he had better get out of the Court of the Priests as fast as possible. He nonchalantly descended the steps to the Court of Israel, trying not to attract attention to himself. Then Jake started to walk further away, attempting to put some daylight between himself and the Pharisee. But the Pharisee had second thoughts about Jake.

"Levite!" the Pharisee ordered. "Come over here. I have a question I want to ask you."

Jake halfway turned back toward the Pharisee. With a questioning expression, he pointed his own finger at himself, as if to say, 'You mean me?'

"Yes, you!" the Pharisee demanded. "Come here."

Jake knew he was caught. But he still assumed his pious pose, head down in prayer-like posture, and walked over toward the Pharisee and the group.

"Levite, who are you?" the Pharisee commanded.

"Sir, I am Jacob of Esdraelon," Jake quietly stated, barely looking up, still with his head bowed.

"Levite, you look very familiar to me. Do you have a brother who lives in this city?" the Pharisee probed. "You remind me very strongly of someone I have seen here in Jerusalem recently. I can't quite remember who that person is at the moment."

"Sir, I am Jacob of Esdraelon," Jake quietly said again still with his head bowed and now with his hands folded partially in front of his face.

"I've never heard of you," sneered the Pharisee. "What Levitical division are you a part of and which echelon are you serving with?"

"I am a very new apprentice just learning how to serve," Jake stated truthfully.

"That does not answer my question!" the Pharisee screeched.

"There is something very odd about this Levite," whined one of the angry men in the group.

"Yes, he is being very evasive," another said.

Saul glared at Jake. "He doesn't sound like a Levite at all!" Saul shouted. "Who are you, man!"

Jake knew his cover had been blown. It was time to escape! Without saying a word, Jake whirled around and ran as fast as he could toward the nearest exit of the Temple grounds. He skittered, in three jumps, all the way from the Court of Israel, down ten feet of steps to the stone pavement of the Court of Women. Behind him he heard the one Pharisee shrieking, "Temple guards! Stop that Levite! Yes, the Levite running for the exit!"

Jake ran in desperation through the Court of the Women, dodging the crowds of worshipers. If he could just get to that one exit – the Beautiful Gate! It was the only way out! But suddenly, up ahead, two burly, red-uniformed Temple guards rushed into the exit out of the courtyard and blocked it. Jake spun around. Here came the Pharisee, Saul, and the gang of hotheads screaming and chasing after him. He was trapped!

Jake quickly whirled back around toward the two brawny guards. He made a split-second decision. "At least I'll have momentum on my side," Jake muttered to himself and charged headlong straight at the two guards, full force. Jake plowed into the pair at top speed, like a fullback hitting the defensive line. The guards both flew backwards, tumbling down the stairs onto the pavement of the Sacred Enclosure. Jake leaped from the top step over the wad of tangled men's arms and legs and kept on running. Sprinting through the Soreg boundary wall out onto the wide, spacious Court of the Gentiles, Jake knew his best chance of escape was straight ahead – out the Temple gate of Solomon's Porch. But instantly it filled up with a half dozen enraged Temple guards.

Jake stopped. Charging guards in front of him. Guards behind him, now scrambling to their feet, rushing at him. The gang of angry hotheads still in full pursuit. Trapped again! Jake glanced to his right. Stretching out in that direction were the wide expanses of the Court of the Gentiles, with its two exits through the Double Gate. His only escape route!

But suddenly a growling guard in front of him lunged at Jake, as if he'd been launched from a catapult. Jake managed to sidestep him, making him miss. In rapid fire, the other guards from Solomon's Porch aggressively swarmed at him. He ducked a diving, attacking guard and Jake shoved the man down hard to the stone pavement. He stiff-armed yet another guard jumping at him from his left. As the guard fell, he grabbed the detective's leg. Jake twisted and wrestled himself free. Instantly, Jake bounced out to his right, looking for clear running room. But the two burly apes from the Temple jumped in and set the outside edge, blocking his route. In desperation, he cut back across to his left, dodging the piles of bodies, toward the broad, wide-open, courtyard – the safe getaway! As Jake ran into the open, another screaming guard leaped headlong at him from behind, trying for a tackle. The sentinel's grasping hands slithered down Jake's back, nearly tripped him. Jake stumbled forward. But he kept his feet under him. The guard landed flat, skidding across the courtyard stones.

Jake turned on the jets, sprinting hard across the spacious courtyard pavement. He dodged bewildered worshippers, weaving in and out between them. He could still hear the angry Pharisee far behind him repeatedly screaming, "Stop that Levite! Stop him!" Up ahead more red-clad guards were running to take up positions at the two courtyard gates, attempting to head off Jake at the exits. All the escape routes quickly were slamming shut.

At that very moment, Jake saw his portly friend Pharisee Obadiah ambling through one of the gates up ahead, on his way into the Temple complex. As he ran, Jake pulled back his Levite turban so

Obadiah could see his face. Obadiah, in surprise, recognized Jake and quickly sized up the desperate situation. Two Temple guards started to block the gate out of the Court of the Gentiles, where Obadiah had just entered. Obadiah pretended to stumble, his black Pharisee robes flailing. He purposely tumbled right into the path of the pair of guards. Obadiah's massive, round body tripped up the two guards and they both sprawled out onto the stone pavement. Jake raced right past the sprawling heap of men and sprinted down the steps of the exit and out of the Temple confines through the Double Gate.

Once in the street, Jake never stopped running until he was safely away. He knew he had to ditch the Levite robes as fast as he could. He and Hannah had planned for a bizarre situation such as this. They prearranged a rendezvous point at a small restaurant three blocks from the Temple enclosure. She would have Jake's old beggar's disguise waiting for him.

The detective dashed the three blocks and ducked into the alley next to the restaurant. As Hannah waited in the café, she saw Jake wiz past the eatery and she rushed out into the alley to meet him.

"Hurry, throw that beggar's cloak over these Levite robes," Jake told the girl, as he pulled off the turban from his head. "I'll tuck the turban under my cloak."

"Here's your ugly mop of horsehair to complete your scruffy look," Hannah smiled. "There, now you look just like your old grubby self."

"Thanks, Hannah," he gasped, still sucking in air rapidly. "You saved my life. They are hot on my tail. Let's get back to the office."

As the two of them emerged from the alley onto the street, two angry Temple guards rushed toward them. The guards were red faced and furious and out of breath. As they ran, they slowed down to give Jake and Hannah a good look. The guards stopped with puzzled expressions on their faces.

Hannah watched them halt and quickly said in a charming voice, "I'm just trying to help this poor, old beggar find his way." Jake had his head down, hunched over, with the mop of horsehair covering most of his face.

Both guards grunted, as they tried to catch their breath. They quickly scrutinized this pretty girl and this ugly tattered beggar man. "Listen, we're trying to catch a fake Levite! So, if you see one, you come and tell us!"

"Okay," Hannah's voice floated in a singsong tone. "I hope you find him."

The guards raced on down the street. Jake looked up at Hannah and pulled back the mop of hair from his face. He glared at her in feigned disgust. "I hope you find him?" he mocked her in a high-pitched voice. "Really? I came this close to having my head knocked off and you go around making jokes."

"Well, I had to do something to throw them off our trail," she countered in a whisper. "They were bearing down on us like a couple of birddogs hot on a scent."

"I know, Hannah, you did the right thing." Jake still was gasping for breath.

"Come on, Jake, we've got to get out of here," she said quietly, as she glanced over her shoulder. "The guards are still in sight"

The couple hurried through streets. "Hannah, you just don't know what I've been through," Jake gasped as they walked quickly. "It's gonna take some time for me to calm down."

The girl's pretty brown eyes softened. "Jake, I'm so very glad you're safe. Let's get back to the office. I really do want to find out what happened to you."

Safely back in the office, Jake, in heated and exasperated terms, spewed out his whole wild yarn to Hannah. He frantically paced around the office, waving his arms, spouting out all the shocking blow-by-blow details. The girl sat in her chair, blown away by Jake's harrowing, near-death tale. Her beautiful suntanned face turned pinkish-white as the horror spread out before her. When Jake had finally spit out all the grisly facts, he collapsed into his leather chair, exhausted. Hannah stared blankly at the detective as she sat braced in the armchair, unable to say a word.

Finally, she mustered the words, "Can I get you a glass of water?"

Chapter 6

SORRY TO DISAPPOINT YOU, SIR

At about four o'clock, later that afternoon, Jake sat at his desk still trying to recover his wits. He was impatiently waiting for Hannah to return. He had sent her on a mission. He heard the door to the main corridor open and he called out, "Hannah, is that you?"

"It's me," she called back. "I did what you asked."

Hannah stepped into the outer office with a guest in tow. Jake could see them come in and he stepped around his desk to greet them. The girl walked through the detective's office door with her visitor.

"Here he is, Jake," she announced. "Pharisee Nicodemus. You asked me to go and bring him here, so here he is."

"Welcome, sir," Jake smiled. "Please come in and take a chair."

Hannah started to close the door to go back to her office but Jake stopped her.

"Wait, Hannah, I want you to stay in this meeting with us," he said with an eager expression. "You've already heard my extraordinary tale, but I want you to hear it again. After all, we're all involved in this situation together."

The girl pleasantly smiled. "Don't you think I should be in my office to guard the door? You know, anybody could just walk into my office and then overhear our conversation."

"You are absolutely right," Jake commended her. "Just lock the door to the hallway and then come back in here."

Hannah hurried into her office and locked the hallway door after first checking the corridor for anyone who might be prowling around. She came back into Jake's office and closed his office door.

"There, I think we're ready, now," Hannah said, as she sat down in a second chair in Jake's office.

"Good girl," the detective smiled at her. Then turning to Nicodemus, "See, that's why I keep her around. She thinks of all the details and keeps me straight."

"And I know you'll be keeping her around for a long time," Nicodemus said to Jake, as he looked over at Hannah.

"Yes, sir, that is very much my plan," Jake smiled. "Now, to get down to business …" Jake started to say but the Pharisee interrupted him.

"Jake, before you tell me anything else, I want to make a statement," Nicodemus said. "On the way here to your office, Ms. Haggai told me that you actually entered to restricted area of the temple, the Court of the Priests. If I had known you would do that, I would never have asked you to go on this extraordinarily dangerous mission."

"Well, that wasn't my original plan. I sorta got roped into crossing over into the Court of the Priests by a real Levite! But it all worked out okay. God protected me and I got the information I needed."

"But you know Jewish law," the gentleman lamented. "You took too great a risk for that information! You were in jeopardy of instant death."

"Sir, I assure you, it was well worth the risk," Jake stated. "The information I did get is very valuable. I know I was in danger. My stint as a Levite was a crazed idea, I admit that. I've never done anything this outrageous before in my whole life. But it was totally worth the risk for the information I got!"

Nicodemus sat in the armchair, slowly, sadly shaking his head. "Still yet, I should have never asked you to endanger your life like that."

"No, no. Don't feel that way. It all turned out okay. Let me tell you what I learned. My Levite experience didn't last very long but it was long enough to discover some troubling news about the way some of the oppressors are thinking. There are several young, elite hotheads in the religious ranks that have extremely vicious plans as to how they can stomp out Christianity. I overheard a small group of them and the indication is that there are many more of them. Maybe a large number of them. And I discovered something else as equally shocking. You remember the young student of Gamaliel that you wanted to speak to about trying to coexist with our Christian movement? His name is Saul of Tarsus."

"Yes, and I did get to speak to him. Saul of Tarsus seems to be a very fine young man and a brilliant Biblical scholar."

"Well, I'm sorry to disappoint you, sir," Jake slowly stated. "Saul of Tarsus may be a brilliant Biblical scholar but he is not a fine young man. He has shown himself to be one of the most violent-minded of all the religious oppressors that I heard speaking this morning."

"No! I don't believe it!" Nicodemus exclaimed bolting straight up in his chair. "You must be wrong, sir!"

"You must believe it!" Jake insisted. "I heard his vicious rantings from his own lips!"

"How can that be?" Nicodemus asked, stunned in shock. "When we spoke together the other day, Saul seemed very receptive and obliging to what his teacher, Gamaliel, had taught him. He also agreed to what I was recommending should be the graceful approach of the religious leaders toward Christianity."

"Well, his attitude in your presence must have been a ruse, acting like he was agreeing with you. I'm sorry, Nicodemus. From what I heard him say today, he may emerge to be one of the major aggressors of the church. His plans are quite ugly toward all Christians. Intimidation. Bullying. Arrests. He is even talking about executions of Christians."

Nicodemus lowered his head and gripped the arms of the armchair tightly. "I can't believe it," he sadly said, shaking his head. "I really thought we had a champion for our cause in Saul of Tarsus. How can this be? He has had the absolute best teacher in all Israel, Gamaliel. How could he betray all of his privileged education, so carefully taught to him by his revered teacher?"

"I guess we all have to make our own choices about what we are taught," Jake stated frankly. "Sometimes, as the Proverb says, 'bad friends corrupt good morals and good teaching.' Maybe something snaps in a person's brain and they flip out into an entirely different course. Who knows what happened to Saul. But the fact is, from what I overheard today, Saul is going to be one of the main adversaries against us."

Nicodemus looked up at Jake. "Then we must pray," Nicodemus stated. "We must pray for wisdom as to how to approach this new threat. But more importantly, we must pray for Saul of Tarsus that God would get hold of him and change his heart."

"We can pray for God to change Saul's heart, but I'm still going to dig into Saul's life and history," Jake stated. "A good detective always needs to know all he can about his target. Data. I need data."

Chapter 7

THE CASE OF THE GOVERNMENT CLIENT

With the specter of a violent Saul roaming the streets threatening Christians, Jake had plenty to think about. His focus on Saul's simmering anger consumed the detective's every waking thought. But suddenly, without warning, a new, menacing threat crashed down right on top of Jake! Out of nowhere, a fiendish, ruthless tyrant invaded Jake's life and demanded that he become the detective's next client!

It had been about a week after Jake's hair-raising Levite caper at the Temple. It was a Tuesday. On this fateful day, Hannah rushed into Jake's office with a frightful urgency graven on her face. In her hand, she clutched a high-grade parchment note. The note had all the trappings of being an official Roman government document. Hannah's pretty face was flushed pink; her brown eyes stark with anxiety. Clearly this note clasped in her hand was much more than a normal business memo.

She slid the note across the desk to Jake. "Jake," she choked, "there is a very large, mean-looking Roman soldier standing in the outer office. He handed me this note and demanded that you come with him ... immediately."

Jake raised his thick, black eyebrows, in surprise, and rubbed his chin with the back of his thumb. "He didn't say what this is all about?"

"No, and this soldier looks very stern, like he really means business. Please read the note. Now."

Jake unfolded the memorandum, which was folded in half. Jake read it out loud, "Governor Pontius Pilate summons you to his residence in the Praetorium immediately."

"This sounds serious. Looks like I'd better find out what this is all about," Jake stated as he stood up.

"Yes. You need to go, right now," Hannah urged. "That soldier out there at my desk doesn't look very friendly and he doesn't seem very patient, either."

"Okay, I hate to delay my investigation about Saul but it looks like I'm going to have to, for the moment," Jake said. Then he jokingly glanced at the girl and teased, "If I don't come back from the Praetorium soon, send my regards to my family."

"Hey! That's not at all funny!" Hannah retorted, with no smile on her face. "Don't forget, I'm family, too – or I will be in the near future. So, no more clowning around. You know how cruel and violent Pilate can be. When you walk in there, you be a perfect gentleman. Be on your very best behavior. Do you hear me? You mean too much to me to be joking around about you not coming back."

"I'm sorry, angel" Jake soothed. "I didn't mean to get you up tight. And I will be on my best behavior when I am around Pilate, as polite and courteous as I know how. I promise. I have no idea what he would want to see me about. Pray for me while I'm gone and the Lord will protect me."

"You know I will do that! I'm always praying for you. When you're out there among the criminals. And now this ... when you've got to go and face our erratic, vicious governor. Until you get back safe to me, I'll be praying hard for you."

"Thanks, I appreciate that. I guess I'd better get goin'. Pilate wants to talk to me. I'll find out what this is all about." As he started to leave, he turned around. "Hannah, keep your nose to the ground on the Saul of Tarsus case. Don't put that case on the back burner.

Don't let it go cold. Too much is riding on keeping on top of that investigation."

Jake nervously waited in Pilate's outer office for several minutes. The menacing Roman soldier who had escorted him there remained standing at Jake's side until the detective was called in to see the governor himself. Several minutes dragged past as Pilate's office military adjutant made the announcement to Pilate that Jake was waiting to see him.

"Mister Jezreel. I am the governor's personal deputy," the military adjutant stated firmly to Jake. "Governor Pilate will see you, now." He ushered the detective toward the governor's office door. As he opened the door, the adjutant quietly growled an order to Jake, "Remember who you are addressing. This is Governor Pilate. You *will* address him with respect and honor."

As Jake apprehensively stepped into the well-furnished office of the governor, Pilate sat behind his ornate desk with two Roman government officials standing nearby. The two officials, dressed in maroon uniforms, both looked like burly body guards.

The military adjutant addressed Pilate, "Sir, this is the private detective, Jacob Jezreel, you wanted to speak with." The adjutant pointed toward Jake.

"Thank you," Pilate's gruff voice rattled. "That will be all."

The adjutant departed and closed the door.

"Mister Jezreel," Pilate stated while remaining seated. He scrutinized Jake with a stern stare. His eyes were hard and black. His mouth set gravely in a firm straight line. Pilate's modest build projected a well put together man, who seemed to be physically fit. Jake had heard stories about Pilate's military service and figured that Pilate's soldier training had contributed to his fit appearance.

Pilate's grating voice continued, "I've never met you in person, but it is good to finally meet you. You have done detective work for me recently and you did a very commendable job."

"Thank you, sir," Jake said, in a subdued voice, realizing he stood before the premier representative of the powerful authority of the

Roman government. Jake remained standing directly across the desk from the governor. "It was my great pleasure to serve you."

"And serve me well," Pilate continued. "It is based on your past performance in doing such a fine piece of detective work for me that I have called upon you once again to ply your investigative skills in solving a particularly thorny problem that I have at this present time."

"It will be my pleasure, sir."

Pilate stood up. His cream-colored tunic was draped with a long, red outer cloak. "Please take a chair," he said, signaling to the decorative chair across the desk from him. The governor then spoke to the two muscular body guards standing next to him. "You two are dismissed for the time being. I want to meet with this man in private. I'll call you when I need you."

The two body guards stared hesitantly at Pilate. Jake could tell they were not comfortable with leaving the governor alone with this stranger.

"Go ahead and go, men" Pilate smiled, gesturing to them to move on out of the office. "I don't think I have anything to fear from this detective."

The two brawny men exited the office and closed the door behind them.

Pilate sat down and looked at Jake for a long moment, surveying the detective's appearance. "You don't look like a detective. You look like a regular guy. Is there no special look that defines you as a detective?"

"No, sir. Sometimes being just a regular guy is my key to success in investigating. I can get into places and not rouse anybody's suspicions."

"That is interesting," the governor mused. "You see, the fact that your appearance is that of a regular guy is the very reason I need you for this job I want you to do for me. None of my people could do this job. They are all too well known around Jerusalem and its surroundings."

"So, you need an unknown face to pull off this job, is that right?"

"Something like that."

"Sir, let me remind you that as a private detective, I have numerous informants and snitches out on the street, who know me by sight," Jake hesitantly stated.

"Could that fact be a problem for you?" the governor asked. "One of them might find out what you are investigating and spread the word?"

"That is the danger I might face," Jake said. "However, if I needed to get information from one of my snitches, I would never tell them the real reason for my investigation. And I would only use my most trusted informants."

"Is there such a thing as a 'trustworthy' informant?"

Jake smiled. "You'd be surprised, sir. I have built up a great friendship with a few of them. They may be a little unethical in their dealings in society but they are reliable when it comes to passing on information off the street. Especially when I slip a few coins into their hands."

"I see," Pilate grinned. "Sounds like the way we do business here in the government. Tell me this, if I were to ask you to do some undercover work for me, how would you go about it?"

"First of all, I'd need to know as much as you can tell me about the problem you are facing. I'd need to know all you can tell me about that person involved, also. Then I'd take it from there as to how I would approach this problem."

"I see," Pilate repeated.

"Sir, what is the problem that I can help you with?" the detective asked, leaning forward in his chair.

Pilate started to speak but stopped abruptly. He stood up. He looked sharply at Jake.

"This is private information. Highly sensitive. The information I am about to tell you must never be repeated to another living soul. Is that understood?" He stood there leaning on his hands on his desk with a menacing scowl on his face, staring at Jake. "I have not told any of my staff or confidants about this. In fact, I have told no one else, except my wife, this information I am about to tell you. No one. Therefore, if somehow this information which I tell you leaks out into public knowledge, I will know that you were the one who leaked it. And if that happens ... well, you can only guess how quickly I will end your life." The stunned impact of Pilate's deadly threat knocked Jake back in his chair. "There will be no room for failure, Mr. Jezreel," the governor's grating voice continued. "You must be successful. You will not fail me."

Pilate stared fiercely at Jake, narrowing his eyes and, from his standing position, tilting menacingly closer, leaning over his desk on his outstretched arms.

As Jake sat there with Pilate hovering over him, he could feel the cold steel in Pilate's black eyes drilling into him. He felt nervous sweat start to bead on his forehead and his hands suddenly grew clammy. Sweat started to run down his back. Pilate's deadly warning was deadly clear.

"Sir, I won't fail you. I stake my professional reputation on it."

"Good man. I need more men like you," Pilate stated.

The governor sat down and pulled a papyrus note out of his desk drawer. He looked squarely at Jake, "I have very powerful political enemies. Some of my political enemies are in very high government places. A man in my position will cultivate many enemies as the years pass. Some of my enemies want to throw me out of power. Not only throw me out but to destroy me. They want my job as governor. They try subterfuge and political maneuvering to try to destroy and defame me. They are dangerous, deceitful, treacherous people. However, I can deal with these people. I can win those political battles.

"But there are other enemies who are even worse snakes. These adversaries attack me from the blindside. They even attack me by attacking my family."

Pilate paused and leaned over his desk toward Jake. "I am being blackmailed," he stated point-blank.

"Blackmailed?" Jake softly asked. "By who? What does the blackmailer have on you?"

"It's not me," Pilate stated, as he fumbled with the papyrus paper on his desk. "The blackmailer says he has damaging evidence concerning my wife and her family. Naturally, the intention of my enemy is to destroy me, if I do not meet his terms."

"What are his terms?"

"10,000 denarii in ransom."

Astonishment flashed across Jake's face.

Pilate saw the shock on Jake's face. "Yes, that is exactly the same shock I received when I opened the note," Pilate grumbled. "10,000 denarii is a princely sum. A lifetime's oncome for the common man. Of course, I can pay it. But I don't trust this snake to honor his word and give me the information in question even if I do pay the ransom."

"So, how can I help you, governor?"

"The blackmailer claims to have certain letters in his possession that would be damaging to me," Pilate forcefully stated, as he stood up. "I want you to get those letters from him."

Jake nearly choked. He swallowed hard. He paused and canted his head as he stared at the governor. "Get the letters?" Jake repeated.

"Yes, I'm not going to oblige this political parasite by agreeing to his ransom," Pilate snarled. "I'll outsmart him by sending you to take the letters away from him!"

Jake swallowed even harder. He could feel his blood draining to his feet. Pilate had just told him that failure was never an option. And Pilate had just emphasized how short his deadly temper could be!

"I believe this extortion note was written by the blackmailer himself," Pilate stated. "I believe I recognize his handwriting. There is no signature. But I recognize his scribble. The extortioner brashly appears to think he is very clever and extremely confident he can get away with his blackmail."

"May I see the extortion note?" Jake asked, as he tried to control his trembling voice.

"I'll do better than that," Pilate gruffly said. "I'll tell you the whole story, so you don't miss any detail.

"Years ago, my wife's father was an officer in the army of Emperor Tiberius. My wife's father at that time was married with a young family but he had a problem of being a little hot-tempered. Rather impulsive. He became irritated with the way the army was being administered. He had been in several battles and had seen some of his friends get killed in action. He determined that the obvious reason for his friends being killed in battle was due to incompetence and gross deficiency of military leadership. He blamed Emperor Tiberius for installing incompetent generals, which led to the incompetent mismanagement of the army, which ultimately caused the death of his friends.

"To vent his anger and frustration, my wife's father wrote several angry letters to a close officer friend in the army. In those letters he criticized Tiberius and his lack of good judgment. He was simply blowing off steam to a sympathetic comrade in arms. Officers will do such things. He got it off his chest. And it made him feel better, even though he knew his letters would not change a thing.

"Now, today, my wife's father … my father-in-law … is a high ranking official in Rome in the government. And he frequently has government dealings with Tiberius. He has a good reputation in his government transactions. He has many sophisticated and cultured friends and associates. His derogatory letters about Tiberius have long been forgotten. Or so he thought."

Pilate rose from his chair and began pacing back and forth in uninhibited exasperation. "Somehow my father-in-law's letters have fallen into the hands of one of my greatest enemies. This enemy's official title is Lucius Taurus. It's a good name for him – he's like a raging bull! I don't know how he got his filthy hands on those letters. Perhaps he found them, bought them, who knows how. My father-in-law thought his letters had been discarded on the trash heap. Perhaps that is where Taurus found them. It would be just like Taurus to squalor around in a trash heap. He is that kind of viper."

Pilate stopped pacing around and squarely gazed at Jake. "Well, detective, does that make any sense to you? Do you get the picture?"

Jake raised his eyebrows, indicating he did get the picture. "Yes, sir, I've got it. You know for sure that this Taurus character could destroy you with these letters?"

"He would and he will," Pilate said flatly. "He knows he can show the derogatory letters to Tiberius and Tiberius would be greatly insulted. Taurus would then prosecute a case for Tiberius to summon my father-in-law to face the Emperor in a trial. And Taurus could then have the ultimate revenge on me and sue to have me replaced as governor and then summon me to Rome to face trial, as well."

Jake thought for a moment, rubbing the back of his thumb on his chin. "So, instead of taking the letters to the Emperor, this Taurus character figures to use the letters to extort money from you," Jake surmised. "He's already put the squeeze on you to apply as much pain on you as he can."

"That is the exact picture of this whole mess. And I know my enemy. He will never stop squeezing me, no matter how much I pay him. He will bleed me dry if he can."

Jake looked at Pilate, not knowing if he should be frightened or sympathetic. He knew the governor was a harsh, ruthless man, at times being brutal in his dealings with the Jewish people. Jake also knew that his own life wouldn't be worth a plug nickel if he failed in delivering the letters to Pilate. But he also saw a man in desperation.

One thing puzzled the detective.

"Why all the animosity between you and Lucius Taurus?" Jake asked.

"Taurus has always been jealous of my success," Pilate said, as he sat back down in his chair. He spread his arms out wide. "All our lives, we both have been rivals. Throughout our military careers, in political life, and even over this position of governor. He is an incompetent, useless rat with the heart of a snake and the brain of the evil one. He never could succeed on his own because of his maniacal ignorance. The only way he has been able to survive is that he finds gullible, benevolent sponsors to pay his way. And now he thinks he has hit upon a goldmine with this blackmail scheme. But he is not going to succeed in extorting money from me. You, Mr. Jezreel, will see to that!"

Jake expression had turned ashen. He could feel Pilate's icy noose tightening around his own sweaty neck.

"What's the matter, detective," Pilate smiled, "you look a little pale. You're not worried, are you?"

"Oh, no," Jake choked. "I'm just sitting here imagining how I'm going to pull off this impossible task."

"We don't use the word 'impossible' around here," Pilate ominously stated, narrowing his eyes again and leaning forward over his desk. "You will get those letters for me. We will cover up this incriminating evidence and keep it from getting spread out to the public. Tiberius will never know those letters existed. He will never see them. Even if Taurus tries to tell him about them, Taurus will have no proof! I will have the letters! My family's secret will be safe. I will be safe! And I will not be publicly humiliated, thanks to you."

Jake shifted uncomfortably in his ornate chair. Pilate's seemingly unreasonable expectations began to crush in upon the detective.

"Sir, where is Taurus at the present time? Will I have to travel to Rome?" Jake asked.

"No, no. Nothing that drastic. He has deliberately come to Jerusalem from Rome to stay for a short time for the sole purpose of harassing and irritating me to blackmail me. He is living right here in Jerusalem at a Pharisee's residence on Hebron Street. The Pharisee's name is Jathniel."

"Hum, I don't know this Pharisee Jathniel," Jake replied. "He may be one of the crooked religious politicians we seem to have in abundance here in Jerusalem."

"I've had Jathniel checked out already," Pilate interjected, "and, yes, he is a crooked politician."

"How does the note say you are to pay Taurus' blackmailer ransom?"

"The note doesn't say. That is Taurus' way of tormenting me. But you'll surprise him and confront him personally."

"Are you not concerned that Taurus might tell Jathniel about the extortion letters?"

"Listen, I know the rat I'm dealing with," Pilate growled. "Taurus wants all the money for himself. In his puny, evil, corrupt brain, he wants to reserve all the pleasure of seeing me tortured by his malicious scheme." Pilate stood up and bared his teeth and his hands deformed into vice-like, ugly claws. "Taurus wants to personally put me in a vice and apply as much pressure to me as he can to hurt me as much as possible. If he shared his devious plans with Jathniel, he would have to share some of the loot with Jathniel. Taurus would never do that. He would never share his maniacal hatred with anybody. Never! So, to answer your question, no, I am not concerned that Taurus would share his blackmailing scheme with anyone else. And even if he did share his plans, you will already have taken the letters from him and he will have no evidence to accuse anyone of anything!"

As Pilate spoke, Jake's mind began churning.

Suddenly a spark of a thought hit Jake's brain! He sat back deeper in his chair, half closing his eyes, visualizing the new idea. He crossed his arms and brought one hand up to thoughtfully rub his chin. As he gazed at Pilate, Jake slowly shook his head, as the thought began to swirl in his mind. He looked down at the floor, squinting his eyes, squeezing the thought through the passages of his brain. There. He could see the plan. It looked like a good plan in the mists of his mind. It was still a fuzzy image but he knew this plan could work. It would have to work!

"Governor, I believe I've got a strategy," Jake said confidently. "I've still got to map out all the particulars in my mind but I believe this plan will work!"

"That is the kind of confidence I want to hear!" Pilate exclaimed, as he sat back down behind his desk.

"I will work out the details and fill you in on what I am going to do."

"No, I don't want to know how you will get the letters," Pilate stated. "Just get them for me. I have all the assurance in you."

"If I might ask, how many letters are there?"

"I have been told by my father-in-law there were four letters all together."

"Hopefully, all the letters are in one place and I can scoop them up all at once."

"My wife will be relieved," said Pilate with a smile. "I'll go and tell her the good news!"

Chapter 8

GRAPPLING WITH A SNAKE

As Jake left Pilate's office, he could feel the governor's ominous noose slung around his neck. There was no time for long deep investigative analysis. Speed now was the top priority. Jake had to move fast. His neck depended on it!

Jake's plan was simple. If Lucius Taurus was tangled up in blackmail against Pilate, he probably was tangled up in some other crooked schemes. So, digging up dirt on Taurus became Jake's objective. The detective knew just the right guy he could count on to get the dirt.

Jake's world brought him into frequent contact with shady, underworld characters. In this criminal environment, the detective relied on several snitches he knew would help him. But he had one particular informant in mind, Pudge the Pickpocket.

Pudge was one of Jake's most reliable snitches in Jerusalem. He was a gentleman, even though he was a thief. Jake was confident Pudge could scour the back alleys and dig up the dirt he needed to solve Pilate's problem. Now the trick was to find the thief.

Jake took a deep breath and plunged down into the bowels of the sleazy, slums of Jerusalem in search of Pudge. Somewhere in the back of his mind Jake remembered that the petty thief hid out on Kidron Street, a dirty, dark alley hidden away from society. Kidron Street reeked of the stench of garbage in the street. The filthy alley meant nothing but trouble but Jake was desperate for help. Every unsavory type of human squalor and deprivation existed in this part of the city. It was a haven full of cut throats and thugs of every description. It was a treacherous place.

Jake saw a shadowy, familiar figure propped up against a grungy brick building next to a stinking gutter filled with black sewage. It was a creepy bum known as Mad Dog. Jake approached carefully, since Mad Dog had his head down, apparently in a daze, looking down at the filthy pavement.

"Mad Dog?" Jake asked in an uneasy manner.

The shadowy figure slowly looked up and slid out a gleaming, iron knife from under his cloak. "Yeah, whadya want?" he growled extending the knife out where Jake could see it better.

"Mad Dog, it's me, Jake Jezreel," he soothed raising his hands.

"Yeah, I knowd who ya is, flatfoot. Whadya want?" The sneering words of the sinister form came from beneath a cloak covering his head. Jake could barely see the thug's grimy face.

"I'm trying to find Pudge," Jake quietly said.

"Why, ya wanna put a shiv into him?" Mad Dog snarled. "I can do dat fer ya fer a few coins."

"No, no! No blade work today," Jake said trying to calm the erratic man. "I've got a job for Pudge. Have you seen him?"

"Whad about me," growled Mad Dog in a low groan, "I kin do any job Pudge kin do. I kin even do it better. And I'll take ya money just as good as he will."

"This job involves a lot of investigation," Jake stated trying to discourage Mad Dog. "It involves tracking down some difficult information."

Mad Dog's blank stare grew even blanker. "Fahget about it," he mumbled, putting away his blade. "I ain't doin' nothin' like that, nothin' that would involve work. Especially some loony snitching where I got ta work hard fah da dough." He glared at Jake a moment longer with his bloodshot eyes and then muttered, "The las' time I seed Pudge he was gamblin' wid some jokers down on da corner."

"Thanks, Mad Dog," Jake said, skirting around the creepy bum and heading down the filthy street.

"Hey, chiseler!" Mad Dog lashed out. "Ain'tcha furgettin' somethin'?" Mad Dog stuck out his grubby hand. "You'd better line my paw with some scratch. Remembah, I still got dis shiv under my cloak."

"Oh, yeah. Sorry, you know I always pay off, Mad Dog", Jake apologized, as he dropped a few coins into the shadowy character's grimy mitt. "Gotta go. I'm in a big hurry. Thanks for the tip."

Down on the corner, Pudge was on his hands and knees, shooting dice with three other unsavory ruffians. Pudge's buddies were all minor league creeps. The alleyway was so narrow that the height of the buildings blocked the sunlight, making the passageway dark, even though it was about one o'clock in the afternoon.

One of the ruffians, Greasy, looked around as Jake approached them. "Watch out, boys, there's a private eye comin'." Greasy stood up and confronted Jake. "Well, I see the gumshoe has come to visit us high class folks of society. Kinda outa your game, ain't ya, shamus? We heerd you been workin' for them Pharisees. You must really be hard up, scrapin' the bottom of the barrel. I pity you, workin' for them hypocrites."

"Yeah, it ain't no picnic, workin' for the religious crowd," Jake said. "Sometimes I think I must have gone delirious for takin' any case workin' with them. Sometimes I think they ain't human." The detective looked down at Pudge, still on his hands and knees. "Pudge. Can I talk to you?"

"Don't you do it, Pudge!" Greasy exclaimed. "He's workin' for them Pharisees. Five will get ya ten he'd sell ya out! He'll get you arrested!"

The other two hooligans, Squinty and Weasel, stood up to confront Jake. "Git lost, flatfoot," one of them snarled. "If you're workin' for them Pharisee clowns, you ain't welcome 'round here, no more."

"Yeah," the other thug growled.

Jake coolly laughed at them all with a nonchalant smile. "Man, I don't know where you cats get your bogus news but you guys are way, way, way behind the times. The Pharisees fired me months ago – a long time ago – for insubordination. They booted me 'cause I wouldn't lie for them and tell them what they wanted to hear."

"Zat so," Greasy schmoozed. "Booted ya, huh. Guess ya wouldn't cozy up to 'em."

"Nah, I wouldn't. The facts that I had discovered didn't match up to their forgone accusations. So, it was, 'scram, get outa here', and I was fired."

The sleazy group backed off. "Oh, okay. Good riddance, I'd say," Greasy muttered. "So, whatsya wanna see Pudge about?"

"The usual stuff." Jake was being evasive. "I'm working a case. I need to see if he'll give me some help."

Pudge stood up. "Hey, Jake. I need to quit dis game anyways. I wadn't winnin' nuthun no way. What's up?"

Pudge was a squatty little man, stocky and plump. Not at all what a person would think of as an elusive, quick-on-his-feet pickpocket. His proud motto was, "I'm short and outa most people's sight. I can git in and outa places before people even knowd I bin there." Such close in "work" required good concentration and attention to details. The job Jake had for the pickpocket required the same focused attentiveness to the task at hand and fit right into Pudge's mindset.

"Pudge, let's talk over here." Jake pointed down Kidron Street to a smelly, rotting garbage pile several yards away. As they walked down the alley, Jake said, "The job I've got for you is a very important one. It involves doing some nosing around, asking questions of some of your associates."

"Associates!" Pudge laughed. "I love it whin ya trow dem big words around about my friends."

"Well, they *are* your associates and I need some important information from them."

"Okay, hit me wid yo bes shot."

"Pudge I've got to find out as much dirt as you can dig up about a crook called Lucius Taurus."

Pudge's face lit up immediately. "Lucius Taurus! He is a snake! He's a four-flusher, a cheat, a swindler! Sure, I knowd all about him. He don't live here in Jerusalem. He lives in Rome. But he does come to Jerusalem from Rome ev'y so of'en. And when he's in town, we all slide him da cold shoulder. We don't want nothin' to do with him. He's poison. We all call him 'Slither' 'cause he ain't to be trusted. He *is* a snake.

"He's one of them pretty boys that's got sponsors backing him. But we all know his main racket is blackmail and being a dirty, low-down rat. He makes the rest of us criminals embarrassed by his sleezy chiseling."

"Sounds like a nice playmate. You say part of his racket is blackmail," Jake stated with a straight face, trying not to act too interested.

"Yah, but that ain't all he does. He swindles money from wealthy merchants and important people on the sly. He don't do it himself. He pays somebody – one of my associates – to steal da money fur him. He pays cold cash for somebody to steal the money. It's quick money. 'Course, if his stooge gets caught, Slither don't know nothin' about nothin'. He leaves his partner-in-crime rot in jail."

"How many of your associates have done criminal jobs for Slither?"

"Not many. There's bin a few. Like I said, Slither can't be trusted. He's poison. So most all of us avoid him like the plague."

"I see," Jake smiled. "And I don't suppose any of these buddies would come forward to testify against old Slither."

Pudge glared at Jake sideways. "Are you kiddin'! That would be suicide – putting their own necks in the noose."

"Sorry, I must have been delusional for even asking such a silly question," Jake laughed. "Do any of your buds have anything that could be solid proof that would put Slither's neck in the noose."

"I don't know. If'n I could find dirt like that, I'd gladly scour it up and give it to ya. Anythun to git old Slither behind bars, whar he deserves ta be. I kin do some checkin' around. I'll hav ta git back wid ya on dat. But I'd wager ya twenty-three eighty that I can come up wit sumpun."

"You're a good man, Pudge," Jake laughed . "I appreciate it much more than you'll ever know."

Pudge stuck his hands up in a defensive motion. "Now, don't you go startin' no ugly rumors about me being good. You'll ruin my repatation."

"I won't. I wouldn't do a thing like that. Reputation is all important. Here, Pudge. Here is some money in advance, just in case you have to buy some information."

As Pudge sauntered off down the dingy street, Jake felt a good sensation knowing that maybe Pilate's noose may be loosening just a little around his neck.

The next morning, Hannah knocked on Jake's office door and stuck her head in the office.

"There's a short, pudgy little man at my desk and he says he needs to see you right away," she announced with an odd look on her face. "Is he one of your snitches? I've never seen him before."

"Yeah, angel," Jake smiled, "He's alright. I hope he's got the information I need. Shoo him in."

Hannah opened the door wide and Pudge moseyed into the office.

"Thank ya, purdy lady," Pudge happily said to Hannah. "It's bin a real pleasure ta meet ya!"

Hannah blushed and closed the door.

Pudge stood there gazing at the girl as she closed the door. Then he turned around with a wonderful look on his face. "Man, I need ta git a job in this here line of work. A purdy girl like that ta look at all day long. Wot a great job to have! I'd never leave my desk if I could look at a beauty like her from sunup to sundown."

"Put your eyes back into your head, Pudge," Jake smiled. "She's not just my secretary. She is my fiancée. And she is pretty, isn't she."

"Ooooeeee, she sure is," Pudge exclaimed. "But since she's yur girl, I'd better just shut my mouth."

"Well, don't shut your mouth for very long," Jake laughed. "I'm hoping you've got some good news for me."

"I believe I just might have something that could put a loop around old Slither's neck," Pudge chuckled. "I tol' ya I'd wager ya twenty-three eighty dat I could fine some dirt."

"And ..." Jake said trying to draw out the evidence

"I got some dirt," the pudgy man snickered.

"And ... is it good dirt?"

"Ooohh, yah!" Pudge's face glowed with the brilliance of satisfaction. "Dat rat made one, big, brainless blunder. He's always struttin' around, actin' so cleaver, but he forgot the basic rule in da crime game, 'cover your tracks'. He just got feelin' invincible and figured he was smarter than eva'body else. I guess he never thought he could git catched."

"C'mon, Pudge, quit stringin' me along. What do you got?"

"Just this. I done some snoopin' around and found somebody who would sell me some damagin' evidence." Pudge settled into the wooden armchair and made himself very comfortable.

"About a year ago, one of my good buds did a blackmail job for old Slither. My buddy saved the hand written instructions that Mr. Lucius Taurus had wrote out fur him. Can you imagine! A hand written note from Slither, hisself, with all the gory details about how my 'associate' wis to pull off da job. That wis Slither's fatal mistake. He should hav never wrote out the instructions. He should hav just told my buddy how to deliver da ransom note and how ta collect the extortion money. Dat hand written note is da clincher! Dat note is all the evidence you'll need ta get old Slither on the hook and send him down the river!"

"That is incredible, Pudge!" the detective exclaimed. "And you've got the hand written note with you?"

"Does Monday follow Sunday? Of, course I got it" Pudge chuckled. "I got it right here in my pouch. It cost me some coin but it was your dough, anyways."

Pudge reached into a small, leather pouch tied to his belt and pulled out a tan, crumpled piece of papyrus. It was folded several times. As Pudge unfolded the papyrus, he announced, "This should be what you're lookin' fur." He handed the paper to Jake.

Jake's eyes grew large and bright. He read the note and reread it to be sure this was the real deal.

"This is it!" shouted the detective, as he jumped up out of

his chair. "And you're sure this is written in Lucius Taurus' own handwriting?"

"Absolutely sure," Pudge proudly announced. "I'd stake my professional repatation on it! And notice at da bottom it's signed by a dude named Maximus. Pro'bly a code name.'"

"Man, you have found exactly what I need!" the detective shouted. "This piece of papyrus is more valuable to me than a million denarii. Maybe more! Pudge you have just saved my life!" Jake shook Pudge's hand vigorously. "Man, thank you, thank you, thank you!"

"Just tryin' to do a good day's work," the pudgy pickpocket smiled. "And did I hear ya say somethin' about a million denarii?" he joked, as he held out his mitt.

By nine o'clock the next morning Jake stood on the front door step of Pharisee Jathniel's residence. After a few knocks on the door, the Pharisee appeared in the doorway.

"Good morning, Pharisee Jathniel. My name is Jake Jezreel. I understand that you have a guest staying with you named Lucius Taurus. I was hoping to speak with him if I could."

Pharisee Jathniel eyed Jake a little suspiciously. "For what purpose do you wish to see my guest?"

"I have something that belongs to him."

"Well, you can give it to me and I'll see that he gets it."

"No, this is something of a personal matter. I think he would really want me to talk personally to him about it."

A little exasperated, Jathniel grumbled, "Oh, very well. My guest is just now rising from bed. I'll let you in but it will be a minute before he can see you."

Jake stepped inside the plush, finely furnished house. *'So, this is where all the temple money goes,'* Jake thought to himself.

In a short while, Lucius Taurus strode confidently into the room. At first glance, Jake was struck by the evil appearance of the man standing before him. He was long and bony and his face had a pronounced v shape from the top of his forehead down to his sharp projecting chin. Even the age lines of his forehead dipped downward into v shapes. The nostrils of his thin, jutting nose were teeny slits.

His eye sockets were sunken, each in the v shape, only sideways, and the sockets hid black, sinister eyes. If Jake had ever seen an embodiment of Satan, this man was it.

Jake spoke first. "Good morning," he said cheerfully. "Am I addressing Lucius Taurus?"

"I am he," spoke the menacing man. "What can I do for you?"

"I have come at the request of Governor Pontius Pilate. He has asked me to come and retrieve some letters you have been negotiating with him about."

"Why have you come to me?" Taurus feigned ignorance. "I don't know what you're talking about."

"No need to pretend. Governor Pilate knows your handwriting and recognized it on the extortion note."

"I see. So, you are Pilate's emissary?" Taurus raised his eyebrows in an aloof expression.

"I am. So, once again I will state my business that I have come to retrieve the letters in question."

"Have you brought the money?" Taurus coldly stated.

"No, no money," Jake said pleasantly. "I don't need it."

"No money?" Taurus bristled. "Then beat it."

"Not without those letters."

"I told you to beat it – while you're still in good health."

"Okay," Jake agreed and turned to leave. But he turned back around to face the threatening man. "Oh, by the way, I have my sources in very low places that tell me that you have dealt with blackmail on other occasions."

"I don't have any idea what you are talking about," Taurus growled and edged closer toward Jake. "And keep your voice down. I don't want my illustrious host to hear these absurd, false accusations."

"Oh, I'll keep my voice down," Jake droned in a softer tone. "I don't need to yell. I'll just tell you straight out that I have in my possession a hand written note which you wrote, providing details to a criminal go-between on how to carry out a blackmail scheme which you devised a year ago."

Taurus choked in surprise. "What are you talking about."

"Just as I said. I've got the note. It's in your own handwriting. You were very helpful in detailing all aspects of how your confidant should carry out your extortion of a prominent citizen here in Jerusalem."

"Impossible. I wrote no such note," Taurus snarled.

"Oh, the note is in your handwriting. I can verify it. And it should be simple enough to get other samples of your handwriting to compare with the script on the note."

"You're bluffing," Taurus stammered, as fear crept over his face.

"No, this is no bluff. Oh, did I mention the note is signed by a person named Maximus?"

Taurus' face instantly turned pasty and white. He began to quiver. "How much do you want for the note?"

"Only the four letters that Pilate has asked for."

"That's all?"

"That's all."

Taurus' eyes glazed over. He dropped his head in defeat. He began to sway back and forth in disbelief.

"I thought I had him this time," he whined. "But no, not this time. My old nemesis, Pilate, has beaten me, once again." Taurus looked down at the floor in disgust. With a wave of his hand in resignation he said, "Just a minute. I'll go and get Pilate's letters."

Taurus, the blackmailer, walked across the room to a locked trunk sitting on the floor against a wall. He unlocked the trunk and pulled out four folded papyrus packets. He walked back over to Jake.

"Here are the four letters," he scowled, as he handed over the letters.

Jake took the letters. "This better be all of them," he commanded.

"It's all of them."

Jake shoved the letters securely into a leather pouch he had hanging from his belt.

Taurus looked puzzled. "Where's my note you said you have?"

"Oh, I've got it," Jake smiled. "But I never told you I would give it to you."

"What!" Taurus exclaimed softly.

"I never told you I'd give the note to you. I think I'll just keep it."

"Why you …" Taurus snarled. He took an angry step toward Jake but stopped short, as his host, Pharisee Jathniel walked into the room.

"Have you gentleman been able to discuss the matter at hand?" Jathniel asked happily.

"Oh, yes," Jake laughed. "Very satisfactorily."

Jake grinned at the fuming Lucius Taurus. "It has been a great pleasure to do business with you." And then he wheeled around and walked slowly out of the residence.

As Jake stepped out into the fresh air of the street outside, he breathed a tremendous sigh of relief. He felt the weight of the world – and Pilate's heavy hand – lifted off of him. He realized that with these letters tucked away in his belt also came his reprieve from the possible wrath of Pilate, if he had failed.

That same afternoon, the detective was welcomed into Pilate's office.

"I have your father-in-law's letters," Jake announced, as he laid the four papyrus packets on Pilate's desk. "I have not opened them to be sure they are the legitimate documents. But I know you will want to check them out. I am confident they are the genuine letters you asked for."

Pilate opened one of the packets and read some of the contents. His face expressed great relief. "Yes, yes! These are the letters I wanted! Thank you, Mr. Jezreel. Thank you very much. My family is indebted to you for saving us from terrible scandal and possible destruction. This indiscretion by my father-in-law can now be covered up forever and our political enemies will have nothing of which to accuse our family. Again, I say, my family is deeply indebted to you. And I am deeply indebted to you. I will not forget this great service you have provided to my family and to me."

"It has been my great pleasure to have served you," the detective halfway bowed.

"I want to pay you for your services," Pilate graciously said. "I will have my treasurer come by your office tomorrow to provide you with a generous payment."

"Thank you very much, your excellency," Jake smiled. "You are too kind." And as he was about to leave, he turned back around to the governor.

"Sir, there is just one more thing. I have here a papyrus note that really might be of great interest to you." From his leather pouch Jake pulled out Taurus' earlier blackmail note that Pudge had gotten for him. He laid it on Pilate's desk.

"This note actually turns the tables on Lucius Taurus. You might want to compare it to the extortion note Taurus sent to you. And you might want to get other samples of Taurus' handwriting and compare his handwriting on this note with other documents which Taurus has written. I can also produce a witness who will put the finger on Taurus as the writer. Do with the note as you wish. But it would seem to me that this note is enough proof for you to do anything you'd like to your old enemy. It looks like you now have the total advantage over Lucius Taurus."

Pilate looked at the note laying on his desk and opened it. His eyes grew bright with satisfaction. And then he looked up at Jake and smiled with a pleased smirk on his face.

"Sir, also notice the paper is signed by a person named Maximus," Jake stated pointing at the signature. "Is that a cryptic code name of some sort?"

Pilate quickly glanced down at the signature and stared at it for a long moment. A delighted smile spread across his face. Pilate looked up at Jake. "A cryptic code name? Yes! Maximus is a code name Taurus used back in Rome. Only a small, select few people ever knew about his code name. But I know it. He figured no one here in Jerusalem would ever connect him with that code name."

Pilate looked down at the note on his desk once again and then back up at Jake.

"Now I know without a doubt that I am truly indebted to you, Mister Jezreel," Pilate gratefully said as he stood up. "I will never forget this favor you have provided to me. If there is ever anything you need in the future, just let me know."

Chapter 9

THE HAMMER FALLS

A week later, Jake still was riding high over the outcome of "The Pontius Pilate Adventure", as he called it.

"Hannah, that case was so top secret I can't even tell you anything about my investigation," Jake laughed. "And I had to burn all my case notes just to get rid of all the evidence."

Jake could not stop smiling. "God, clearly gave me His wisdom and the help I needed to solve Pilate's problem."

The girl smiled. "Judging by the sack of silver coins that Pilate's treasurer dumped on my desk, I'd say that God truly did help you in that investigation!" she giggled.

"It was an incredible experience to watch God at work," the detective stated. "I could see Him guiding me in my thoughts. God is faithful."

"Well, if Pudge the Pickpocket had anything to do with the case, I know it had to be a real 'incredible experience'," Hannah laughed.

Several weeks after the Pilate Case, Jake and Hannah decided to enjoy a late lunch at a sidewalk table outside Josiah's Deli. The beautiful warm afternoon sunshine felt good. It was satisfying to get away from the office and take a break from Jake's current case, involving a bad-tempered family squabble over the estate of a deceased relative. One infuriated member of the quarrel had attacked some of the others and then fled the scene. Jake's job was to ferret out the attacker.

As they enjoyed Josiah's Blue Plate Special, the couple reveled in the miraculous ways the church of Jesus Christ was multiplying by leaps and bounds.

"Every day more and more folks are being added to the church," Hannah beamed. "It's fabulous!"

"Fabulous is right! I have heard some church leaders say they estimate there are over 200,000 Christians in Jerusalem!" Jake exclaimed.

"Bible studies and home churches keep popping up all over Jerusalem," the girl laughed.

"What surprises me is the unity among the believers," Jake said. "People from all different backgrounds and nationalities are coming to Christ. You remember just a few months ago, the number of Greek-speaking believers became so large that the apostles had to choose seven godly men to manage the ministry affairs of those Grecian believers."

"I do remember that," Hannah recollected. "They called them deacons. Stephen was one of those prominent men who were chosen."

"You know, I've heard good things about Stephen. He's proven to be a man of integrity. He is doing a great job ministering to the widows in that synagogue. That part of the church is growing so fast they're busting at the seams!"

"That's a great problem to have!" Hannah smiled. "When the numbers get too big and you have to get more help to manage each group of members, that is a really great problem!"

Jake and Hannah both burst out in laugher. The church was alive! Growing like wildfire!

Suddenly, right in the middle of their joyous laughter, the wonderful early afternoon bliss exploded into a fierce firestorm of chaos. A fellow Christian came running wildly down the street toward them, screaming. As he dashed past the man shrieked, "Stephen has just been stoned to death! God help us!" The man kept on running down the street and disappeared around a corner.

Jake stared at his secretary. "Stephen stoned to death?" the detective asked in disbelief. "We were just talking about him. Why would anybody want to stone him? He's a good man. His only desire is to help people."

Another man rushed desperately down the street in Jake's direction, "Stephen is dead! Stoned to death!"

Jake leaped out into the street and grabbed the man's arm to make him stop running.

"Man, what is going on?" he exclaimed.

"They just killed Stephen!" the man screamed breathlessly. "Lemme go!"

"Wait! Why was he killed? Who killed him?"

"The religious leaders!" the man gasped. "I don't know all that happened. I do know that Stephen was accused of some terrible crime and he was dragged in front of the Sanhedrin! Stephen witnessed to them about the Lord Jesus and the religious leaders went insane! Then they dragged Stephen outside the city and stoned him to death! I don't know what's gonna happen next but I know I'm gettin' outa town!" The man yanked away from Jake, wheeled around, and fled the scene in panic.

Jake walked slowly back to the sidewalk table where Hannah was now standing up. "Angel, I don't know what to think about all this. Probably the best thing to do is get back to the office and just lay low for a while."

As the couple started to head for the office, another man sprinted past them shouting, "Saul of Tarsus has gone mad! The religious leaders have all gone mad! They're coming after Christians! Run for your lives!"

"That does it!" Jake exclaimed to Hannah. "Saul's on the loose! Let's get outa here and off the street!"

As the couple reached the stairs leading up to Jake's office, fellow Christians were running and screaming in all directions, helter-skelter in terror. The streets swirled in a frantic uproar.

"Get up the stairs quick!" Jake yelled to Hannah.

At the top of the stairs, the pair ran down the second story corridor and ducked into the office. Jake locked the door behind them.

"We can lay low here for a while until we get this thing figured out," the detective quietly said to the girl.

Hannah's expression was set firm. "I guess we could see this day coming," she said matter-of-factly. "Nicodemus, Obadiah, Asa, they all warned us that the lid was about to blow off. The warning signs were all there. The jealousy and rage of the religious leaders has finally hit its limit."

"Yeah, but how far will they go in venting their anger?" Jake asked as he crawled across the floor of his office and peered over the window sill out into the street below. "How long will their harassment last?"

"Good question," Hannah answered as she crawled over and sat on the floor next to Jake with her back leaned up against the wall under the window. "Still sounds like a lot of screaming and yelling out in the street," she said listening to the chaos outside. "What do you think is happening?"

"Our friends are being chased down like dogs," Jake said in a hush. "All over the city ... hunted down like criminals."

"Oh, Lord, please help them and protect them," Hannah whispered.

As the couple sat on the floor frozen in time, listening to the pandemonium right outside their window, Jake sighed and looked up at the ceiling, deep in thought. "I can visualize the banner headline story in *The Jerusalem Times* tomorrow. 'On the very same day that the rebel Stephen was stoned to death, a great and oppressive persecution lashed out against the criminal Christian church in Jerusalem.' You're right, angel, we could have seen ... we should have seen this day coming. I should have ..." Jake's voice trailed off.

Several hours dragged past. Jake and Hannah sat quietly in the office on the floor leaned up against the wall under the window. They could hear turmoil outside their perch most of the afternoon. Toward the evening as darkness fell, the commotion below in the street seemed to subside.

Hannah looked over at the detective. "Jake, it's getting dark. What do you think we should do?"

"I think I should get you back home to the safety of your father and mother," he said quietly. "Surely those vicious hunters won't break into citizens' homes."

The couple cautiously crossed his office and then the outer office. Jake carefully eased open the main office door and checked the hallway. Nobody there. The faint evening light shrouded the corridor in black and gray tones. Everybody in the building had already left work for the day.

"I'm counting on the darkness being a good shield of protection for us," Jake said. "Come on."

The pair ventured out into the dark corridor and silently made their way to the stairs.

"Let me go first," he told Hannah. "I'll go downstairs and check to see if the coast is clear."

"Nothin' doin'," she said in a feisty tone. "We're in this together. Where you go, I go."

"Oookaaayy."

Down the steps and they paused at the bottom. All seemed to be safe. Quickly the couple hurried down the dark street and within a few minutes they safely had reached Hannah's home. A knock at her parent's door, a quiet call through the door to identify who was knocking, and Hannah was whisked safely inside the protection of her parent's home.

"Don't come to work until I get word to you," Jake instructed the girl as they parted. "Just lay low. Stay here under the protection of your father. You should be safe here."

"Are you sure you wouldn't rather stay here with us?" Hannah's father asked with alarm in his voice. "You're very welcome to stay. They won't break into our homes. We should be safe."

"Thank you, sir," Jake stated. "I'll be alright. I need to be able to roam."

Jake figured it would not be a wise idea for him to go home. The gang of temple thugs just might be waiting for him there. So, he doubled back to his office in the dark. He still had some cinnamon doughnuts from Caleb's Doughnut Shop leftover from the morning, so he ate them for supper as he sat in the darkness of his office. He found Hannah's shawl and made a pillow of it. Jake slept the night on the bare floor of his office.

The next morning, the turmoil outside seemed to have gone. Jake got up enough gumption to poke his head up over the second story office window sill and scan the street below. Activity seemed to be back to normal. He wanted to leave the office to do some probing around. But Jake decided to not take any chances, so he slipped on his dingy beggar's disguise and risked stepping out into the street below. As he had hoped, most people looked right past him and his disguise, treating him as the panhandler they thought he was. He decided to try to make his way to the home of Nicodemus and find out if the gentleman could shed any light on the desperate situation.

Jake reached Nicodemus' home on King David Boulevard. The Pharisee answered the door. He quickly recognized Jake in his costume and yanked the detective into the home.

"Jake, what are you doing roaming around the streets?" Nicodemus quietly exclaimed. "The long-expected persecution of the church has started. The religious leaders have sanctioned this harassment and authorized the oppression of anyone who calls himself or herself a follower of Christ."

"Anyone! You mean they are going after both men and women?"

"*Anyone.* All of us who name the Name of Jesus and claim Him as Messiah. None of us is safe. And I hate to say it but that young scholar, Saul of Tarsus, is leading the onslaught against the church. You warned me about him. Saul has received the full authority of the High Priest and the Sanhedrin to spearhead this persecution. And the religious rulers are fully behind him. He has a free hand to do whatever he pleases."

Jake grit his teeth. "Nicodemus, what has made Saul so angry with Christians?"

"I have discovered some terrible facts about Saul since you did you foray into the Temple disguised as a Levite," Nicodemus sadly stated. "Those new facts are very disturbing. Saul has become a flaming crusader to stamp out Christianity."

"But why?"

Nicodemus shook his head sadly. "Saul is a Pharisee. You have to understand that being a Pharisee sets Saul's mind into a particularly, narrow prism. As a Pharisee, Saul has embedded into him an overpowering love for Israel and Judaism and the Law. Pharisees believe acceptance with God is based on obedience to the Law. Obedience to the Law is supreme! Pharisees have faith in their good works being the only way for God to accept them. Legalistically following the Law of Moses and all the additional volumes of oral teachings handed down through the rabbis is most important for a Pharisee's acceptance by God.

"On the other hand, we Christians don't legalistically follow the Law. We live by faith in Christ and the Law is our guide to learning to follow God more efficiently. The Law is not our taskmaster. Saul, just like most Pharisees, opposes this teaching of Christianity as sacrilegious and heretical.

"Also, Saul's exposure to the teachings of his fellow Pharisees has deeply rooted a nationalistic spirit in him. No other nations are allowed. In fact, a wall of separation between other nations and Judaism is firmly in place both culturally and theologically. We Christians gladly accept believers in Christ from all nations. Saul would call that concept heresy and cause him to aggressively fight against that."

"Saul does have a problem," stated Jake.

"Yes, he does," the gentleman continued. Nicodemus paused to get his thoughts collected.

"You see, Saul is like the rest of his fellow Pharisees. The whole Christian movement is upsetting to the Pharisee's stable, orthodox Judaism. Belief in Christ has created tension between the intrenched politician, religious leaders and what they consider to be an upstart, outsider religious cult. In their minds, Christianity could eventually cause Judaism to be corrupted. The political, religious leaders could be toppled from their prestigious positions. I have begun to realize this is Saul's position on Christianity. I know how Pharisees think, because I once believed that way, too. But then, at the cross, for the first time, I realized that Jesus is the true Messiah that He is! And I believed!"

Nicodemus paused for a moment and his eyes widened as a new thought illumined his mind.

"It's about the cross," he said matter-of-factly. "The cross could possibly be another major reason for Saul's violent opposition to Christianity."

"The cross? Why would that be?"

"Saul is steeped in our Jewish traditions, like all the rest of us," Nicodemus continued. "The popular thinking is that Messiah will come to fight and defeat the Romans and liberate Israel. I'm sure in Saul's mind he is wondering how Messiah can liberate Israel from the Romans if He is crucified on a cross. It is the cross Saul must deal with! The cross doesn't fit the popular image of Messiah. In Saul's mind, a dead Messiah, hanging on a cross, can't save anybody. I'm sure Saul must struggle with this truth, like the rest of us, because Jesus doesn't fit the popular mold for Messiah. To Saul a crucified Savior is ridiculous and absurd."

"But that false idea ignores the fact that Jesus is raising from the dead!" Jake exclaimed.

"Exactly! That's the crux of the matter!" Nicodemus exclaimed. "The false concept of a dead Messiah doesn't take into account the resurrection of Jesus! You and I both are witnesses to Jesus' resurrection. We've seen Him alive from the dead! We know that Jesus had to suffer on the cross to take our sins upon Himself! By raising from the dead, He carried our sins far away!"

"And Jesus *is* alive!" Jake stated. "Saul doesn't realize that Jesus is not dead, hanging on the cross! He's alive right now!"

Nicodemus shrugged his shoulders. "I am sad to say it but I think these are some of the reasons Saul may be so hateful to the followers of Christ," the gentleman stated. "He now feels that it is his call from the Lord God to stamp out all remnants of heretic Christianity."

Jake heaved a heavy sigh. "Hannah even told me that we should have seen this attack on the church coming. All the warning signals from the Sanhedrin and the religious leaders were there is plain sight." As Jake talked, he pulled off his beggar's disguise.

"You mentioned Hannah," Nicodemus said. "Where is Hannah now?"

"She is safe with her father and mother."

"Have Hannah's father and mother become believers in Christ?"

"Yes, they have, I'm happy to say."

"Then they are in danger, as well."

"What! How can that be!"

"I know for a fact that Saul and his gang of bullies have authority to raid the homes of Christians," Nicodemus sadly stated. "I've already heard that some believers' homes have been broken into and the Christians dragged off to prison. The religious persecutors are not playing nice, either. They are resorting to violence and cruelty."

Jake's face turned white in terror. "You mean Hannah and her family could be in danger right now?"

"We are *all* in danger right now," Nicodemus stated trying to help Jake keep perspective. "There is nothing we can do at the moment. We just need to keep hiding for the time being. Because of my place on the Sanhedrin, I don't think they will bother me, yet. So, you should be safe here with me. And we can pray. We must believe in the power of prayer. We do have the Lord Jesus and we can pray for Hannah and her family that God would protect them during these treacherous times."

Jake stared at his gentleman friend. "Nicodemus, this crisis is the first real test of my faith in Christ," Jake sadly said. "I'm not passing this test very successfully. My faith ain't doing too good right now. Help me learn to pray, brother. I'm not much of a man of prayer."

"We will pray together. Stay here with me today. You will be safe here with me."

For all the afternoon, Jake stayed with the gentleman Pharisee, but in the late evening he desperately wanted to check on Hannah. He dumped his beggar's disguise. "I'm going to face this threat as Jake Jezreel, not a beggar," he told Nicodemus as he stepped out into the inky black night.

"Jake, be very careful," the Pharisee whispered to him. "Every shadow may hold danger."

It took several minutes and a lot of slinking along darkened walls and corners to reach Hannah's home. As Jake approached her home, he realized there was something strange going on. There were no lights on in the windows of her home. Jake crept up to the front door. Pale, grey moonlight etched an eerie design on the oak threshold. He glanced all around him to be sure he had not been followed. He gently knocked on the door. No answer. He knocked again. Still no answer. His heart began to pound in fright. *'Where could she be?'* Immediately, his brain filled with terrifying images of Hannah savagely being dragged off to jail. The detective became frantic. He pushed open the door and peered into the pitch-dark house. From the faint, gray moonlight outside the home, Jake could see that much of the furniture in the room had been overturned in what appeared to have been a mighty scuffle. Chills run up his spine. *'Where is Hannah?'* he asked himself. *'Where is her family?'* He sank down to the floor in despair. "Dear Lord Jesus, where are they?" he prayed. "I must find them. Help me find them."

Jake's analytical mind began to click. "Maybe she escaped and ran to a neutral place where the home invaders wouldn't search, like the office," he said out loud. "Maybe she's there!"

The detective crept through the night streets silently and reached his office building at about midnight. The dark, gloomy stairs were difficult to navigate but Jake climbed them in the dark and felt his way down the black obscurity of the corridor. He fumbled for the door, office number 211. Jake eased open the door. Darkness engulfed his office. A faint glimmer from the moonlight outside dimly illuminated the office area.

Jake stiffened abruptly in shock! A scene of devastation slapped his eyes. The entire office had been trashed! Every piece of furniture had been upended. Filing cabinets thrown on the floor and rifled through. File folders strewn everywhere. Case notes scattered all over the place. Everything of value smashed in pieces on the floor.

But the worst shock ... all the precious papyrus notes which Jake and Hannah had carefully documented and filed about the life of Jesus Christ were ripped up and torn to shreds!

Jake gasped at the sight. The attackers had been here looking for him! And when they couldn't find him, they decided to take out their vengeance by looting and wrecking his office.

"They did a thorough job of destroying everything" he growled out loud, as he scanned the devastation. "And my precious notes about Jesus' life … my precious notes … Those valuable notes …" His voice trailed off.

"Now I'm getting' sore!" Jake blurted out. "First, they take my girl and then they take away my livelihood! And then they destroy my most prized property, my history notes about Jesus!" Jake's blood pressure hit the top! "They've gone too far! They just don't know who they are dealing with! They've crossed the wrong guy!" In anger, he slammed his fist into the palm of his other hand. "Somebody's gonna get smacked!"

Then Jake caught hold of himself. "Hey. Hey. Take it easy, man," he told himself out loud. "The worst thing you can do is to lose your head. Don't let your emotions run away and drive you to do something idiotic. I'll just stay here for the night, amongst the trash. Those thugs won't come back here tonight. They've already been here looking for me and been disappointed. No, they're done for the night. I'll sleep here. The only problem is I don't have any more cinnamon doughnuts."

Chapter 10

DOWN INTO THE SLUMS

Night emerged into a glorious, bright new morning. Yellow shafts of sunlight streamed into the office through the windows. Jake peered over his second story window sill to the street below. Bands of marauders were again roaming the cobblestone thoroughfare. He watched the religious thugs break down the door of a Christian family just across the street.

Jake ducked down below the window sill. "I've got to find someone who can tell me what has happened to Hannah," he said out loud. "Oh, how I wish I had my beggar's disguise, now. Jake Jezreel is too big of a target."

As he sat there amidst the mess on the floor, Jake heard other people stirring in the building. "Folks are beginning to come to work. And they all know I'm a Christian. I've got to get outa here."

The detective quickly stepped out into the hallway. Some people were just coming up the stairs to his right. He immediately turned to his left and darted down the corridor to the back staircase. Hurriedly Jake walked out onto the front street. He held his hand up to his forehead pretending to have a headache, as if shielding his eyes from the sunlight. This trick helped cover his face. It was a good shield – but for how long?

'I've got to come up with a better plan than this,' Jake thought. *'I just can't keep walking around. Where can I go to escape the bullies?'*

For an hour Jake dodged in and out of doorways and corners of buildings, trying to hide in the shadows. From his flimsy hiding spots he watched the religious tyrants patrolling the streets. Occasionally they would snag an unsuspecting Christian and arrest him. At a distance, he watched as the religious tormentors broke into any and every home where they suspected believers in Christ may be hiding. Jake's blood boiled at the twisted misery smeared out before him. Innocent people dragged off to prison for doing nothing wrong. Their only crime was loving Jesus!

The detective had to turn away from the judicial carnage taking place before his eyes. He was a hunted man, too. Hiding is back alleys seemed to be the only strategy for survival at the moment. He knew he couldn't go home. The enemy would be waiting for him there. There seemed to be nowhere to go.

Then his survival instinct kicked in. "Where is the most unlikely place for the religious zealots to go? In the slums! Of course! They wouldn't allow themselves to get dirty in that filthy place. That will be the perfect place to hide out. It certainly can't be any more dangerous than being accosted here on the city streets."

The plan made perfect sense to Jake. Maybe he could find Pudge the Pickpocket again and see if he could hole up with the petty thief for a while. Destination: Kidron Street.

By way of the labyrinth of back alleys, Jake made his way across the eastern side of the city to the center of town. When he reached the fringes of the ghetto and Kidron Street he descended into the dingy slums in search of Pudge. Kidron Street still smelled of garbage and waste. That fact hadn't changed any. But somehow the stench and vile surroundings didn't seem to bother Jake very much. This was going to be his hideout for a while.

Warily the detective walked the dirty, dark alley. The same cast of unsavory desperados still hid out in this grimy slum. Jake had no idea where Pudge lived, so once again he knew he would have to ask one of the sleazy cutthroats of Kidron Street where the pickpocket lived. Fortunately, on this occasion, Pudge was standing out in the open, propped up against a slimy green brick wall, talking to a buddy.

Jake ambled toward Pudge. Pudge saw him coming and laughed.

"I bet I knowd why yur here," he said with a smirk. "You on da run from da law! Ain't dat right. That religious bunch. Ain't they justa barrel o' laffs?"

"Yeah, just a barrel of laughs," Jake said, shaking his head. "I see you've heard about the chaos against all the Christians." Jake started to rub his head. "I really do think I have a headache."

"I've got sumthun to fix that," Pudge smiled.

"What I really need is a place to stay, outa sight, until this mess blows over," Jake said. "Could I lay low at your place for a few nights?"

"Sure, not a problem," the pickpocket laughed. "You kin flop wit me. Ya're one of us, now, man. Ya're now a criminal type on da run and laying low, just like us."

"Pudge, you're a lifesaver and a good friend. I'll be forever grateful to you."

"Man, I toad ya before. Don't be aspreadin' dat Mister Goodness junk around too much about me," Pudge whispered. "I got my professional repatation to protect. Come on, I'll show ya where I lives."

"Pudge, I feel right at home here with you already. You wouldn't happen to have an extra cinnamon doughnut on ya? I'm starving."

Two days passed. Jake hid out at Pudge's place biding his time.

"Any news from the outside world?" Jake asked Pudge after the third day. "I've got to find out whatever happened to my secretary."

"Yur worried about dat purdy lady of yours, yur bride-ta-be, ain't cha," Pudge said.

"Yeah, I really am worried. I went by her home. She had disappeared and the place was turned upside down."

"I've got some feelers out. I sent Squinty over to the prison area. He's got a pal who works at the jail and maybe he kin get a line on your purdy secatary. Relax, Jake. I'm sure she's okay."

"Thanks for all your help, my friend," Jake said. "I'm going to walk around a bit, Pudge. I'm getting cabin fever, all cooped up here in your lovely bungalow."

"Don't stray too far. You know, some of the inhabitants of Kidron

Street don't like nobody re-motely 'sociated wit law enforcement. You wouldn't wanna git yar throat cut."

"Naw, I don't think I'd like that. I'll stick close."

The detective stepped outside of Pudge's small flop house, which he shared with a couple of other unsavory characters. Once out in the dirty street, Jake walked a few feet. He noticed the suspicious looks on the faces of some of the denizens of the dreary place. He decided that walking around may not be too healthy, so he started back toward Pudge's dwelling. But as he turned around, Mad Dog, the shiftless bum, stood staring into his face.

"Watya doin' here, shamus?" Mad Dog growled in a guttural, low voice.

"I'm here for my health. Every once in a while, I need to come here in your wonderful neighborhood to get invigorated."

But another creepy bum named Nails spoke up, "Ain't ya heard, Mad Dog? This here private gumshoe is layin' low at Pudge's place. This guy is hidin' out from the religious cops. He's one of them goody-goody Christians!"

Mad Dog's grungy, sunken face seemed to brighten up. "Yau're hidin' out from da cops. Well, well." Mad Dog looked at Jake with an evil eye and smirked. "Well, well," he repeated and walked off.

As the eerie figure slinked away, Jake was not sure what was on Mad Dog's mind.

In the early morning, Jake woke up to a scuffling commotion outside in the street. He saw Pudge leap out of bed and dart to the front door. Suddenly Pudge yelled, "Jake, jump up! Run for it! Out the back way! It's the cops!"

Jake threw off his blanket just in time to see two large, armed religious guards slam open the front door. Mad Dog stood right outside in the street pointing into Pudge's house. The muscular guards shoved Pudge aside, knocking him to the floor, and forced themselves into the room.

Mad Dog pointed at Jake. "Dat's him! Dat's him!"

One of the guards bellowed at Jake, "Are you Jake Jezreel?"

"Yeah, dat's him and don't let him de-ny it!" Mad Dog hysterically screeched.

"Yes, I'm Jake Jezreel. I surrender. I'll come peacefully."

"Where's mah money!" Mad Dog whined to the guards.

"You'll get paid. You'll get paid," one of the burly guards snarled back at Mad Dog. "Now, shut up!"

"Come with us!" both burly guards roared at Jake in unison. Then they yanked Jake into a standing position and tied his hands tightly behind him.

"I told you I would go with you peacefully," Jake said to the two guards in disbelief. "Why all the ropes?"

"Shut up, Christian!" one of the guards yelled. "You deserve even worse!"

They manhandled Jake out the door of Pudge's house and into the grimy street.

Pudge scrambled to his feet and yelled out the door, "I'm sorry, Jake! I really am sorry!"

Mad Dog stood across the narrow alleyway next to his stinking gutter filled with black sewage. He sneered and grinned a twisted grin, as he watched the guards shoving Jake down the street. With sadistic satisfaction, Mad Dog laughed, dreaming of the reward money he would soon be clutching in his dirty mitt.

There was no trial for Jake. No other Christian had received a trial. Neither would Jake. The burly guards dragged the detective to his grimy, gray stone jail cell and threw him in with the other fifteen prisoners crammed into the tiny tin can.

Jake sat down on the grubby floor to collect his wits and rub the rope burns on his wrists. Every aspect of his life had collapsed in a heartbeat. *'What happened?'* he thought to himself. *'Where is God now? Where is Hannah? Is she safe? In prison? Is she still alive? Will I ever see her again? What horrible thing will Saul do next?'* The detective had no answers. Only depressing, lingering questions.

And for now, this murky, gray stone jail cell – this dungeon – would be his home.

Chapter 11

DUNGEON

The crushing closeness. Men smashed together. The oppressive heat. The pungent smell of sweat and grim. The persistent monotony. All this within a ten by fifteen foot gray stone vault.

There may be worse places to be than a dungeon. But Jake couldn't think of one. Hours and days and weeks of bread and water in this tiny, dirty, stone cell was not what Jake would call a resort vacation. Personal hygiene became impossible. The small compartment stunk. But eventually a person can get used to it – somehow.

The only saving grace about prison was the fact that so many other Christians were jailed along with the detective. Even though sixteen men were all crammed into the little, cramped space like sardines, the brothers in Christ continued to praise Jesus for the opportunity to suffer for their Savior's sake.

While the days of prison misery dragged on, frequently the prison guards came to the cell and would wrench one of the brothers out and haul him away to be punished in one of the synagogues. "This is by order of Saul of Tarsus!" the guard would command. Then the guard would snarl at the prisoner, "Saul is waiting for you. He is going to have you beaten to within an inch of your life. Then he's going to make you renounce this false Christ you believe in so much!" Then the guard would thunder with laughter. This ugly twisted, torment repeated itself daily, as the weeks dragged on.

One Christian staggered back into his cell after his grilling, black and blue and bleeding. "Saul of Tarsus was there. He conducted the inquisition. He is a mad man! He is a very bitter, hateful man against Christians! But I didn't renounce Christ! I promise you of that! I would never forsake my Christ! They couldn't make me deny my Lord Jesus! Never!"

Day after day the torment continued, each man got his turn in the barrel. Even Jake. But the maniacal torture couldn't break the men. Nobody, not one of them, cracked under the beatings. Every man pledged his loyalty to Jesus. Not one man deserted his faith!

"Listen, guys, we've got to pray for Saul of Tarsus," Jake reminded the men, as he nursed his own cuts and bruises. "He's a tool for the religious authorities. They recognize that Saul's got a seething hatred for Christians, so they have turned him loose upon us. But God can change his heart. Saul can find the love of God just like we did. Once his heart is changed, God can put a new desire in Saul. Who knows, Saul might stop persecuting us for good!"

The group agreed heartily. As the days passed, as the torture reminded them, the bedraggled band of Christian cellmates began a fervent prayer campaign for God to transform their tormentor. They soon found that they could not hate someone they honestly were praying for in love.

As the daily suffering stretched on, the prisoners all tried to encourage each other by recalling different sayings that Jesus had once taught about suffering for their Lord.

Since Jake had spent so much time with Jesus during the Nazarene's Galilean ministry, he tried hard to remember the predictions the Savior had made.

"One thing I remember Jesus teaching in a sermon up on a mountain dealt with persecution," Jake stated one day. "He said, 'You are blessed, when men shall abuse you and persecute you and say all manner of evil against you falsely, for My sake.' And then Jesus said, 'Rejoice and be extremely glad for great is your reward in heaven.' Listen, guys, when Jesus made those statements during His sermon on the mount, He clearly was letting us know that this persecution we are experiencing right now is obviously for His sake. It's due to the fact that we belong to Jesus. Belonging to Jesus should comfort all of us. And when we are persecuted, He is also being persecuted right along with us. He told us to rejoice because we are suffering along with Him!" Jake paused and looked around at his jail buddies. "Doesn't that encourage you?"

"Sort of," said a sad cellmate. "I guess so."

"What Jake told us is true!" another Christian said. "Before all this persecution started, one of the apostles – you all know Nathaniel – well, he told me a statement Jesus privately taught them on the very night our Lord was betrayed. Jesus flat out said to them, 'If the world hates you, you know that the world hated Me before it hated you. If you were part of the world, the world would have loved his own. But because you are not part of the world and because I have chosen you out of the world, the world hates you.'"

"Yeah, we're gettin' plenty of that," a forlorn soul whined, rubbing the bruises across his shoulders.

Another Christian piped up, "I remember something else Jesus said when He preached here in Jerusalem. He said, 'The servant is not greater than his master. If they have persecuted Me, they will also persecute you.' So, it seems pretty clear. The only reason we are being persecuted is because the enemies of God persecuted Jesus first."

One young confused believer dejectedly sat over in the corner and cried out, "But I didn't think becoming a Christian would be this rough."

The Christian men in the cell gathered around the distraught young believer.

"We understand," said one fellow prisoner trying to calm him down. "It ain't like the false teaching that some dishonest preachers are peddling. They preach 'accept Jesus and all your troubles will go away.'"

Jake knelt down to be more on the young believer's eye level. "This jail cell is certainly a reversal of all the fabulous days when everything in our Christian life was delightful," Jake quietly said.

"But the dark days will not last forever. They can't last forever! We have too great a God!"

"That's right. We've got to see beyond this unpleasant time," another man declared. "There will be a moment when Jesus will come back to take us with Him to Heaven!"

"But that seems so long from now!" the young man cried out.

"Maybe not so long," encouraged one brother. "Jesus said He would come back for us. Maybe it's today!"

"And when Jesus comes back," another prisoner laughed, "he will validate that He is in charge! And in His glorious power He will gather up all of His followers and declare them as His own!

"We've got to trust in God's providence," said another. "God's hidden hand is working and moving in the shadows. We can't see His greater purposes. Sometimes what happens doesn't make any sense. We may not understand but we can trust God to be working out His purposes."

"Knowing God is in control, should give us inner peace," said another.

"Yes, He is the Master planner," remarked one man in the back.

"But I don't like it," the young believer whimpered. "This jail, the beatings, this rotten food, this living in a tiny, dark stone box. How can I have peace in this dump?"

"Take heart, my man!" added another prisoner. "Peace comes from your personal relationship with Jesus. He individually singles you out to be your faithful companion, right here in this stinking cell. Then He gives you His peace. Remember, His peace He gives to you comes from His close inner contact with you. Not from this mad world. Jesus gives you the peace you need – His divine peace. He is always with you in your heart."

Another man from across the cell piped up. "And remember, Jesus told us He has overcome the world! When you're in the depths of despair, you need to turn *to* your faith in Jesus, knowing you too can overcome this world, through His power!"

Another kindly man sat down beside the young believer. "Listen, friend. Listen to these men. Their advice is right on target. You've got to open your heart to the reality of God's presence in your life, right here, right now with you. Sensing God's close presence with you will give you courage beyond measure."

An older gentleman standing nearby spoke up. "Listen, all of you! All of us need to take these spiritual truths to heart, for our own encouragement! Think of what the prophet Nahum said in his prophecy in Nahum 1:7. He said, 'The Lord is good, a fortress in the day of trouble! And He knows them that trust in Him!' That is the Lord's promise to each of us! The Lord knows those who trust in Him and He knows each of you personally! He is our strong fortress in times of trouble! Take heart in those glorious facts!"

"Yeah, the psalmist wrote that God never slumbers or sleeps," remarked one man. "So, He's always watching over you."

"And God said in another place that He will never leave you or forsake you," said the man at the back of the cell.

All these scriptural truths heightened spiritual exhilaration among the prisoners. Men started shouting praises hilariously.

One of the cellmates was a scribe who had recently surrendered to Christ. "Listen, men, in all my study of the Scriptures, one truth has always jumped out at me," he stated. "That truth is that our God is more powerful than any earthly enemy. I'm thinking of one Bible episode when King Sennacherib, king of Assyria, attacked King Hezekiah, our king of Judah. In that fearful time King Hezekiah encouraged his people by proclaiming, 'Be strong and courageous, be not afraid or dismayed for the King of Assyria, nor for all the vast army that is with him. There is One who is with us Who is greater than all the hordes who are with Assyria's king. With that king is the arm of flesh, but with us is the Lord our God to help us. He will fight our battles.' And we all know the great ending to that story! The Lord God Himself defended Jerusalem and saved His people, bringing glory to His Name! The Angel of the Lord swept through the Assyrian camp and killed 185,000 soldiers and drove off King Sennacherib back to his homeland! God is all powerful! We must never forget that!"

Jake turned his attention back to the young man sitting on the floor. "Can you hear what these men are saying? All this is true. God is all powerful! We must believe that God will defend His people today in the same way He did back in Bible times. But while you wait for the Lord to act, you've got to face the facts of your present situation.

"I spent the better part of a year and a half with Jesus when He ministered here on earth. He made it clear that if we followed Him, we could expect the same mistreatment that He got. But He also made it clear that it was a privilege to not only have faith in Him for salvation but also to suffer for Him. Try to remember that, brother. It is a wonderful privilege to suffer for Him. But the sweet part of the deal is that Jesus is all powerful and He promised to always be with you."

The young Christian sat on the floor blankly staring at the detective.

As Jake sat down next to the young Christian on the grungy floor, he put his hand on the man's shoulder.

"Just know this, friend. My girlfriend, my fiancée, was taken captive, just like we were. She is locked up somewhere in this city. I haven't a clue where she is or what her condition is. I haven't seen her for several weeks. I don't like that, either. I don't know if she is alive or dead. But I know she belongs to Jesus. I know He cares for her much more than I ever could – He died for her. That proves He cares for her. So, I know I can trust Jesus. I can trust Him to hold her and take care of her. That is what faith in Christ is all about."

The young believer continued to stare at Jake. "Wow, I didn't know all that. Compared to you, my problems look small," the young man said. "And you say you have no clue where your fiancée is locked up."

"No, I have no idea," Jake stated. "I don't know anything about her prison conditions, who she's with. But I do know Jesus is with her. That's all that counts. That's the comfort I have."

Other men began to recall their similar family stories, explaining that many of their family members had been dragged from their homes, separated, and locked up. Each story seemed to add comfort in the Lord to the young man and to the whole assembly of Christian men.

A pastor in one of the house churches in Jerusalem spoke up, "It truly is a blessing to repeat the words of Jesus, 'You shall be hated by all men for My Name's sake.' I don't mind being hated by men as long as our suffering puts a pleasing smile on our Lord Jesus' face!"

"Man, that will preach!" shouted one of the prisoners.

"Amen!" came the resounding echo through the overcrowded prison cell.

A full-blown revival meeting broke out. More testimonies began to flood the captive congregation. Men sang songs of victory in Jesus and His salvation. Preaching of Scripture rippled throughout the group. Who cared that all they had to eat was bread and water when they were feeding on the Living Bread from Heaven and the Living Water of Life!

Somehow the first days in prison seemed to not be so miserable when those brothers in misery shared the scintillating joy of the Lord! Fellowship sparked a bond of Christian love and cohesion. This persecution by the religious leaders had actually now welded these Christian men into a unit, ready to attack the enemies of Jesus with the potent Gospel message of Christ!

But time dragged on … and on … and on … and on.

And time slowly began to take its eroding, demoralizing toll.

Chapter 12

DEATH IN THE CAMP

Day by day the wretchedness of the dirty, stinking prison began to wear on the Christians. The cesspool of filth they lived in began to play on their minds. The loneliness for loved ones. Being crammed together with no breath of fresh air … the fresh air of freedom. The boredom. It became harder and harder for the prisoners to maintain the positive Christian mindset amidst the dingy, nasty, gray stone walls. Days stretched into weeks … with no end in sight.

As those dark days stretched out, even Jake's faith began to wobble. He missed his sweetie greatly. His heart ached for Hannah. He had moments of deep yearning for her. After all, they had spent nearly every day working closely together for three and a half years. Jake missed his close, affectionate confidant. He longed for her wispy voice; her happy, breezy energy. She filled that cavernous void in his heart … that emptiness … that he felt every day in this wretched cell without her. Without her touch. Without her warmth. Without her encouraging words. Without her beautiful smile. Without her lovely presence.

'Man, you've got it bad,' he thought to himself, as he sat propped up against the grungy back wall of his prison cell. 'I wish I could see Hannah. Be near her. I get so tired of clutching at past memories. I want the real thing! Where can she be? Every day I'm worrying about her safety, wondering if she's okay. I'm tired of longing for her. I wish she was right here with me!'

And then Jake caught himself in the middle of his personalized pity party. *'Hey, get hold of yourself, pal!'* he scolded himself. *'I can't just throw away all the truthful words my cellmates have been saying in these past weeks about the Lord. I've got to stay focused on Jesus. A good detective always stays focused on his objective. Somewhere in all this is the will of God, disguised as misery, just waiting to be discovered.'*

Sometimes God sends just the right man, at just the right time, with just the right message. One of the new deacons in the church, whose name was Nicanor, had been thrown into the same jail cell as Jake and the others. One day, when the mood among the jailed Christians began to sag into discouragement, Nicanor spoke up. To get everybody's attention, he began banging his tin cup on the cold, dingy stone prison wall.

"Hey! Listen up, you guys, listen! We've got to snap out of the doldrums we have fallen into!" Nicanor exclaimed. "Come on guys, where is the joy of the Lord? Remember, in Nehemiah 8:10, Nehemiah told his people during Israel's time of trials, 'Do not sorrow, for the joy of the Lord is your strength!' Think of it! God's joy is in your heart! Think of the strength that fact brings into your daily experience! Do not sorrow! The Lord's joy in your hearts confirms you are secure with Him, centered on Him!"

"We know what you're sayin' is right," one man said. "But these circumstances … you know, can begin to get ya down. Explain how the Lord's joy is my strength."

"The joy of the Lord is a holy joy," Nicanor explained. "His joy comes when the Lord becomes the center of your life. The very center. You cannot descend into self-pity. Turn your attention fully upon Jesus. Feel His closeness right in the center of your relationship with Him. In the security of your relationship with Jesus you begin to know that He cares for you. All this brings you joy and in that joy you find new strength you never knew you had!"

"Sounds reasonable. But I'm not feelin' it."

"The joy of the Lord will come as we begin to encourage each other with the truths of our salvation," Nicanor stated. "Try it. Turn your attention to each other and away from your own self-absorbed doldrums. Start reminding each other of the fabulous promises of the Lord, about His presence with us, and His overpowering love for us. Go ahead. Try it!"

Slowly a low murmur began to ripple through the cell. Then as the men began to encourage one another the murmur became more of a masculine swell of praise.

Nicanor sounded out, " This is more like it! You've focused upon Jesus! Jesus' love is real love. His love is true love. Jesus dying to pay the penalty for all our sins is proof of His powerful love for us. What a wonderful gift He has given you! Isn't that truth in itself enough to lift our spirits far above these prison walls up to the heavens in thankfulness to God? So, be thankful for Jesus' love for you. Be thankful to Him for all He has given you!"

Nicanor's speech on the joy of the Lord certainly did prop up the sagging spirits of the men. It gave them new focus. It gave them a godly point of reference to hang on to. The joy of the Lord brought a new remembrance of their gratitude for God saving their souls from eternal destruction and Hell. This dungeon might be like Hell but it was all the Hell these men would even experience, thanks to Jesus' saving grace!

As one prisoner put it, "Thankfully I know I have the Lord's joy in my heart and eternal life to boot!"

But suddenly, one ominous day, the genuineness of their joy of the Lord came under merciless attack.

On that ominous day, a sadistic prison guard poked his sneering face up against the bars of the cell. "Hey, all you goody, goody Christians. I've heard you guys yapping about being so happy and thankful. Well, bite on this! I just heard the news that several Christians died recently in prison. They were executed! Yeah, exterminated! And I can tell you this fact! It was because your good buddy Saul of Tarsus authorized their executions! How do you like that? Kinda makes ya feel all warm and tingly inside, don't it!" The guard burst out in hideous laughter.

The guard continued to stand jeering at them. "And from what

I've been told, there's gonna be even more of you Christians bite the dust! One by one. Maybe even one of you in this here cell will be next! Haw, haw, haw!" he laughed sadistically as he walked away. "Wrap your tiny, little brains around that!" was his parting shot.

Shock descended upon the jail cell. Christian brothers dead? The joy of the Lord plunged out of sight deep into the horrifying abyss. Christians dead. Executed. Somber oppression swept over Jake's cell. Were these dead Christians some of their friends? Would one of Jake's cellmates be next to be executed? Fear gripped each man. Despair filled the tiny compartment.

One prisoner cried out in terror, gasping for breath as if he'd been punched in the stomach. He fell to his knees and stretched out his hand upward, like he was trying to hold off an invisible attacker and shrieked, "I am doomed! They are coming to kill me!"

Several of the Christians grabbed the man and attempted to comfort him. His hysterical cries soon defused into a low, mournful moan.

The shroud of death spread its insidious fingers over every men in the jail cell.

Some inmates bowed in sorrow and stunned silence. Some men cried. Some folded up into a cocoon of withdrawal. Others flashed rage. "Where is God, now?" some fumed.

"Why didn't God protect our brothers from death!" one man asked in disbelief. "Tell me how to be joyful for that!"

"Will God let us be executed, too?" another cried out.

Nicanor spoke up. "Brothers! Have you lost your faith? Don't you trust Jesus to be your Savior in both life or death? Remember, Jesus told us that the way they treated Him would be the way this evil world would treat His followers. The evil world murdered Jesus. This evil world hates us because we follow Jesus."

A Christian brother stared up at Nicanor from his bowing position. "You are right. Where is our faith? This is now the true test of our faith. We must believe in faith, nothing wavering, that Jesus is here with us, no matter what happens to us."

"Yes, thank you, brother, for you testimony," Nicanor stated.

"We can expect no better treatment than Jesus got. Remember, no matter what happens, let your minds dwell on how very much Jesus loves us. Focus on Jesus' love for us. He loved us so much that He died to take away our sins. That kind of love covers all events, even death!"

Nicanor's words, however, seemed to bounce off many of the shocked, stone-like faces in the cell.

"Listen, brothers!" a house pastor exclaimed. "We must pray for the families of our dead brothers. We should grieve for our deceased friends. We must do that. But we also have hope – hope that our fallen brothers are right now in the glorious presence of Jesus. And we will see them all one day in heaven! And if God chooses to allow one of us to be executed, it will be a gift! God will free us from these bonds and welcome us to be with Him in His presence forever!"

Some of the men seemed to take courage from those thoughts.

"Listen, guys," Jake exclaimed. "Don't just sit here and take it on the chin. We've got to fight back!"

"Fight back!" one prisoner yelled. "With what?"

"Fight back with prayer!" Jake proclaimed. "We've still got the power of prayer! Our God is still alive, isn't He? Don't you think He's listening? Let's take that power of God and wield it toward Saul! Pray for Saul! Pray that God will grab ahold of Saul and break his heart. Saul's vengeance against the church must be stopped. Prayer can do it! Only our Father in heaven can stop him. God can change Saul. We can't … but God can."

But the dark days stretched on. Nothing changed. Time in "the slammer" wasted away. News of the continued assault on the church occasionally reached the ears of the prisoners. More prison beatings and more deaths occurred. Somehow, by God's miraculous grace, none of Jake's cellmates were extracted for execution.

Encouraging reports also filtered in to the men in the prison cell that many Christians had fled Jerusalem to escape the persecution and had scattered to the wind. They also received word that the Christians, wherever they ran to, scattered the seeds of the Good News of Jesus and His salvation everywhere they traveled. When

Jake's cellmates heard this encouraging report, they all rejoiced! "Our Lord God has outwitted His enemies once again!"

Weeks of prison life turned into months ...

And then ... out of the blue ... a bizarre event occurred. Staggering is more like it! It was during the eighth week of Jake's prison sentence. As the detective slumped dozing in his cell, bundled up in a dirty blanket, one of the guards timidly approached the cell. On this day, this jailor was not his typical abusive self. In a hesitant manner, the guard halted in front of Jake's jail cell.

"Ahem," he cleared his throat. "Which one of you is Jake Jezreel?" the guard asked in a halting and very polite tone.

"Hey, Jake," one of the Christian brothers called to the dozing detective. "Wake up. The guard is calling for you."

Jake roused from his sleepiness along the back wall and stood up. As he stepped toward the guard, the brothers parted so he could get to the bars of the cell door.

"I'm Jake Jezreel," he said sleepily. "Is it my turn in the barrel again?"

"No, sir," the guard courteously said. "Governor Pilate has ordered your release from prison immediately."

Jake looked sideways at the guard, in shock. "You're kidding me!" Jake stated in surprise. "Pilate? What's he got to do with this?"

"He will explain it all to you when I take you to his office," the guard said graciously as he unlocked the cell door. "Please come with me."

The cell door groaned on its rusty hinges as it swung open. As Jake exited his cell, he turned around and waved to his buddies. "I don't know what this is all about. Maybe I'll be back and maybe I won't. But just know this, brothers. Jesus loves you. Know Him and make Him known! See ya!"

Chapter 13

SURPRISING NEW BEGINNING

Jake's dazed brain was still spinning. His sudden and baffling release from prison seemed like a fantastic illusion.

As Jake and the guard walked down the prison corridor, the guard began to plead. "I'm so sorry for this mistake of having you imprisoned, sir. It was not my fault. I was only carrying out orders. Please don't tell Pilate that I am at fault in any of this, sir." The guard chattered on and on nervously.

Jake knew something strange was up, when the guard kept calling him "sir".

"Pilate was very angry when he heard that you had been arrested and incarcerated," the guard blathered on. "He is still very angry. And it is a bad thing for Governor Pilate to be angry. Please remember, I never beat you. All I ever did was carry out the orders that were given to me. I only did what I was told."

Jake smiled at the jailer. "I'd never squeal on you," he said as he shuffled along. After being crammed unto such a tiny space for so long, Jake was having trouble getting his legs to function correctly. "What I will do is show you the God-given love that our Lord Jesus showed to everyone He met. I know you've heard us talk about Jesus time and time again in our cell. Jesus loved all people so much that He died for their sins on a cross. Then He overpowered death and is now alive waiting to save you from your sins. Try to believe this fact. Jesus loves you. You can become a Christian, right now. It only takes your willing surrender of your life to Him."

The jailer stared blankly at Jake, as they walked. "I've heard this story before. From you men. I'm gonna have to chew on it some more."

"I was just like you. I was skeptical until I met Jesus. When you get back to the prison, have a discussion with the guys in my cell. They'll be glad to fill in the blanks and help you get a better understanding of salvation through Jesus Christ."

The pair reached Pilate's office door. Jake glanced down at his filthy clothes. "Shouldn't I clean up a little before I walk into the governor's immaculate office?" Jake asked the guard. "I look a mess."

"No, no! Governor Pilate insisted that you be brought immediately to see him," the guard said with urgency in his voice. He snapped opened the door to Pilate's headquarters. "If you would please, go on in to his adjutant's office and I'll follow you."

Jake walked into the Pilate's headquarters. Pilate's personal military adjutant jumped up and dashed across his office to heartily greet Jake.

"Mister Jezreel, it is a pleasure to see you again," the adjutant smoothly stated. "Please take a chair here in my office. I'll let governor Pilate know that you are here." And then he disappeared into Pilate's main office.

'Quite a difference in the adjutant's smug attitude from the last time I was here,' Jake thought. *'Maybe Pilate has told him to treat me with more respect.'*

In a moment the military adjutant reappeared through the door. "Please, sir, come in. Governor Pilate is anxious to see you."

Jake rose from his chair, a little wobbly, and looked at his grimy prison cloths. "Are you sure I can't clean up a little before I meet the governor?" he asked the adjutant.

"No, he wants you just as you are. You may go in," the adjutant smiled and swept his hand toward the open door into Pilate's inner sanctum.

Before he entered the door, Jake turned back to the prison guard.

"Now, be sure and have that talk with the boys back in my cell," he reminded.

"Thank you, I will."

Jake smiled, turned, and entered Pilate's office door. Pilate was standing up behind his desk as the detective walked in. The governor came around the end of his ornate desk and enthusiastically greeted Jake, shaking the detective's hand.

"Mister Jezreel, I am so very glad to see you, alive!" Pilate laughed. "And I am so very sorry that you were imprisoned. I regret that you had to go through all the torment caused by these so-called religious elites! Are you okay? Are you well?"

"Yes, sir, I'm a little thinner now but I probably needed to lose a little weight, anyway."

"You are too gracious," Pilate smiled. "Please sit down and rest yourself." Pilate's military adjutant still stood at the door. "Get this man some food, and I mean good food. He looks nearly wasted away."

"Yes, sir!" The adjutant immediately wheeled around and exited the office, closing the door behind him.

"Mister Jezreel, I only learned of your imprisonment this morning," Pilate sadly said. "I had no idea that you had been arrested and imprisoned. The chief priests have not kept a very good record of who they have arrested. So, I was totally in the dark about your arrest. To keep the peace with the Jews, I've tried to stay aloof, watching from a distance, letting the religious leaders play their ghoulish games. I've been observing the way they have targeted the Christian community. But I've tried to stay back and let the Jewish authorities self-govern their nation. I've always tried to be conciliatory to the Jewish nation and its elite class. But sometimes these people ..." Pilate shook his head in disgust and disbelief.

"Here lately, the religious elites have been treading on very thin ice," Pilate stated firmly, as he sat down behind his desk. "They murdered this fellow Stephen several months ago. Stoned him to death. I did not sanction that killing. And the religious authorities know that I alone hold the power and authority to sentence a person to be executed. That killing disturbed me. But I couldn't find out who was responsible for Stephen's murder. It was a mob action. A spontaneous killing.

"I would have investigated Stephen's killing but that very same day, the great persecution against the Christians was launched by the religious authorities," the governor stated in contempt. Pilate leaned over his desk and rested his arms, palms down, on the desktop. "That is when this whole city went insane," he stated in a low disgusted tone. His eyes narrowed. Then he looked down at his desk, shaking his head again. His eyes slowly rose and sympathetically looked at Jake. "Once again, I watched closely the shenanigans of the religious authorities. They appeared to me to be self-governing the nation in whatever foolish persecutions they undertook. I realized it all stemmed from that preacher, Jesus of Nazareth, and His followers. Months ago, during Passover I agreed to the Nazarene's crucifixion but since then, I've heard stories that Jesus of Nazareth is alive again. It is very hard to believe. But these Christians believe it."

"Governor Pilate, the reports that Jesus is alive are absolutely true," Jake stated. "I've seen Him alive. I've spoken to Him. And that is why I'm a Christian."

"*You* are a Christian," Pilate said looking squarely at the detective. "I see. So, in the future you will have that mark on you. In the future you will continue to be persecuted by these religious nuts just simply for being a Christian."

Pilate stood up and began to pace back and forth behind his desk. His cream-colored tunic draped with a long, red outer cloak flowed behind him as he paced rapidly. "I'm going to have to do something about that."

The governor stopped pacing and sat down again. "Let me get back to what I was saying. I went along with these mad, unbalanced religious authorities and their pious disruptions until they started killing more people. Granted, I have given some latitude to the Sanhedrin when it comes to religious punishments. Even when the punishment is determined to be the death sentence due to religious reasons. When the Sanhedrin started requesting several executions based on religious problems, I approved their requests. But then more and more requests came to me, authorized by the chief priests. I began refusing these requests. I found out that the main instigator who signed off on the execution requests is a brash upstart named Saul of Tarsus. None of this wholesale execution is allowed by Roman law. And I've determined to totally put a halt to these executions. As a result, I'm currently placing particular attention on investigating this character, Saul of Tarsus.

"Now, let me get back to my story and how you fit into all this," the governor continued. "Mister Jezreel, the only way I found out about you being in prison was through my personal military adjutant. You met him moments ago. Something caused my adjutant to think about you in investigating these executions of Christians. He went by your office and saw your wrecked facility in a complete shambles. It was then he realized you must have been arrested by the Jewish authorities. He did some checking around and found out what prison you were in and immediately came to me with the information. I want you to know, that my adjutant's report infuriated me! And I acted immediately upon his report. Without any hesitation, I sent word to the prison for you to be released."

"Well, sir, I will be forever grateful to your military adjutant and to you, sir," Jake stated.

"Yes, my personal adjutant is a fine officer and a fine man," Pilate stated. "He is very service minded and does his duty. I depend upon him in everything. He's the kind of man you can depend upon to get things done."

"I am grateful," Jake said. "It sounds like he is the right man to have taken the effort to diligently searched me out."

"He is the right man. The right man for whatever job I ask him to do."

Pilate again stood up and began pacing back and forth. "You know, I've been thinking as we've been talking. I've got to do something about those insane religious authorities coming back and arresting you again. I never want you to go through that punishment again. The thought has occurred to me that there is a way to protect you and stop them from ever arresting you again."

Pilate's words spiked Jake's full attention and he perked up in his decorative chair.

"You have become a very important person to me and my family," Pilate stated. "I hope you know that. We owe you a deep debt of gratitude because of the great service you performed for us, regarding the Lucius Taurus affair. You saved our family and myself from great personal destruction. Because of that, I am indebted to you and I will do all that is within my power to protect you. I think I have come up with a way to block these religious nuts from ever laying their hands on you again."

Jake stared at Pilate in disbelief. "Sir, that would be marvelous. It's beyond my comprehension as to how that could be possible."

"I know it is beyond your comprehension," Pilate said smoothly. A confident satisfaction swept over his face. "The idea just came to me and I know I can do it and how I can do it."

Jake gazed at the governor in anticipation.

"It is really a very simple solution," Pilate said with a wave of his hand. "It is called … Roman citizenship. I am going to make you a Roman citizen. And I have a plan as to how I can do it."

"A Roman citizen!" Jake blurted out, his voice piquing in happy delirium. "How can that ever be?"

"You see, I know the Roman laws. Once I declare that you are a Roman citizen, the Jewish authorities had better not touch you or they will answer to me!"

"Sir, I would be very grateful for such protection. But I'm a Jewish Christian. Not at all a Roman."

"Roman law provides several methods for acquiring Roman citizenship," Pilate stated confidently. "The method I am thinking of is a common means of securing citizenship. There is a provision in the law that allows a member of an auxiliary militia or a member of the Roman army to be granted citizenship. As far as I'm concerned, you acted as my own personal auxiliary militia when you performed the special service to me and my family in the business of Lucius Taurus.

Therefore, I am going to write up a commission establishing you as my special, personal auxiliary militia, assigned to me, stating that you acted under my orders to provide a confidential service for me. Along with that I will write up a citation stating that you acted with great valor and courage in fulfilling your mission. That should do it!"

The governor paused and looked at Jake with a satisfied expression. "Well, what do you think?"

"Sir, I am totally speechless." Jake truly was surprised. "You are too kind."

"Roman citizenship is my gift to you for your saving my life," Pilate smiled. "And remember, from now on you will be under my full protection. If any of these religious nuts even touch you, I will drop the hammer on them."

"Thank you, sir," Jake said in humility, his voice shaking in disbelief. "I will be forever grateful for you saving my life."

"It is the least I can do," the governor smiled. "I will have that commission letter written up and I will sign it. Then I will inform the Sanhedrin and the chief priests of your Roman citizenship and tell them in no uncertain terms to keep their hands off of you. Your citizenship will be recorded in our local court filings here in Jerusalem, in Judea, and then in our court filings in Rome. Everything will be official, I promise you."

Jake sat limp in the chair overwhelmed with emotion. He was so stunned by all that Pilate had promised to do, he couldn't move for a moment.

"Well, Mister Jezreel, what do you think you will do with your new found freedom?" Pilate asked with a laugh.

Jake shook his head, as if to fling the cobwebs out. "I guess I'll go back to doing detective work," Jake whimsically said. "It's all I know how to do. 'Course I'll have to clean up my office before I can start work."

"I'll take care of that," Pilate stated firmly. "I'll have some of my people recruit a labor team comprised of religious leaders and their cronies. I'll make them clean up your office facility. And I'll also make the religious leaders pay for all the repairs. Anything else?"

"Well, sir, there is one more item that is the most important to me. You see, my secretary who is also my fiancée, is in prison somewhere, I don't know where. Could you …"

"Say no more," Pilate interrupted. "I'll take care of that, too. What is her name? I will immediately get my military adjutant to track down the prison she is in and have her released before close of business today."

"Thank you, sir. Getting her back means more to me than anything else."

"I know exactly what you mean." And then Pilate looked up as his adjutant opened the door and entered the office. "Well, Mister Jezreel, here comes your food. And I see this is some of my very favorite foods. Eat up while I write out your commission statement and the Roman citizenship citation."

Pilate then looked at his adjutant, who had just placed the delectable food in front of Jake on a small table. "I have another assignment for you that requires immediate attention," he stated to his adjutant.

"Yes, sir. What is your assignment?"

"Mister Jezreel's secretary has been imprisoned. I want you to locate the prison in which she is incarcerated and order her immediate release. And her name is …?"

Chapter 14

SHIFTING SANDS

Jake could not contain his excitement as he followed Pilate's military adjutant down into the prison to release Hannah. The detective was still weak from his own imprisonment. But right now, he felt like a million, knowing he would soon see his girl again.

As Jake walked along side Pilate's military adjutant on their way to the prison, Jake remarked to the adjutant, "I understand that it was you who took the time to find me in prison and report back to Governor Pilate."

"Yes, I was able to find out the cell where you were incarcerated," said the adjutant, slightly glancing over at Jake. "When I learned of your imprisonment, I knew Governor Pilate would want to know of your plight."

"Well, I want you to know how very grateful I am to you for caring enough to get me released," Jake said. "You are a good man."

The adjutant said nothing, just looked straight ahead. He wasn't quite sure how to respond to Jake's compliment. Finally he stated, "It was my pleasure. I knew you had done a great service for his excellency in the past. I knew he would want to secure your release."

"Well, all I can say is thank you, thank you very much." Then in a flash of genuine gratitude, Jake asked the adjutant, "I've never known your name. May I call you by your first name?"

The adjutant continued to look straight ahead as they walked, with a rather stoic expression. Then he half smiled and without looking at Jake said, "My name is Marcius."

"Marcius," Jake repeated. "That is a good, strong sounding name. Pleased to meet you, Marcius."

"My mother seemed to like the name. I've lived with it for years," the adjutant stated with a smile, still looking straight ahead.

Pilate was right when he said earlier that the Jewish authorities didn't keep good records of where prisoners were jailed. Adjutant Marcius had to search diligently in tracking down the correct jailhouse where Hannah was confined. But through his due diligence, the adjutant finally found her prison. And as they approached the cell where Hannah was caged, a scintillating thrill shot through Jake's body.

Finally halting at her cell, adjutant Marcius spouted out his command.

"Jailer! We are here to release Hannah Haggai!" he demanded, as he handed over Pilate's official release orders to the prison guard. "Release her immediately! And be quick about it!"

The guard scrambled into action! His keys hurriedly rattled in the jail door lock. The barred door swung wide open. In the dim light, Jake could see that the tiny, canister size cubical was crammed with women who had been imprisoned for their Christian faith.

"Hannah Haggai!" the guarded yelled into the dingy darkness of the cell. "You are released! Please come out! Please come out as quickly as you can!"

A few tense moments passed. "Hannah, they are calling for you!" the other imprisoned ladies called toward the back of the jail cell. "They are letting you go! Hurry!"

Jake impatiently took a few steps toward the open cell door. "Hannah!" he called into the murky compartment. "It's me! Jake! You're free! Come on out!" The dim lighting made it nearly impossible for Jake to see anything in the cell but shadowy figures. "Hannah!" he called again in desperation.

Finally, Jake could see some of the ladies helping Hannah make her way to the front of the tiny cubicle. In a moment,

Hannah stumbled her way to the cell door. Jake gasped. Hannah looked as if she was half-starved and emaciated. Her face was ashen white. Her eyes sunken; half-closed. But when she saw Jake, she brightened up.

"Hi, honey," she said trying to put a lilt in her weak voice. "It is so wonderful to see you." Though she was malnourished and sickly, she managed to put a happy twinkle in her eyes.

Jake ran to her and scooped her up into his arms. He didn't care about the proper Jewish rules of etiquette at this moment. He held her tightly in a loving embrace. And as he did, he felt her collapse into his arms.

"Hannah! What's wrong!" he exclaimed, as he lowered her to the floor, still holding her.

"I feel kinda weak, right now," she quietly said, her eyes still half-closed. "But I'm gonna be okay now. You're here." Then she faintly smiled at him, her sense of humor drifting to the surface. "I sure would love to have one of your cinnamon doughnuts, right now," she softly breathed, in a delirious laugh.

Jake looked up at the women still in the jail cell. "What is wrong with her!?" Jake demanded.

"She is so loving," one of the woman said. "She always is giving her food away to others who weren't getting enough. In this tiny cell there never is enough food to go around. She always shared hers."

Another woman spoke up. "We tried to get her to not give away so much of her food but she insisted that they needed it more than she did. She said she was young and strong and the older ladies needed food more that she did."

Jake looked down into Hannah's half-closed, listless eyes and smiled. "Listen, girl, we're going to get you outa here and nurse you back to health. I'll get Caleb to hand-deliver some cinnamon doughnuts right away!"

Her listless eyes opened slightly more. "Sounds wonderful to me," the girl weakly said, her words slurring together. For a moment her eyes brightened. "It is so good to see you, Jake."

"Sweetheart, I've got to get you home." And then he remembered.

"Oh, we've got no place to go. Your home, my home, our office have all …" And then he cut off the rest of his statement.

Adjutant Marcius stood by, watching and listening. He spoke up. "Mister Jezreel, we have emergency quarters in the governor's mansion. I'll take it upon myself to house you and the lady in those quarters, that is until we can get your office and your residences back in order."

"Would you do that for us?" Jake asked in shock.

"I have the authority," adjutant Marcius stated. "The governor has told me to accommodate your every need, so I am authorized to do this. But first, allow me to help you both get back to the governor's mansion. Your lady friend is very weak and I will assist you in getting her there."

"Thank you so very much," Jake sighed in admiration. "You and the governor are so very gracious."

The adjutant halfway bowed. He gestured to a Roman soldier who had escorted them from Pilate's headquarters. "These people need our help in taking them back to the Praetorium. Soldier, we will be as careful and gentle as if they were own family members."

And then Adjutant Marcius, himself, knelt down, tenderly scooped up Hannah in his arms, and began carrying her back to the Praetorium. Hannah looked up into Marcius' face and smiled. Then she laid her head on his shoulder and crooned, "Thank you soldier. You're a wonderful man. You have been sent by God to help me."

Safely housed in Pilate's quarters, Adjutant Marcius spoke to Jake and Hannah. "You are under the governor's personal protection, now. None of the religious leaders can or will harm you here. I know you both are still weak from your time in prison, so my fellow Roman soldier who escorted you here will make all the preparations for your stay here."

"Thank you, sir," Hannah faintly replied. "We thank God for you taking a hand in getting us released."

Marcius halfway bowed again. "We Romans do have our good points. Just to let you both know, Governor Pilate has also authorized me to order the release of Ms. Haggai's parents. I have located the prisons where they are being held. So, upon your leave, I am off to the prisons where they are confined to order their immediate releases."

For the next few weeks, Jake and Hannah had the run of the "emergency quarters" in Pilate's mansion. The governor made sure that his guests got the best of service and all the nourishment needed to get them back to tip-top health.

"Spare nothing to provide for my trusted friends," Pilate told his military staff. "This man has done a great service for me. Nothing is too good for this man whom I have the greatest respect for."

Most importantly, Jake and Hannah also enjoyed the comfort of being together again after being separated for so many months.

Jake and Hannah continued to gain back their strength as the days passed. They also were able to spend a good deal of time together renewing their relationship and making plans for the future. Pilate's gracious hospitality allowed them to live in safety. But it finally came time for the couple to leave the governor's haven and venture back out into the ugly world. Jake's new Roman citizenship, granted by Pilate, guaranteed that the religious leaders would not harass him. So, it would be safe for him and Hannah to get back into society.

Pilate also got his own little dig at the pompous religious leaders. He demanded that the Jewish leaders refurbish Jake's destroyed office and home. And they had to foot the bill! Pilate also ordered the religious elites to be personally involved is making the repairs. Pilate's orders were emphatically clear, "The religious leaders will pay for all the repairs – to both facilities – out of their own pockets! And just for good measure, make some of those highbrow leaders get their dainty hands dirty and do some of the hard labor!"

The religious leaders were forced to eat their humble pie. They grumbled about it but with much humiliation, they forked over all the necessary cash needed to fix the devastation they had created. The Roman official and soldiers in charge of overseeing the reconstruction projects took their cue from Pilate and made every effort to humiliate the religious leaders every way they could. The supervising Roman official insisted that the finished work on Jake's office and home had to exceed the previous standards.

So, when the renovation projects were finally completed, Jake's detective agency office and his home exceeded all expectations. The facilities ended up as top-of-the-line facilities – better than ever before!

Finally, the big day came! On that first day back in the detective's renovated office, Adjutant Marcius, escorted Jake and Hannah into the premises.

"Mister Jezreel, here are the keys to your brand-new office," Marcius stated as they paused in front of the office door, Door 211. "I hope you will find everything satisfactory."

Jake took the door key and turned it in the lock. As the office door swung open Jake hesitated. He couldn't believe his eyes. A bright, immaculate workplace lay just beyond the threshold.

"Wow! Now, that is cool!" Jake exclaimed.

"Ohhhh …" was all Hannah could say, as she covered her mouth with her hands in excitement.

"Go on in," Marcius said with a smile on his face. "It's all yours, compliments of Governor Pilate."

"I am just amazed," Jake said, looking around, as he walked into his new office.

Marcius followed them. "We put all your files back in the filing cabinets, as best we could. Ms. Haggai, you will probably want to refile them since I realize you more than likely have your own filing system. But at least the files aren't scattered all over the floor like they were when we first started the cleanup."

Marcius then reached over and picked up a burlap bag from the top of Hannah's brand-new secretarial desk. "When work first started on cleaning up your destroyed office, I noticed papyrus papers scattered all over the place. I also noticed certain papyrus notes that had been purposely ripped up and strewn everywhere. These particular papyrus notes seemed to have a specific importance because I noticed there were frequent references to Jesus of Nazareth in the writing. So, I gathered up all the shredded pieces of these particular papers and put them in this burlap bag. My thought was that maybe you could piece the notes back together and salvage the information preserved in these records."

Stunned and shocked by the adjutant's surprise announcement, Jake and Hannah stood motionless in disbelief. "Those are the Jesus files!" Jake said as his voice elevated in excitement. "I thought those files about Jesus were destroyed and lost forever." Slowly Jake reached out for the bag. His hands began to tremble in anticipation, as he clutched the burlap sack. "Sir, you just don't know how much this means to us. The treasure that you have recovered," Jake said slowly to Marcius. His hand now was visibly shaking. "In this ordinary sack you have preserved our most valued possession. This is my recorded history of the life of Jesus Christ!"

Pilate's adjutant seemed to already understand the intrinsic value of the notes. "I realized as much," he proudly said with a blissful expression. "You see, I read some of your notes as I picked them up off the floor. I even began to piece some of the notes together and began to read about this fascinating Man named Jesus. What few notes I read, convinced me that Jesus is a Man worthy of surrendering one's life to."

"And what decision have you made?" Jake asked.

"I will continue to seriously consider the matter." Marcius smiled and nodded his head signifying he really meant what he said.

"I truly want to thank you, Marcius, for rescuing these valuable notes," Jake stated. "From the bottom of my heart, you have my undying gratitude. We thought these notes were destroyed and lost forever. Now, you have recovered them. You have given the Christian community a great gift; provided us a great service."

"It is my great pleasure," Marcius said. "However, now comes the really hard work of piecing all these fragments of notes back together."

Hannah spoke up. "Oh, it won't be hard work at all! In fact, it will be our delight! We will have fun reading about Jesus' life all over again and taking each piece of the puzzle and putting it all back together again. Oooh, I'm already excited! Thank you, sir. You are too kind!"

Beyond the walls of Jake and Hannah's safe haven, Saul of Tarsus still stormed around the city ravaging the church members that still remained in Jerusalem. He attacked like a savage beast. It was all too clear that Saul's burning desire in life was to destroy all remnants of the Christian movement in the capital city. Those Christians who dared to stay remained at their own peril. Jesus' apostles remained holding the nucleus of the church together. Many believers eventually fled the city, scattering to the wind. Scattering throughout the Roman Empire.

Under the protection of Pilate, Jake still was able to operate his detective agency. But his detective business began to drop off. His Jewish clients learned of his new found faith in Christ and stopped coming to him. He was "blacklisted" by the Jewish population. The little bit of investigative work he did pick up was primarily from Roman citizens who lived in Jerusalem or from foreign clients. Business soon became almost nonexistent. But when a person produces a fine product, worthy of attracting attention, people will find out about it and start coming back. Jake could only hope.

Chapter 15

THE DISGRACING OF NICODEMUS

The onslaught of persecution not only decimated the common Christian citizens but it also ravaged the ranks of the religious leaders. Those religious leaders who dared claim Christ as their Savior found harassment, as well. This fact became all to painfully real, late one morning. As Jake sat at his desk with Hannah in the newly renovated office, Nicodemus appeared in the office doorway.

"Hello," Nicodemus said cheerfully. "No one was in the outer office, so I just invited myself in."

Jake jumped up in respect and greeted his honored guest. "Well, hello. You are always welcome," he said with a smile. "Work has been kinda slow lately and we weren't expecting any company. Please come in and sit down."

Hannah also stood up. "We were just sitting here talking. Talking about those wonderful days when Jesus was here and we could hear His voice and listen to Him teach."

"Sounds like a great discussion," the gentleman said. "Those were wonderful times."

Nicodemus looked at Hannah. "Please sit back down in your chair. I'll sit in this other armchair across the desk from your boss."

As the gentleman took a seat, the three of them sat looking at each other for a long moment.

"The persecution has been devastating, hasn't it," Jake stated trying to fill the silence.

"Yes, it has." Nicodemus' voice was uneasy.

Jake sensed a nervous tone in the gentleman's voice.

"Nicodemus, is something wrong? There is a note of sadness in your voice. Are you downhearted?"

"Actually, no, I'm not downhearted. In fact, it is the best thing that could have happened to me."

Jake scooted closer to the man across the desk. "What has happened?"

"I have been permanently removed and expelled from the Sanhedrin," Nicodemus flatly stated. "I have been barred from ever holding a position on the High Court. All the religious authorities knew of my loyalty to Jesus even before Jesus was crucified. But when I made a public profession of Christ as my Lord and Savior, that was too much for the Sanhedrin to endure. They stripped me of my seat on the council."

"How could they do that!" Jake exclaimed. "You are one of the most respected and honorable men in the Sanhedrin!"

"None of that matters to them, anymore," the gentleman sadly said. "These men have been my friends for many years. At least, I thought they were my friends. Now, they have turned into a pack of ravenous wolves. So ravenous that when they threw me out of the Sanhedrin, their final act of judgment upon me was to have me beaten. So, they dragged me outside of the courtroom and they beat me."

Jake jumped to his feet in horror. His chair flung back against the wall. "What! They beat you! They actually beat you! How could they! The animals! The barbarians!"

Hannah jumped up out of her chair, too. "Sir, are you all right?" she cried out. "How badly did they hurt you?"

"Oh, it was a usual beating … with rods. I'm black and blue but I'll live. No bones broken, I think."

"I just cannot believe how vicious our religious authorities have become," Jake fumed.

"They have become quite vicious. Hatred is a deadly poison," Nicodemus' voice choked. Tears welled up in his aged eyes. "That is the reason I have come by your office. I've come to say good-bye."

"Good-bye? Where are you going?"

"The antagonistic Jewish authorities have given me twenty-four hours to get out of Jerusalem," Nicodemus' voice flooded with dejection. "I have been banished from Jerusalem. I am not allowed to ever set foot in Jerusalem again. Never to see God's holy Temple again. Never to see these blessed streets or my comfortable home again. All my wealth has been stripped from me. It is all gone. I have nothing left of this world's goods. That great statesman, Gamaliel, has offered to let me stay at a home he has in the country. I'll be living on the good graces of my friend, Gamaliel."

"How can they do that to you?" Jake exclaimed, still standing but now leaning on his extended arms on his desk. He bowed his head. He was hiding the anger on his face from Nicodemus.

"Jake, it is an honor to suffer for my Lord and my Savior. I consider it to be an honor for the Sanhedrin to punish me in this way," Nicodemus seemed to drift off into a wonderful trance. "From the very first evening when I spoke to Jesus privately, I knew He was a very special Man. He told me then that I needed to be 'born again'. Eventually, I figured out what He meant. He was telling me that I needed to be born spiritually through faith and trust in Him. Well, I've trusted in Him completely. I am born again spiritually. And I openly let my faith in Jesus be known. I knew what would happen, but I didn't care anymore. I love Jesus more than anything and that's all that matters. 'Let the chips fall where they may', is how the old saying goes. So, I'm glad they threw me out of the Sanhedrin. I'm glad to be done with all that religious hypocrisy. I've got Jesus Christ as my Savior. Nothing else matters!"

Jake shook his head in admiration. "I admire you, sir. Your faith is truly built on Jesus Christ!"

Hannah gazed at the gentleman. "What will become of you? Will you live in the country forever? Can you never come back to the city to see us?"

"Oh, the Lord Jesus is not done with me, yet," Nicodemus smiled. "Thank you for your concern, Hannah. Jesus is just planting me in a different spot. As long as I draw breath, I'll proclaim my Lord Christ to anyone in the country who will listen to me! But please feel free to come and visit me anytime. Our fellowship is not over, by any means."

"So, when will you be leaving town?" Jake asked. "You said you have only twenty-four hours."

"As soon as I leave your office, I will be departing Jerusalem," Nicodemus sighed. "I have some helpers who are assisting me with my luggage and baggage. We will be leaving for the country momentarily. The chief priests are watching me right now, at this moment. They are waiting for me, not to help me but to make sure that I leave the city today."

Jake stood straight up. "Well, I'll be going with you, sir, to help carry your luggage," Jake stated abruptly. "They aren't going to run you out of town without me helping you and supporting you. I know it's a quick decision but I really want to help you. And I won't have it any other way."

"Thank you so very much, Jake," Nicodemus quietly said. "That means a lot."

Jake smiled at the sad gentleman. "Sir, it will be my greatest personal honor to help such a good friend and brother Christian as you. Besides, by going with you, I'll find out where you'll be living and we can come and visit with you in the future."

Jake turned to Hannah. "I know this is a quick decision, kinda spur of the moment," he said to her. "But I think it's the right thing to do,"

"Honey, you must go. You must help our friend," Hannah said, her voice filled with compassionate love.

"Besides, we don't have any business goin' on, anyway," Jake smiled. "And you might as well go on home for the day. We'll get back to doing nothin' tomorrow."

Nicodemus stood up and paused, staring at the detective and the girl. "Before we part, let me mention something that is heavy on my heart. There's one more person I implore you to pray for." Tears now flowed down his cheeks and onto his silvery beard. "Please pray for my good friend and fellow Christian, Joseph of Arimathea. Joseph risked his seat on the Sanhedrin as well when he buried Jesus in his own tomb. All he wanted to do was show his loyalty to Jesus by giving our Lord a decent and respectable burial. Now, Joseph is probably going to be stripped of all his authority and his seat on the Sanhedrin. I don't know what will become of him. Do pray that the Lord will give him strength through this time of testing in his Christian life."

Chapter 16

TARGET: DAMASCUS

The next day, as Jake returned to Jerusalem from helping Nicodemus move into Gamaliel's country home, he had to pass the Sanhedrin council building. He noticed a beehive of activity in the street around the building. "I wonder what all that fuss is about?" he asked himself. Very quickly he found out.

As Jake opened the door to the office, Hannah jumped to her feet immediately when she saw him.

"Jake, you're back!" she exclaimed. She ran over to the detective and grabbed him by the arm. "I was getting antsy waiting for you! Governor Pilate has been desperately trying to find you! All morning, he's had couriers frantically running in and out of our office. He wants you at his headquarters immediately."

"Why, what's the big emergency?"

"His envoy said Pilate has urgent business with you. Something to do with Saul of Tarsus! The governor needs to talk to you right away! His people have been searching for you last evening and now this morning! You need to get over to his headquarters right now! Go!"

"Okay, thanks, angel. I'm on my way."

When Jake reached Pilate's headquarters, Adjutant Marcius jumped up out of his chair and rushed to greet him.

"Thank you for coming," he stated eagerly. "Governor Pilate needs to talk to you! Please follow me."

They hurriedly crossed the adjutant's office and opened Pilate's main office door. "Sir, Jake Jezreel, the investigator is here," he announced.

"Mister Jezreel, you have finally come," Pilate stated while sitting behind his ornate desk. "I've been looking all over Jerusalem for you."

"Sir, I was out of the city helping Pharisee Nicodemus move his belongings. The Sanhedrin threw him out of Jerusalem permanently."

"Yes, I heard about that. Nicodemus is such a good man," stated Pilate. "The religious lunatics are showing their true maniacal colors, again. They are once again revealing how hateful they are. In fact, it is for that very reason I need to see you. They are now forming up a caravan of their accomplices to go to Damascus to track down and arrest Christians who have fled there for safety."

Pilate gestured to the armchair across the desk from him. "Please, Detective Jezreel, have a seat while I explain to you what is going on."

Pilate then stretched his arms out and placed his palms flat down on the desk top. His sharp eyes narrowed as he emphasized the severity of the situation.

"I have discovered, through my sources, that the leadership here in Jerusalem is determined to crush the spread of Christianity. They don't want Christianity to become established in Damascus, since that city is a major trading center. Their fear is that from that trading hub, Christianity could quickly spread throughout the Roman Empire. So, their scheme is to capture all the Christian believers in Damascus and drag them back here to Jerusalem to imprison them."

Jake looked bewildered. "Sir, can they do that?" he asked.

"Saul of Tarsus has received authorization from the chief priests to make these arrests," Pilate stated. "I try not to interfere in the Jews religious squabbles. However, I am concerned about any violations of Roman law in this particular trip.

"As I said, I have found out that this whole expedition is spearheaded by that zealot Saul of Tarsus. He is the main person who keeps stirring up most of the trouble. The best I can tell, Saul is out to eradicate Christianity off the face of the earth. I really don't care one way or the other. But I know Saul is a troublemaker and

I'm going to have to deal with him sooner or later. That is why I've called upon you."

"Your excellency, I am at your service," Jake declared.

"I knew you would be," Pilate stated with a smile. Then the governor stood up and began to slowly pace back and forth behind his desk, as he carefully unfolded his story.

"From my informants I have found out that Saul of Tarsus went to the high priest and asked for letters to be presented to the synagogues in Damascus. These letters give him full authority to seek out and arrest any Christians who have escaped Saul's reign of terror here in Jerusalem. In fact, Saul and his gang of cohorts will be leaving early tomorrow morning on their search-and-capture expedition. That is why I've been diligently searching for you. I need you to go along with them to keep track of all of the group's activities. I know these people can be ruthless, so I want you to report back to me anything that they do that would violate Roman law."

"Yes, sir, I'm ready to serve you," Jake affirmed. "But what will be my cover? Won't Saul be suspicious of me as an outsider and not a part of his close confidants?"

"Not a problem," Pilate said confidently. "I've got that all taken care of. I'm going to give you a letter that authorizes you to travel with Saul's entourage, as my personal Roman governmental representative. With that authorization, he cannot deny you from traveling with him. It is vital for my purposes that you accompany Saul. I need your powers of observation to detect any suspicious activities by Saul and his henchmen that would be violations of Roman law. Of course, you will not tell Saul the real purpose of your traveling with them. Your purpose on the surface would be only as a Roman government escort representing the governor."

"Sir, you know that most of the people in the group will know who I am and that I am a private investigator."

"All the better," Pilate smirked. "That will add authenticity to your escorting them as a government representative."

The governor opened a desk drawer, pulled out the official letter, and handed it to Jake. "Here, this document gives you full authority to travel with Saul and his group. He cannot question your right to travel with them. I have sanctioned your authority to go along on their trip."

Pilate then reached over to the right corner of his desk and picked up a small tan leather bag from the desktop. "Here is some money for your needs while you are on your trip. You'll be gone probably for several weeks, so you'll need this cash to sustain you. Saul surely won't provide for your needs while you're on the trip. So, the Roman government will provide for your needs."

Pilate smiled at Jake. "Now, you'd better hurry. You need to get ready to leave with Saul in the morning. They will be leaving from the Sanhedrin council building at the crack of dawn."

"Governor," Jake said confidently, "I won't disappoint you."

After leaving Pilate, Jake quickly made his way back to the office.

"Hannah, I'll be leaving on an investigation for Governor Pilate tomorrow," he told the girl. "For now, let's keep this info on the down-low. I'll be out of town for several weeks in Damascus. I need you to 'hold the fort' while I'm away."

"You know I can 'hold the fort'", Hannah said. "But you know I'll miss you a bunch."

"I'll miss you, too, honey. I'll be thinking about you every minute."

That evening, Jake threw together a few extra clothes in a burlap sack, along with some food for the trip.

The detective arrived at the council building bright and early the next day as the sun peeked over the Mount of Olives to the east. He found the Damascus entourage forming up. Jake searched for Saul. He could never forget Saul's penetrating face. In a moment, the detective heard the distinctive, snarling voice of Saul barking orders to his people. Without hesitation, Jake strode up to the growling Pharisee.

"Saul of Tarsus?" Jake asked already knowing the answer.

Saul turned around slowly, deliberately. "Yes. And what do you want?" he snapped in a defiant tone.

"My name is Jake Jezreel. I have been ordered by Governor Pilate to escort you on your journey to Damascus. I will be acting in an official Roman capacity as the governor's personal representative to ensure that there are no hindrances to your trip along the way."

Saul glared at Jake with steely-eyed suspicion, his hands on his hips. "I didn't know Pilate took such a vested interest in my campaign," Saul sneered, squinting his black eyes. "Since when did the governor decide to involve himself in what is purely a Jewish matter?"

Jake handed Saul Pilate's letter of authorization. "I can't answer your questions. Here is my full, official authorization by the Roman governor to proceed with you to Damascus. Read it yourself. There are no ambiguities in the wording of the document. I am ordered by Governor Pilate to escort your expedition."

One of Saul's henchmen standing nearby said, "Saul, I recognize this clown. He's a private investigator. Pilate must have hired him. What's your game, gumshoe?"

"Pilate needed a representative to escort your group. Since my detective work has been rather slow lately, he ordered me to be his representative on this trip."

The henchman glared at the detective. "So, you've sold out to Rome! You work for the Roman government! You betray your own people!" he growled. "You're a turn coat and a traitor to your own country. You're worse than a tax collector, siding with the enemy."

Another rabble laughed, "This makes you a government man. A dirty Roman government man."

Jake felt their hot anger and the hesitation in all of the group standing around him. He decided to counter attack and lay out the facts.

"Either I go with you, as authorized by the governor in that letter you hold in your hand or I'll shut down this whole expedition. That letter gives me that authority. Either I go or you don't go." Jake stood there with his arms folded in front of him with a confident smile on his face. He knew he had the full might of Rome on his side.

Saul's expression quickly changed to exasperation. His face turned into a scowl and he glared angrily at Jake. For a long moment the two men stared at each other. Then Saul handed the letter back to Jake.

"Okay. You may come along," Saul mumbled. "Just stay out of my way."

The expedition pulled out of Jerusalem at about seven AM on the 140 mile journey to Damascus. The trip required several days, estimating about 25 miles a day. There were a couple of routes the group could have traveled but Saul chose the road that hugged the Jordan River. This route finally emerged into Galilee. The trip brought back many happy memories for Jake, as he retraced his steps and recalled the last time he ventured along this route. On the previous trip, his objective was to investigate Jesus. Fond memories flooded back to him. He remembered meeting Jesus for the first time. And with great satisfaction, he savored the memories about how that encounter with Jesus had radically changed his life.

The group arrived in Galilee on the third day of the journey. The route skirted the western shore of the Sea of Galilee. They traveled past the nearby city of Tiberias, nestled on the sea shore. The city had been built by Herod Antipas, who named it after Emperor Tiberias. The city also was the capital of Galilee. From there the group traveled through Magdala, the hometown of Mary Magdalene. When the entourage reached the northern shore and the city of Capernaum, they stopped for the night. They even stayed in the same hotel where Jake had stayed on his earlier investigative trip.

As Jake walked the streets of Capernaum, overwhelming love welled up in his heart! Just being back in Capernaum invigorated all the past fond associations with Jesus and specific places in the town. Everywhere he looked, he could visualize wonderful pictures of Jesus teaching here, teaching there. The images of Jesus filled the city streets.

That night Jake could not sleep. His excitement meter pegged out! His mind spilled over with so many delightful memories! Jake soon found himself escaping out of his hotel room and walking the very same streets where Jesus had taught.

So many wonderful, heartwarming recollections. Every street

held a treasured memory. But Jake had to wrap up all those wonderful remembrances and put them to bed. It was time for the detective to get a little shuteye.

The next morning, Saul and his gang got back on the road. Jake had to tuck away all of his happy memories, as the group left Capernaum. Silently Jake thanked the Lord that He had led Saul to choose this route to get to Damascus. The short time spent in Capernaum had been a wonderful time of refreshing, reflection, and remembering.

The entourage continued on the road to Damascus. North of the Sea of Galilee, the road turned right and angled northeastward. Once they passed the city of Chorazin, ahead of them lay a sixty mile stretch of road, before they would reach Damascus. After they crossed the Jordan River in northern Galilee and climbed out of the valley, the terrain undulated but lay relatively flat. They could make good time.

As the journey progressed, the patience of everybody in the group began to wear a little thin. Everyone was hot and irritated and annoyed. All during the entire trip, Jake could hear the angry discussions about Christians circulating among the rabbles traveling with Saul. It was obvious these men pressed on, totally driven by their hatred and their contempt for Christians. But now, as the angry mob trudged the final hot, dusty miles, their exasperation began to bubble over.

"These disgusting Christians!" one hot and tired rabble complained. "Why do they have to cause so much trouble! We wouldn't have to undertake this lousy trip if those useless Christians would just give up this phony cult they belong to!"

"Yeah," growled another. "I'm dog-tired. I hope when we catch these crumby Christians, we just throw them *under* the jail forever!"

On top of all this simmering discontent, the members of the mob still showed their suspicion of Jake and his role in the expedition. So, no one really talked much to the detective. That was just fine with Jake. He didn't want to talk with them, either. All he cared about was focusing on his job of spying on Saul to see if he could catch the zealot violating Roman law in this location far, far away from

Jerusalem. He even secretly hoped he could gum up the works of Saul's plans by somehow warning the Christians in Damascus about the approaching danger.

As the miles ground along on the fifth day, the group left Galilee behind and entered the province of Bashan. In the far distance to his left, Jake caught sight of the dark, gray conical shape of Mount Hermon off to the west. Though the mountain lay on the faraway horizon, it still was imposing in size, standing tall for all to see. Jake recalled the story that Peter, James, and John told about the earth-shattering event on Mount Hermon when Jesus was gloriously transfigured before their very eyes. During His transfiguration, Jesus' godly glory shown out from His human form and His clothes gleamed a dazzling white.

As Peter told the story, he remembered, "A cloud covered the sky above us and a voice sounded out from the cloud, announcing to us, 'This is my beloved Son. Listen and obey Him.'"

As Jake looked over at Mount Hermon, he wished he had been there that day to see Jesus' transfiguration. *'But I'm glad Peter told the story,'* he thought to himself. *'It is even more proof positive evidence that Jesus truly is the Christ – the Son of God!'*

By the time the group camped at the end of the fifth day, Saul's entourage had crossed over into Syria and the Ituraea. Now they were within range of Damascus and an easy half day journey.

As the sixth day of the mission dawned, everyone woke up eager to get back on the road and get this torturous expedition over with. There were only a few miles left to travel. Their target was almost in reach. Even though everybody in the mob was tired and disgusted, their mission to eradicate Christianity from Damascus drove them on. All they could think about was getting a glimpse on the distant horizon of the city walls of Damascus.

"Are you tired of your escort job by now, shamus?" one of the group chided the detective.

"No, I'm thoroughly enjoying myself," Jake laughed. "The fresh air. The 'fine' food. The splendid companionship. You know, the perfect trip!"

"Very funny, shamus. You're just a laugh a minute. Well, we'll be getting to Damascus today a little after lunch time and I'm looking forward to getting some real food in the city."

"I'm glad to hear that," Jake said. "We've come a long distance to capture Christians. 140 miles. That is quite a long journey just to arrest some folks who aren't even bothering you. Saul must really hate these followers of Jesus."

"We all hate them. Otherwise, none of us would have come on this stinkin' journey into this foreign land. We believe like Saul does, that Christianity should not be allowed to exist in Israel or any other place on earth."

"And you think there are Christians in Damascus?"

"Oh, yeah! We know they're there! We have reports they are huddled in the city like a pack of dirty dogs. And we know what to do with dirty dogs," the man laughed out loud.

The entourage got started moving at around eight o'clock that morning. The sun began to quickly heat up the day. The desert road was dry and dusty. Mile after mile trudged by. Closer and closer to Damascus the expedition marched.

Around noon time, the group approached Damascus. The city loomed ahead. A happy, brighter attitude swept over everyone in the group. About another half hour and they would be walking through the city gates.

Suddenly, in a blinding flash, the sky lit up in an explosion with intense light! The glaring light blazed brighter than the noon day sun! So powerful was the explosive shock wave of light that it knocked Jake off his feet. As he lay knocked down onto the sandy dust of the road, Jake shielded his eyes from the blinding glare of the intense rays. And then he noticed that everyone else in the group also lay sprawled out flat in the road. The blast of light had sent a powerful shock wave through the air, striking all of them.

As he lay in the roadway, Jake thought he heard a sound, almost like a voice, emitting from the sustained brilliant light overhead. But he couldn't make out anything that was recognizable about the voice-like sound. Then Jake felt a presence – a wonderful, familiar presence. It had the sweet aroma of heaven. Jake lay there, face down, not wanting to look up. He just bowed his head and felt at peace.

Then Jake heard another strange sound. It was Saul of Tarsus, who also had been struck to the ground by the flash of light. He was on his knees and seemed to be talking to the brilliant light from heaven, though he was bowed down to the ground.

"Who are you, Lord?" asked Saul in a quivering voice.

Jake realized there was a brief pause, as the strange sound continued, as if speaking to Saul.

And then Saul spoke again. "What shall I do, Lord?" he asked, still bowed in a fetal position to the ground.

Again, Jake noticed a pause but longer this time as Saul appeared to be listening to the mysterious sound from the dazzling light.

And then ... suddenly ... the intense light was gone. There they all lay, all the band of travelers, sprawled on the ground. Everyone was visibly shaken by the sudden and frightening incident. As they lay there, they all looked over at each other.

One of them exclaimed, "What in the world was that? What just happened?"

"I don't know. It was like the sun exploded!" another groaned.

One man looked at Jake. "Hey, man, are you okay?" he asked Jake.

"Yeah, I think so," the detective replied starting to stand up. He began to dust himself off and check for any broken bones. And then suddenly, Jake realized something was wrong with Saul. He rushed over to the man from Tarsus.

Saul staggered to his feet, his hands fumbling in the air, as if he was blind. "Saul! What is wrong?" Jake exclaimed.

"I can't see! I can't see!" Saul cried out. "My eyes! My eyes! The blazing light blinded me!"

Saul tried to take a step but stumbled over a rut in the road and fell to his hands and knees. "Someone help me!" he cried. "I must get to Damascus! Please help me!"

Jake and another man, named Brutus, grabbed Saul under his arms and hoisted him into a standing position. Saul still clutched at the air as if struggling to find a solid surface to cling to. "Please take me to Damascus! I can't see! You must help me get to the city!"

Jake and Brutus held Saul steady and started walking toward Damascus about two miles away. The rest of the group had finally recovered their wits about them and they trailed along behind. Jake noticed that Saul kept muttering, "I must get to the city. I must get my new orders."

Always the curious detective, Jake quietly asked Saul, "What happened to you back there on the road?"

"I can't talk about it now," Saul softly said. "I've got to sort this out in my mind first."

The visibly shaken expedition slowly shuffled their way into Damascus. Finally, at about two o'clock in the afternoon, the group made their way down the main street in the city, a street called Straight. There they found lodging at a house belonging to a man named Judas in the center of town. They were all very tired from their long, arduous journey. But adding to their physical stress, their frightening experience just outside of town had cascaded them all into a semi-shocked psychological state.

Jake and Brutus helped Saul to his room in Judas' house. But Saul seemed very detached from his surroundings. He appeared to be in a trance, adrift in another dimension. His eyes were open but he could see nothing. Saul sat on his bed with his head slightly bowed, hands folded in front of him, and he rocked backward and forward in tiny, methodic movements. He seemed to be praying.

"Saul, why don't you lay down and get some rest," Jake soothed, making an effort to get Saul more relaxed on his bed.

Saul looked up in the direction of the detective, climbing back into reality and calmly said, "No, I'm fine. Just fine. I must meditate and pray for a time. I'll be fine."

Some of Saul's traveling companions looked at Saul with disturbed expressions. "Something is very bad, wrong with Saul," they discussed among themselves. "He acts like he was hit with a ton of bricks. He acts kinda looney. Has he gone batty?"

"Well, how would you feel after being the target of that blinding light back there on the road," Jake said to them all.

"Target? What are you talkin' about? What do you mean ... target?" they all asked at once.

"Didn't you hear Saul talking to the mysterious sound coming from the light? Like he was specifically singled out and targeted by the light."

"Yeah, we all heard him talking. We just figured he was crying out in fright."

"I don't think that was it, exactly," Jake replied. "His words seemed to be part of a conversation."

"Conversation? You mean he was talking to a spirit?"

"I can't exactly say," Jake said, shaking his head. "But you must admit, Saul seems to be a changed man. Something powerful happened to him back there on the road that has altered his demeanor."

The group of men stood in a circle around their stunned leader. They all hung their heads. They were worried. Some had their arms folded in front of them, others their hands hung limply at their sides.

"What are we going to do, now?" one man asked. "Our leader is disabled. He had our only plan of attack. We have no strategy without Saul. None of us has any authority to arrest people, only Saul. What to do? What to do?"

A happy thrill ran through Jake's body as he heard the persecutors in confusion about their future attack plan. Without their leader, they were hopelessly crippled in their campaign of terror. Jake smiled a great big smile inside and praised God under his breath.

"Well, boys, let's give it some time," Jake feigned encouragement. "Maybe whatever has sidelined Saul will pass and he will eventually recover."

"Okay, detective," one of the crowd conceded. "That's all we can do. And I'm glad to hear that the Roman government man can give encouragement to us people."

"We government men always try to be helpful to our citizens," Jake smiled.

Chapter 17

SOMETHING'S VERY DIFFERENT

For three days Saul sat in his room, praying. Sometimes in a chair. Sometimes on his bed. Most of the time on his knees. But he always was praying. During those three days, Saul would not eat any food or drink anything. He seemed to be waiting ... for something.

During those three days, Jake occasionally visited Saul. "How are you doing today, Saul?" he would always ask. Their conversations began to take on the flavor of friendship. Saul seemed to have lost his usual snarling edge. His whole persona melted into a less combative demeanor and a more gracious behavior. The self-described persecutor of the church now actually started to emit an air of warmth and humility.

But one day as Jake came into the room, while Saul sat on his bed, Saul blankly stared into space in Jake's direction. He then asked an odd question. "Who are you?"

"Who am I? I'm private detective Jake Jezreel, emissary for governor Pilate."

"I know that is what you told me," Saul stated staring off into space. "But who are you, really?"

"I'm a private eye needing work and Pilate hired me."

"But you're more than that. I can sense it. There is something strangely different about you. You're not like the other men on this mission."

"I'm just a man earning his paycheck."

"I didn't know you when we started out from Jerusalem. But now after my encounter on the road, I have a sense that we have something in common."

"Encounter? What do you mean encounter?"

Saul paused, seemingly sizing up the situation. "I believe I can trust you. I can't see you but none the less, I believe I can trust you. The encounter I speak of is my encounter with the Lord Jesus Christ."

Jake jolted and staggered backward a step in shocked surprise. "You ... you saw Jesus Christ?" he asked, his voice shaking in exhilaration.

"Yes, I encountered the Lord Jesus Christ. He spoke to me from that blinding light out on the road to Damascus. He told me I was persecuting Him. I thought I was serving God by trying to destroy the Christians. But Christ made it very plain to me that because I persecuted the church, I was personally attacking Him. Jesus told me that He is so completely intertwined with His church that my attempts to destroy Christians actually were attempts to destroy Him. The Lord told me my attacks against Him were like me kicking against the sharp cattle prods used to drive cattle. He made it clear that my kicking against the sharp sticks was only injuring and destroying myself. Nothing good would come of it if I continued to attack Him.

"Then the Lord Jesus told me to come into Damascus and he would send me further instructions. I've been waiting these three days for those instructions."

Jake could hardly contain himself as he listened to the marvelous words of Saul. "Saul! All I can say is praise God! What a fantastic testimony! From what you've told me, we are brothers in Christ!"

"I knew it! I just knew it!" Saul exclaimed, leaping up, still unseeingly gazing off into space. "After my encounter on the road, I just had this sense that you and I had a common connection. It is Jesus!"

"This is fantastic!" Jake laughed. "I can't believe it! We Christians have been praying for you all these many months! This is a true miracle of God! God has marvelously answered our prayers!"

"I can't believe it myself!" Saul declared. "After all the horrible destruction I have done to the church and to all those Christians, I don't deserve any of the mercy of Jesus. And yet ... He still gives me His grace and mercy!"

"When Jesus transforms a guy, He really transforms him totally!" Jake exclaimed. "This is unreal!"

Saul's expression changed as he deliberated on his sudden metamorphosis. "I know this is only the beginning of my transformation. I know I've got a long way to go. But Jesus told me as He spoke to me along the road that He would give me further instructions as to His future plans for me."

"So, are you telling me that Jesus has called you to a new mission?" Jake asked.

"It would appear that way. He will let me know where to go from here. I may have to go as a blind man, but I will go wherever He tells me. I don't want to fight my Lord Christ any longer."

Later that same day, after lunch, Jake came back to visit the man from Tarsus. Immediately, Jake noticed a delightful, refreshing change had come over Saul's behavior. Saul was sitting in his chair with a gigantic smile on his face.

"Saul, what has happened? You look so very happy!"

"I've heard a word from the Lord Jesus," Saul said in a giddy tone. "Jesus has shown me a vision of a man named Ananias who will be coming to me to lay his hands on me so I can receive back my sight. I think this man will also give me further instructions."

As Saul finished speaking, there was a knock at the door. Saul tensed up when he heard the rap on the door. Jake did too but quickly ran to the door and opened it.

A very well dressed man stood outside the door. He appeared to be quite nervous. "I was told that Saul of Tarsus resides here," the man stated in a unsteady voice. "May I see him ... talk to him? My name is Ananias."

When Saul heard the man say his name was Ananias, he shot up straight in his chair in surprise. He half turned toward the sound of the man's voice in anticipation of God's next move.

Jake invited Ananias into the room. "Nothing to worry about, friend," Jake said calmly. "The Lord Jesus has already been here ahead of you. Welcome. Jesus has already spoken to Saul about you."

Ananias smiled and walked cautiously into the chamber. He knew who Saul was – the destroyer of the Christians. He was fully aware that Saul had come on a search-and-capture mission. In an edgy yet confident manner, Ananias walked up to Saul and stood right beside the man from Tarsus.

"Brother Saul, look up at me," Ananias stated in a calm voice. "The Lord Jesus who intercepted you as you traveled on the road, has sent me to you so you may recover your sight. Also, the Lord Jesus will fill you with the Holy Spirit, so you may be empowered to do His work." Ananias paused and then commanded, "Receive your sight once again."

Immediately, in an instant, Saul's blindness evaporated! He could see again!

"It's like great scales just fell off my eyes!" Saul exclaimed loudly, rubbing his eyes with the back of his hands. He looked up and saw Ananias and shouted, "Hallelujah! I can see again! Praise God! Praise Jesus! His mercies endure forever!"

Saul jumped up and shook Ananias' hand vigorously. He looked over at Jake, standing there in shock after seeing yet another miracle of God. Saul grabbed Jake's hand and heartily shook the detective's hand, too. Saul began to tremble in his happy exhilaration.

Ananias smiled in relief at Saul's genuine joy. He tried to calm down the emotions of the man from Tarsus.

"Brother, Saul, I have a message for you from the Lord Jesus."

Saul immediately calmed down, as best he could, and sat back down in his chair, anticipating God's further instructions.

Ananias began, "The God of our fathers has chosen you, that you should increasingly know His will, and know the Righteous One, the Lord Jesus Christ. You also will learn to hear His voice and recognize the very words of His mouth. For you shall be His witness unto all people of all the things you have seen and heard.

"The message from the Lord Jesus is this, 'Rise, and stand upon your own two feet: for I have appeared unto you for this purpose. I will make you My minister and a witness both of what things you have seen Me do, and of those things in which I will reveal to you. Delivering and rescuing you from the Jewish people, and also from the non-Jews, to whom I now am sending you. Your message will open their eyes and turn them from darkness to light, and from the power of Satan unto God, that they may receive forgiveness of sins, and inheritance among them which are sanctified by faith that is in Me.'

Ananias concluded his message from the Lord. Saul sat in his chair with a glorious expression on his face. But Ananias was not quite finished.

"And now, brother Saul, why do you sit here waiting? Arise, and be baptized, calling on the name of the Lord Jesus!"

Saul jumped up. "Why *am* I waiting around! Please baptize me. There is much work to be done!"

The next few hours erupted into a happy delirium. Word scattered like wildfire through the Christian community that Saul had become a follower of Jesus Christ and was about to be baptized. The pressure of Saul's persecution suddenly released in a hilarious display of joy throughout the believers. They now rejoiced that their old enemy was "dead" and existed no more! Now, Saul lived as one of the Christians who called Jesus Lord. The huddling Christians flocked to come and watch as Saul of Tarsus was baptized in Jesus' name!

Excitement filled the next several days. Saul began to become acquainted with his new Christian companions. Abounding elation filled those days. A new and wonderful relationship began to form between Saul and the Damascus Christians. Saul truly enjoyed his new Christian friends. And the Christian friends truly enjoyed their new brother. But he also began to connect his vast knowledge of the scriptures with the rock-solid truths contained in those scriptures about the Messiah, the Christ. Day after day Saul went to the synagogue to pour over the scrolls of the scriptures and to make notes.

One day, after a very productive study session, Saul commented to Jake, "I was so blessed to have had such a superlative teacher in Gamaliel. He grounded me in the divine nature of the scriptures. He generated a hunger and thirst for the scriptures in my soul. I grew to love the scriptures. They were my spiritual food. Now, I can see the connectivity of the entire Biblical discourse. The Biblical treatise points to the coming Messiah and it pin-points Jesus as the Messiah! This is the message I must preach. And preach it to every man, woman, and child that I come in contact with!"

One evening in the midst of a meeting with the believers Saul stated, "I have settled my past with the Lord! I know I'm forgiven! And God made it clear to me that He has entrusted to me the glorious Gospel of Jesus Christ. I am so thankful to God, Who has granted me strength and given me ability to preach the Gospel. He has counted me faithful, appointing me into the ministry. God has done this for me, a former blasphemer and a persecutor, who acted so arrogantly, insulting Jesus in my aggression. Jesus' grace has flooded over me. Jesus is supplying faith and love that can only come from my Lord Christ.

"I have come to realize that this is a faithful saying and worthy of all acceptance, 'Jesus Christ came into this world to save sinners.' And of those sinners, I am the absolute worst! But I have obtained mercy so that in me, who is the worst of sinners, Jesus Christ might reveal His overpowering patience as an illustration to those who will believe in Him for life everlasting."

Finally, it was time. The Sabbath day dawned. It was time to launch out into the deep and begin fishing for men. Saul stated to Jake, "I am going to synagogue today. Are you coming with me?"

"Absolutely, I wouldn't miss it! So, what is your plan?"

"I am going to preach Christ and that Jesus is the Son of God."

"You're going to preach Christ as Messiah in the synagogue?"

"In the synagogue."

"Sounds very provocative, my friend."

"I would submit to you the fact that Jesus Christ Himself is very provocative. He provides eternal life … but only if people will surrender to Him."

"Then let's get going. The Lord goes before us and great things are going to happen!"

The large cream-colored limestone synagogue stood only a few blocks down the way on the street called Straight. As the two men reached the large, structure, they entered and found the building about three-quarters full. Jake noticed the synagogue rabbi busying himself at the front on his elevated platform. Saul and Jake walked the center aisle toward the front and found seats on the third row. Quiet and silent prayer hovered over this solemn, Sabbath meeting.

More men were making their way into the synagogue when the ministering rabbi began the worship service. Prayer and scripture reading started the worship meeting. After a short time, Saul stood up and asked the rabbi if he could read scripture.

"Yes, sir. We are honored to have you with us, Pharisee Saul from Jerusalem," the rabbi stated. "You are most welcome to share the deep truths you have discovered from your diligent study of God's Word."

"Thank you."

"What scripture would you like to read?"

"The Book of Isaiah," Saul replied.

The rabbi looked puzzled. "Which scroll?" he asked. "The entire volume of Isaiah is composed of five scrolls."

"For today I'd like to read from the last scroll. I believe there are some real gems in that scroll."

The rabbi stepped over to the rack of parchment documents and thumbed through them until he found the last scroll of the Book of Isaiah. He carefully slid the selected document out of the rack and cautiously laid it on a study table at the front of the synagogue. The table had two scroll rests to cradle the two ends of the parchment roll.

"Now, you must be very careful with that scroll," the rabbi warned. "It is the only one we have. In fact, it is the only one in Damascus."

"I promise you I will be very careful with it," Saul soothed.

Saul opened the scroll and unrolled it. He found the passage from which he wanted to preach and then looked up toward the congregation. "Men of Israel, here is a passage I have long puzzled over. In fact, we all have. It is Isaiah 53." He said this as he carefully settled the parchment into the scroll rests. "Scholars have long believed this is describing the Messiah. But we have always wondered how the triumphant King Messiah could be a Suffering Servant, as well."

From that moment for the next fifteen minutes, Saul launched into a well-constructed message as he read from Isaiah 53. As he passionately preached, Saul emphasized how Messiah would be humiliated and despised and rejected by His very own people. Saul pressed home the fact that Messiah would be a man of sorrows. Then Saul masterfully correlated the facts of Jesus' life, overlaying those facts onto the truths found in the Isaiah 53 description of Messiah.

Saul paused to sense the crowd's response. There were some very puzzled faces in the congregation.

Turning back to the scroll, Saul continued reading. "'All of us like sheep have gone astray. Everyone of us have turned to his own way and the Lord purposely has laid on Him the sinfulness of us all.'

Saul looked up at the crowd. "Men of Israel, is it not plain? This scripture tells us that the Messiah will be the person upon whom the Lord God will heap all the sins of mankind. We have all gone astray from God– every last one of us. We are hopelessly lost because of the depth of our sins.

"But Messiah willingly has taken our sins from us, so our spiritual relationship with God may be healed. Jesus of Nazareth has fulfilled everything that these scriptures tell us Messiah will do. On the cross, Jesus carried our sins, placed upon Him by the Father. His sacrifice satisfied the anger and wrath of the Father against us due to our sins. Jesus has completed all the work of Messiah as defined in these verses. Therefore, Jesus of Nazareth is the Christ! He is the Son of God!"

When Saul made this last statement, an unsettled rumble surged across the synagogue congregation. One man stood up with a very puzzled look on his face.

"Let me get this straight. You are Pharisee Saul of Tarsus, is that correct?" the man asked in a bewildered tone.

"Yes. That is absolutely true."

"We know you are the main persecutor of Christians," the man continued. "You are a Pharisee. We have viewed you as a hero and defender of our Jewish faith. You are the very man who has been trying to destroy the Christians in Jerusalem. We also know that you came here to Damascus on a mission from the chief priests with the main purpose of capturing and arresting Christians. We fully believed you would seize them in chains and drag them back to the chief priests. Then why, as the guardian of Judaism, would you now do a complete reversal and begin preaching that Jesus of Nazareth is the Christ? We know that Christians are undermining Judaism by trying to drive a wedge into our religion and deceive Jews to run after this false cult. You are only encouraging our fellow Jews to chase after a false religion!"

"Your argument would be true, if we did not have these scriptures we have just read to be convincing evidence that Jesus has fulfilled these predictions about the work of the Messiah," Saul defended. "You see, God has changed my heart! He has accomplished a great transformation in my soul and spirit. He has revealed to me the truths of the scripture and their direct connection to Jesus of Nazareth. Jesus *is* the Christ! Our Messiah!"

An agitated rumbling murmur rippled across the synagogue congregation.

"We've never heard anything like this before!" exclaimed many of them angrily.

More angry discontent surged. "Ridiculous foolishness!" screeched others in disgust.

"Saul of Tarsus, you tried to destroy Christians," one protester shouted. "How can it be that you now are promoting this false cult. So, what does this reversal mean?"

"I am a Christian!" Saul exclaimed. "The Lord Jesus, Himself, spoke to me as I was on my way here on the road to Damascus. He revealed to me that He is Lord and when I persecuted Christians, I actually was persecuting Him."

"Nonsense!" yelled another man, jumping up in the front and pointed angrily at Saul. "You are hallucinating! You have become hysterical!" He turned around to his fellow worshippers. "This man claims to see visions and apparitions and then comes and tells us we must now follow an already known deceiver like Jesus of Nazareth! Don't listen to him! He's lying! This man, Saul, who once was a brother, a protector of all we Jews hold sacred, is now a traitor to our faith!"

Another worshipper stood up. "Gentlemen, what if what Saul has revealed from scripture is true?" he passionately exclaimed. "What then? We have longed for years for Messiah to come. Pharisee Saul has prepared his argument solely from the scriptures. Should we not at least consider what he has said directly from the holy rite? We need to meditate and pray about these Messianic claims that have been presented from our sacred scriptures?"

The synagogue rabbi raised his arms to quiet the congregation. "Men, please calm yourselves." he soothed. "The supposition that this visitor has raised is very interesting. These scriptures from Isaiah have long been debated and discussed. They are believed to be Messianic verses. The question is whether these Messianic verses can be attributed to Jesus of Nazareth. Let us adjourn our meeting

for now and return to our homes and pray and ask God to reveal the truth to each of us. We can discuss this subject more intelligently next Sabbath day."

With that declaration, the meeting broke up. In small gaggles of worshippers, the men drifted out of the synagogue, murmuring and quietly discussing the debate they had just witnessed.

Jake looked at Saul with a questioning expression. "Well, what do you think?"

Saul smiled. "I think we have planted some seeds in some hearts today. Let's cultivate those seeds this week."

Chapter 18

SYNAGOGUE GOSPEL

The next several weeks became like undulating storm-tossed waves! Exhilarating, plunging, soaring, plummeting. Saul's repeated attendance at the synagogue worship services created consternation in some but glorious praise in others. Saul's skillful expounding of the Scriptures proved the undeniable truth that Jesus is the Christ.

"Gentlemen, time would fail me if I try to include all the scriptural proofs.," Saul explained in his preaching. "I will try to be brief.

"Isaiah 9:7 tells us the Messiah would be an heir of King David. Jesus of Nazareth comes from the kingly line of David.

"Micah 5:2 tells us that Bethlehem would be the birth place of the Ruler in Israel, the Messiah. Jesus of Nazareth was born in Bethlehem. He was born in Bethlehem during the census decreed by Caesar Augustus, while Quirinus was governor of Syria.

"From his birth in Bethlehem emanated many fulfilled prophecies. Numbers 24:17 describes the coming of King Messiah. It says, 'I see Him, but not now. I behold Him, but not near. A Star shall rise out of Jacob. A Scepter shall rise out of Israel.' At the time of Jesus birth, there are reports of a mysterious Star appearing in the sky. These reports also tell us that the wonderous Star attracted a group of wise men from the east.

"When these wise men made their long journey from the East following the star, they fulfilled another prophecy about Messiah found in Isaiah 60:6 where it says, 'All those from Sheba shall come. They shall bring gold and frankincense. And they shall proclaim the praises of the Lord.' These wise men from the East came bringing these same gifts – gold and frankincense and myrrh. Gifts for a King.

"Isaiah 9:1,2 says that the One who would bring Light to those who live in darkness and the shadow of death would come from Galilee. Jesus' hometown is Nazareth in Galilee. He grew up and ministered in Galilee. And the people saw the great Light of hope shine upon them through Jesus' ministry.

"Deuteronomy 18:15 calls the Messiah 'the Prophet'. Moses calls Messiah 'the Prophet' who would come and be just like Moses. Jesus came and He alone was exactly like Moses. Jesus' life was identical to Moses as a mediator, in His closeness with God, in His countless miracles, and in His establishing of a new covenant – a covenant of grace. And when men saw the miracles Jesus was performing, they proclaimed that He was 'the Prophet'.

"Zechariah 9:9 states that the King Messiah would ride into Jerusalem on a donkey. One week before He was crucified, Jesus rode triumphantly into Jerusalem on a donkey. The crowds cheered Him as King!

"But to me, Psalm 22 is the one most compelling of scriptures connecting the Messiah to Jesus. We Pharisees have long believed that Psalm 22 is speaking about the Messiah. On the cross, Jesus quoted the first line of Psalm 22, 'My God, My God, why have you forsaken me?' It was like Jesus was telling us 'Look in this Psalm and see me! Read it!

"The Psalm reads like this:

"Psalm 22: 6-8 states 'I am a worm ... a reproach of men ... despised ... they laugh and scorn ... they mock and insult me.' Jesus suffered all of these horrible things – reproached, despised, scorned and mocked. The Psalm foretold that all this would happen to Jesus.

"Psalm 22: 11-13 says 'trouble is near with no one to help ... bulls surround me ... they snap at me like a ravening lion.' Jesus died surrounded by His ravening enemies. They were like bulls and lions, encircling Jesus, viciously insulting Him, enjoying watching Him die.

"Psalm 22: 16 states 'they pierce My hands and My feet.' The Psalm accurately predicts how Jesus would die. Jesus' hands and feet were pierced by the spikes that nailed Him to the cross. When David wrote this Psalm, he knew nothing about crucifixion by being nailed to a cross. Only God could have foretold of spikes piercing Jesus' hands and feet.

"Psalm 22:18 says 'they part my garment among them and cast lots for my cloths.' The Roman soldiers who crucified Jesus cast lots for Jesus' clothing there at the foot of the cross."

Saul paused for effect. The room simmered with colliding mixed emotions.

"Much learning has made you mad, rabbi," one man seethed. "Messiah will be a conquering victor over our oppressors not dying on a cross."

"You read the scriptures for yourself," Saul exclaimed. "See for yourself that the scriptures clearly tell us that Messiah will come first as a Suffering Servant before He will come as a Victor."

The man sat stupefied in his seat.

Saul spoke up. "Sir, read these scriptures which I have just cited. See if these scriptures are indeed proof that Jesus fulfilled the prophecies pointing to Messiah. I have more scriptural examples, if you can take it!"

"It is all too wonderful!" one man called out. "Say on, rabbi!"

"Are we all in agreement?" Saul asked.

"Yes, teacher, please tell us more!" resounded the overwhelming response from the crowd.

"I will gladly tell you more! I will be brief.

"Zechariah 11:12 tells us the Suffering Messiah would be betrayed for thirty pieces of silver. Jesus was betrayed by one of His close disciples for exactly thirty pieces of silver.

"Zechariah 12:10 states that Israel would stare and gaze at the Messiah whom they pierced, the very One who poured God's grace out upon them. The people of Israel shall mourn for their Messiah whom they have pierced ... Jesus, whom they pierced with nails and a spear when Israel crucified Him.

"Zechariah 13:7 tells us that the associates of Messiah would rise up and strike and kill 'The Shepherd'. Jesus' fellow Jews struck and killed Him, who was their 'Shepherd' sent to them by Jehovah.

"And, brothers, we must impress upon you the vital study of Isaiah 53. Isaiah 53 is filled with overwhelming Messianic truths which we must explore. Isaiah foretold that Messiah would be despised and rejected by His people and given no honor. Yet, Messiah would carry our sin burden and be afflicted for us, taking our place of punishment at God's hand. And by Messiah's wounds, we are healed! He was cut off from the land of the living to take the wrath of God for our sins upon Himself.

"Fellow Jews! There are so many rich truths in these verses from Isaiah 53. I beg you to study these verses diligently. Contained in that scripture passage is the precise picture of Jesus Christ and the suffering He endured to be our Messiah that He might save us from our sins!

"But the most compelling evidence that Jesus is Messiah is the fact that He once was dead but *now* is alive! In Psalm 16:10, the scripture states that God's Holy One would not remain in the grave and see corruption but would resurrect from the dead. Who is this 'Holy One' mentioned in the Psalm? The 'Holy One' is Messiah, who lives forever with His saints to reign! And who is this Messiah? It is Jesus of Nazareth, who was crucified, dead and buried and who God raised from the dead. Jesus is alive! It is Jesus' resurrection that is the greatest proof that He is Messiah, the Christ! Jesus is the 'Holy One' spoken of in the Psalm. He is truly alive and there are hundreds of eye witnesses to His resurrection."

Because of Saul's proficient exegesis of the Scriptures, large numbers believed Saul's convincing message of Jesus as Messiah. Wholehearted trust in Jesus as the Christ enthusiastically flourished in the new converts, as they began following the teachings of their new Savior.

It was a spectacularly wonderful time of salvation and revival in

Damascus! Hardened hearts softened. Obstinate minds blossomed into loving souls! Lives centered on the Lord Jesus through faith in Him!

But ... in such a great city like Damascus, the majority of the population remained unconvinced. The doubters were divided. Some residents still couldn't understand how Saul could suddenly flip his loyalty from being a persecutor of Christians to becoming a "traitor" to the Jews. Others ridiculed Saul's claims that Jesus is the Messiah. Still others sunk into a deeper hatred for Saul because they could not refute the truth of Saul's claims about Christ. The atmosphere between Saul and his many opponents grew increasingly edgy.

And then came the fateful day ... the lethal tipping point. One Sabbath in the synagogue, with all the animosity swirling around him, Saul introduced the teaching that Jesus Christ had come to be the Messiah for all people of all nations of the world.

It was like an explosive, fiery blast ignited right in the middle of the synagogue!

"Wait just one minute! Explain your statement?" several Jews stood up in protest. "Christ is to come as Messiah for the Jews! This is what we have always been taught! Our teachers have always taught us that! Because of this, we've also been taught to always shun the heathen!"

"Brothers," Saul declared, "I have explained this before. Remember the original promise to Abraham in Genesis 18:18 stated that God's plan from the start was to bless all nations. God promised that Abraham would, 'surely become a great and mighty nation and all the nations of the earth shall be blessed in him.' And again, God told Abraham in Genesis 12:2, 3 'I will make you a great nation ... and you shall be a blessing ... and in you all the families of the earth shall be blessed.' And once again God promised our father Abraham in Genesis 22:18, 'In your seed all of the nations of the earth shall be blessed.'

"Now the promises were made to Abraham and his Seed," Saul contended. "But God did not say, 'To all your seeds,' as if He was speaking of many. No God spoke of Abraham's One 'Seed', who in reality is Christ!

"Jesus Christ Himself is our peace and unity, who has made both, believing Jews and believing heathens, into one unit. Christ has broken down the wall of separation between the two groups and has destroyed in His flesh the hatred and hostility that has long divided the two. Christ has created in Himself a new creation, one new people of faith from the two."

"Blasphemy!" shouted many of the Damascus Jews. "Saul, you may be a scholar but you have just crossed the line into lunacy! Your interpretation of scripture is wrong! You have gone insane!"

One self-righteous scholar screeched, "How can you even think of intermixing the holiness of Judaism and mingling dirty heathens into that holiness!" he shouted. "It is absolutely unthinkable! The purity of our religion cannot be mixed with heathen, pagan worshippers!"

"But think on the scriptures I just quoted," Saul responded. "The scriptures prove what I say!"

"We don't care about that!" they screamed.

"But God's original promise was that He would bless all nations through Abraham!" Saul answered.

"No! No! No! Don't try to confuse us!" the protesters argued. "We have been taught by our religious leaders to shun pagan people. This beloved oral teaching comes from centuries of Jewish traditions! That is what our leaders have always taught us and that is what we believe!"

"Your Jewish leaders have been wrong!" Saul countered bluntly. "They know nothing of the love of God! Let me help you understand God's great purposes."

"How dare you insult our respected religious leaders!" many in the synagogue shouted in anger.

"We will not hear anything else you have to say!" many others howled, jamming their fingers into their ears.

The synagogue erupted in rage and the men stormed out of the building. Saul had deeply offended them. Their deep-set traditions suddenly were threatened by actual Scriptural truths that Saul had preached. A thick, invisible curtain of dark hatred between them and Saul and the Gospel descended immediately. It was the final curtain.

Days passed. The Jews aggression against Saul gained greater intensity. Saul quickly became a despicable, hated man throughout the city. Jake's detective instincts told him this kind of hatred could soon lead to a dangerous situation for Saul. It felt like the lid was about to blow off.

The detective knew it was time to get busy snooping around. What he discovered proved to be even scarier than he first imagined! He discovered a brand new, even more sinister enemy. This new terror come from an entirely unexpected evil.

Armed with this new chilling evidence of this unforeseen threat, Jake made a b-line to Saul's room on Straight Street.

"Saul, I've got news that you must hear right now," Jake warned emphatically. "I've been doing some snooping around. Talking to lots of people in the city. I've talked to Christians and Jews, and even the Arab residents who live in Damascus. I've dug up distressing information that blindsided me totally!"

"Blindsided? How? In what way?" Saul asked.

"It turns out that you have made a new, powerful enemy here in this territory, other than the Jews!"

"I knew I'd make enemies," Saul stated. "What do you mean by 'a new powerful enemy'?"

"Yes, a new enemy," the detective said. "Damascus has a mayor, they call him a governor, and he is under the control of an Arabian king named King Aretas," Jake explained.

"Yes, I've heard of him," Saul replied. "King Aretas and King Herod Antipas were involved in a family squabble that resulted in fighting between them. Herod was married to the daughter of Aretas, then divorced her, and King Aretas became so angered that he went to war with Herod."

"Well, that's the old news. Here is the new news," Jake said. "It turns out King Aretas has learned about you and your Christian revival here in Damascus. And he does not like it. He is the king of this territory. He is the big cat of this jungle. With the spreading of the Gospel of Christ, King Aretas feels extremely threatened that someone like you would just waltz into his kingdom and grab all the headlines. King Aretas wants to be *the* top dog in his kingdom. Aretas wants total control of his own territory. He will not allow any rivals. And he considers you to be a threat to his power. So ... he is making plans to eliminate you. He has teamed up with the governor of Damascus and has plotted to capture you and to kill you. The king has instructed the governor of Damascus to carry out his plan. Aretas wants you dead."

"Dead? The Lord Jesus may have something to say about that," Saul firmly said.

"This threat by King Aretas comes on top of the fact that many of the Jews in the city already hate you. They can't refute the scriptural claims that Jesus is the Christ. In their madness, the Jews have thrown in with the king and the governor. They are cooperating in their plot to kill you. It's the age-old problem. If a group can't win an argument, they just deny the truth, and kill their opponent."

"Do you know when this plot is supposed to be carried out?" Saul asked.

"The best I can understand it, they will spring their trap as soon as possible. Maybe even today or tonight. So, we've got to hide you. And we've got to move you out of this room, somehow, very quickly. The governor knows exactly where you are living here on Straight Street.

"Maybe my friend, Ananias, can provide a hiding place for me," Saul considered.

"Yah, that's a great idea," Jake stated. "Ananias lives over on the perimeter of the city and out of the central part of town. Let me get some Christians together. We will move you right away."

Within the hour, in a carefully laid out plan, the Christians of Damascus secretly moved Saul out of his residence on Straight Street in broad daylight!

"Brother Saul, we meet again," Ananias said cheerfully, as he greeted Saul and safely closed and locked his house door. "I know why you have come. I have heard the rumors of the threats to your life."

"Brother Ananias, the threats are more than rumors," Jake stated firmly. "The threats are real. Can you hide Saul until we can come up with an escape plan for him?"

"Of course, I will hide him. You are more than welcome, brother Saul."

Chapter 19

MIDNIGHT ESCAPE

Jake ventured back out into the city streets. He knew he had to find out more about the plot of King Aretas. Hopefully he would discover the timing of how it would be carried out. He wandered over to the market place – always a good spot to eavesdrop and overhear gossip. It wasn't long before Jake got an earful of info.

Two red clad Arabian military soldiers stood talking to two Jewish leaders near a vegetable stand. Jake eased over in their direction, pretending to be inspecting the vegetables. One of the soldiers was bragging about capturing Saul.

"Yeah, we've got all the city under surveillance," the soldier confidently crowed. "We've got all the city gates guarded. The whole town is in lockdown. There is no way Saul can escape the city. We'll catch him. And, by order of King Aretas, we will kill Saul." The four men roared with laughter.

"We've already raided Saul's room where he was staying, but he dodged us," the other soldier stated. "No problem. Saul is hiding somewhere in this city. But he can't hide forever. He cannot escape. All the city gates are heavily guarded. The whole city is sealed up tight as a drum."

Jake now had all the data he needed. Saul was trapped in the city. Jake had to quickly get this urgent message to Saul.

'Lord, help me get this warning back to Saul,' Jake prayed silently.

As Jake turned and began walking casually away from the four men, one of the Jewish leaders spotted the detective. He shouted at Jake, "Hey, you, didn't I see you in the synagogue with Saul?"

Jake didn't even turn around. He ignored the man's challenge.

"Hey, you! I'm talking to you!" the Jewish leader shouted.

Jake kept on walking trying to get as much daylight between him and the four men.

"Stop! Stop! You were spying on us! Stop!"

Jake never looked back. He broke into a run and darted around the first corner he could get to. As he rounded the corner he glanced back. The four men were in hot pursuit, one of the red clad soldiers was gaining on him. Down a half a block and Jake dashed into an alley to his right. Jake could hear the soldier right behind him … getting closer. He could almost feel the warrior's hot breath on the back of his neck. In the middle of the alley, Jake spied a pile of wicker baskets full of garbage, stacked up against the wall. As he ran past the baskets, Jake snatched the top basket down and slung it behind him into the middle of the narrow alley. The entire stack of garbage baskets tumbled across the alley. The charging soldier plowed right into the pile of refuse and fell face down into the slop.

Jake turned another corner. As he rounded the corner, he found himself in a crowded market plaza. Jake blended in with the mass of people milling around, shopping in the market.

From within the safety of the packed crowd in the market plaza, Jake could see his pursuers searching for him. One of the soldiers was a real mess! He was covered with putrid-looking gray muck. His royal red uniform wasn't red anymore! And he looked flaming mad! Jake kept his head low and jostled his way through the mass of humanity to the other side of the market plaza. There he slipped into a side alley, safely skittering away and escaping.

Jake made sure he was not followed. He made his way to bustling Sargon Avenue. Up ahead was Abana River Street, where Ananias lived. Still wary that he may have been followed, he turned slightly and surveyed over his shoulder. For several moments, he scanned the crowd behind, to be sure he had given all adversaries the slip. Cautiously, the detective turned onto Abana River Street with one last glance behind him. Jake quickly approached Ananias' home, several doors down the passageway. One last scan all around him and Jake knocked on Ananias' door.

"Who's there?" came Ananias' muffled voice through the wooden door.

"Jake. Open up."

Once inside the safety of Ananias' home, Jake breathed a welcomed, heavy sigh of relief.

"Wow, that was some adventure!" the detective exclaimed. "I did find out the information I needed to know. It's not good."

Everybody in the home gathered closer.

"We have got a real problem," Jake stated. "I have just discovered that there is no way for Saul to get out of Damascus. All of the city gates are guarded day and night. I just overheard some Arabian soldiers and Jews bragging about how Saul will never get out of Damascus alive. They also said that a house-to-house systematic search has been started throughout the whole city trying to find Saul. I heard those same Arabian soldiers say that they have already raided Saul's quarters on Straight Street searching for him. Good thing we got outa there. They may be scouring the streets right now, searching every place. We've got to figure out a way to get Saul out of Damascus tonight."

Ananias smiled and exclaimed, "Hey, my friend across the street has a two-story home. And he lives on the city wall. His house has a window upstairs that looks out through the city wall!"

"That's it!" Jake stated. "The Lord has shown us the way of escape He has provided! Saul can escape through that window in the city wall"

"We can't do this in broad daylight," Ananias warned. "But we must wait until night under the cover of darkness and when most of the city is asleep. I've got a rope. And I've got a wicker basket large enough for Saul to fit into. I will go across the street right now to ask my neighbor to help us."

Several hours passed. The shroud of darkness descended outside.

It was night in the city. The tension in Ananias' home that night grew more intense.

"We must continue to wait until the darkness can fully shield Saul's getaway," Ananias cautioned.

The night hours dragged slowly by. Minutes ticked by ever so deliberately. Every noise outside the door carried a potential danger with it. Each person in the home knew the risk of harboring a wanted man. If the governor's men or the king's soldiers stumbled upon Saul's hideout, what would happen to Saul? What would happen to all of those found with Saul?

Saul stood and reassured the Christians. "Listen, everyone, please, don't be anxious. The Lord Jesus didn't confront me on the road and save me just to let me be captured and killed. He told me He has a future ministry waiting for me beyond these walls. He told me He would deliver me from the Jews and cause me to be a minister to the Jews and the non-Jews. I am to preach Christ and His salvation, opening the eyes of people so they may turn from darkness to Light. Do not worry. Jesus will deliver me with your help."

Suddenly heavy footsteps sounded in the darkness right outside Ananias' door. The commotion of a crowd of throaty voices snarled ominously in the street!

Terror was right outside the door!

"Open up! Open up in there!" a menacing, cruel voice bellowed in the street. Then a brutal fist began pounding repeatedly upon the door. "Let us in or we'll break down this door!" roared the brutish voice in the street.

Again and again the powerful fist bludgeoned the door with increasing ferocity.

"Break it down!" yelled a defiant voice from out in the street. A strong, determined shoulder slammed against the door from outside. "Break it down!" Again, the shoulder slammed against the door. The door bolt began to give way and rip loose from the doorframe!

Quickly, one of the brothers shoved Saul into a corner of the room, down on the floor, and hurriedly threw a pile of blankets over him. Then the brother sat on the pile!

"Open up in there!" yelled the terror outside the door.

"Just a moment, please," Ananias said through the door. "Let me get it open."

The wooden door yawned open, now askew on its hinges. Beyond the door stood a mob of red clad Arabian military soldiers, holding blazing, yellow torches. The captain, dressed in his royal, red colored uniform, growled at Ananias, "What took you so long to open up? Are you hiding something?"

"We were having an evening of fellowship and prayer," Ananias answered. "It took me a moment to get up from the table."

The captain determinedly stepped inside the home, scanning everyone in the room. "We are going door to door searching for a man named Saul. The city governor and King Aretas want us to bring him in for … questioning."

The captain started to walk around the room, gazing intently into each of the seven faces in the home.

"I know what Saul looks like," growled the captain. "None of you look like him. Have any of you seen Saul?" he asked.

Jake stood up. "Sir, I did see him earlier today. It was over on the street called Straight. I think he has a room over there."

"We've already checked there," snarled the captain. "Saul has fled the premises."

The captain's eyes swept over toward the man sitting down on the pile of blankets. "Are you tired? Too tired to get up?" the captain questioned the man.

"Yes, sir, quite tired," the man said, "But I'll get up in respect for you as a military man." He started to stand but the captain sneered, "Never mind. I wouldn't want to put you to any trouble, tired boy."

The captain slowly turned and let his eyes drift around to study all the faces. Satisfied, he gradually stepped over to the doorway, turned around, and very deliberately swept his eyes around the room one more time. Then his curiosity refocused his attention back on the pile of blankets in the corner.

"Why so many blankets?" the captain asked narrowing his eyes.

"I am a manufacturer of blankets and other cloth items," Ananias quickly stated. "I deal in the textile industry. There on that side of the room is my loom on which I weave my blankets."

The captain folded his arms across his chest and bit his lip. "I see," he said. Still unconvinced, he started to step over toward the pile of blankets again, squinting his eyes as he glanced over the pile once more.

"And you, tired boy. The blankets are real comfortable, I suppose," the captain chided the man sitting on the blanket pile.

"Yes, sir. Soft as can be," the man said casually. "Would you like to look at them?"

The captain edged closer.

"They are of the finest quality," the man feigned a sales pitch, running his hand smoothly over the velvety material. "The best in Damascus. Here, let me show you some of the premium items of our stock." The man stood up and began to peel off the top delicately embroidered blanket. "Feel the texture and notice the exquisite needlework of the embroidery."

"No. No, don't bother me with a sales pitch," the captain fumed. "I haven't got time for frivolous things at this hour of night! I've got far more important matters to deal with at this moment!"

The captain turned and again slowly stepped over to the open doorway. He pivoted around and once again deliberately swept his eyes around the room.

"You men continue with your … wonderful evening of fellowship," the captain scoffed. "But don't get to praying too hard. We just might be back."

In a moment, the military man stepped back out into the glare of the torches in the street. He and his troop of hooligans began banging on the neighbor's door across the street. As the captain began yelling for the neighbor to open up his door, Ananias slowly slid his slightly skewed door closed.

All the brothers stared at each other in amazement. Each man held his breath. "God has protected us." they all whispered to each other. "But we must be sure they're gone."

Several minutes dragged by. The terror outside the door still lingered as the troop meticulously made its way door by door down the dark street.

After several more minutes everybody in the room could hear Saul under the pile of blankets. "Are they gone, yet?" his muffled voice called out.

"Yes, they've gone," Jake said as he began to peel off the layers of blankets from the pile.

Saul emerged sweating profusely, gasping for air. "I thought I would suffocate. It was getting really hot in there, especially when somebody sat on me!"

"That was me," grinned the man who had sat on Saul. "That was the best I could do with what I had."

"Well, that was quick thinking," Saul laughed. "I do believe you just saved my life."

More long hours passed. Midnight came. The moment of action.

"Dowse all the lamps in the house so we don't attract attention when we open the door," Jake whispered. The detective slid open the door of Ananias' home to check the dark street outside. Patch blackness shrouded the narrow passage between the row of houses. The troop of soldiers, with their bright, glaring torches was gone. "A perfect cover," Jake muttered to himself.

"Let's go, everybody," the detective whispered to the group in Ananias' home. Silently all the men in the home crept across the street, Saul with them. Ananias' friend had purposely extinguished all the lamps in his house, so as not to backlight the men as they entered the doorway.

Once all were safely inside, the new host lit several lamps and welcomed Saul to his residence. "This way, please, brother Saul. This way to the stairs. We must do this quickly."

Everyone climbed the stairs to the second story. The starry, night sky shown gloriously through the upper room window. Below the window was a thirty-foot drop to the ground outside the city wall.

"Looks like the time has come, brother Saul," Jake said. "We've got six strong bodies here ready to lower us through that window and to the ground outside the city. Let me go first. I'll get on the ground outside to be sure the coast is clear. Then you follow. Then I can go back with you to Jerusalem. I can help the Christians there understand how you have converted to be a follower of Christ."

"No, Jake, you're staying here," Saul stated somberly. "I'm not going back to Jerusalem. At least not just yet. The Lord has told me to go out into the Arabian desert where He will instruct me. He has made it clear to me that I am not to receive my future message from man but through direct, personal revelation from Jesus Himself." Then turning to all those in the upper room. "Thank you all for your gracious help," Saul said warmly. "Without you I could not escape. You are truly my ministers for the Lord."

Then pausing for a moment. "It is time," Saul said. "Thank you all. May God bless you all."

Ananias had tied two ropes to the handles on the large wicker basket and eased the contraption through the window. They tied off the ropes to a wooden pillar in the rafters of the room and Saul gingerly snuggled into the basket. The man from Tarsus now dangled outside the city wall, with the ground about thirty feet below. The men in the room grabbed the ropes, untied them from the pillar, and gently began to lower the basket with Saul aboard down into the night. As he disappeared from sight, Saul whispered back to them all, "Thank you all. Jesus is Lord."

Chapter 20

HANNAH

When Jake left Damascus, the city was still buzzing about Jesus Christ's saving grace. King Aretas' oppression had eased. Excited Christians, who were dispersed by the persecution in Jerusalem and Damascus, scattered out across the entire region. Jesus' kingdom continued to thrive and expand. And as the Christians scattered, they continued to spread the Gospel of Jesus Christ everywhere they traveled. Satan's human cohorts could not stop the expansion of the Good News of Christ. Jesus Christ came to save the lost!

As Jake trudged the last few miles in his long 140 mile trek back to Jerusalem, his thoughts swirled around all the events of the past year. So much had happened to him, to Hannah, and to the church.

But now only one obsession possessed Jake's mind … Hannah! Nothing else mattered right now! He was about to see his girl again! Once he hit the Jerusalem city limits, Jake headed straight for the office and his sweetie pie. He knew he had to report to Pilate about the Damascus trip. But that report could wait. As he made his way down the second story corridor of his office building, he found the much awaited door up ahead, Office 211. In tantalizing delight, Jake slowly opened the office door a crack. There she was! Faithfully holding down the fort from behind her desk.

Jake flung the door wide open. "Hannah!" he shouted throwing his arms open wide.

Hannah grabbed at her chest in surprise and lurched back in her chair. She jumped up, her eyes smiling, as she gasped in unexpected delight.

"Jake!" was all she could say.

He hurried in to gather her into his arms. They held each other for a long time, both of them laughing in gladness. After several minutes, he slowly released his embrace of her and looked in her eyes. "Did you miss me?" he joked.

Hannah pushed him back and swatted him on the shoulder. "You goof!" she laughed. "Of course, I missed you. I missed you every day, every hour, every minute."

"And I missed you, too, so very much," he said sincerely. "I've come to realize I need you around every day, every hour, every minute."

"You've been gone for weeks, now," she stated matter-of-factly. "I had no idea if you were still alive or dead. You left here traveling with that horrible monster, Saul, the worst enemy the Christians have ever known." Hannah's voice became resolute. "I know that Governor Pilate granted you Roman citizenship, but I didn't know if Saul would even care about that. He hates all Christians, Roman citizens or not. I didn't know what he might do. He might have decided to kill you on the road to Damascus, just because you're a Christian."

"Well, honey, you had every right to believe that. But there is a new twist to the saga," Jake calmly said to her, trying to sooth her ruffled emotions. He cupped his hand under her chin and held her pretty face until their eyes met. "I've got a shocking tale that will knock your socks off. And you're probably not going to believe it at first," Jake said. "It's going to rock your imagination, but listen to me. Are you ready?"

Jake paused; his voice hung suspended in teasing silence.

Hannah stared at the detective in anticipation. Then she twisted her face away from his grasp and blurted out, "Okay! Ready for what?"

"Saul of Tarsus has become a Christian!"

"What!" she exclaimed. "Saul is a Christian!" she repeated. "You've got to be kidding me!" Then she slowly sank down into her chair in disbelief.

"I am absolutely not kidding," Jake laughed. "And let me tell you, Saul's transformation to Christianity is so radical that now he no longer wants to be called Saul, which is his Jewish name. He told me emphatically that he now wants to be called by his Roman name, Paul. The name Paul means 'little' and he feels that the name Paul best describes his new life in Christ. Paul wants to be thought of as the 'little one'.

"Paul wrote me a note explaining his thoughts about himself. Here, Hannah, let me read it to you." Jake pulled out a papyrus paper from his leather belt pouch. "Paul slipped this note to me just as he slid out of sight over the wall in Damascus to make his escape into the night. It reads, 'Jake, I am the least in God's kingdom. I am not worthy to be called anything else because I persecuted the church of the Lord Jesus. I am what I am by the grace of God. Because of that I am going to work harder than all the apostles by the grace of God in me.'

"Hannah, God's conversion of Paul has so completely flipped his life over from being the worst enemy of Jesus, that now Paul has become the greatest champion of our Lord Christ!"

Hannah still sat in her chair, too stunned to speak. She shook her head in disbelief. Finally, when the words came, she said, "The Lord Jesus is so very powerful. Thank you, Lord." That's all she could say.

"I've got so much to tell you, but first I want to spend some time with you, just talking," Jake smiled. "Tell me. How've you been doing? How are your folks? What is the temperature of the persecution of the Jerusalem Christians ..."

For several hours Jake and Hannah sat and talked and relaxed together. Eventually they drifted over to Caleb's Doughnut Shop to enjoy Caleb's warm cinnamon doughnuts and his tasty coffee. The couple sat at a small table in the back corner of Caleb's shop. They talked. No one else existed in the world at that moment. Back together again ... their world was safe and secure again.

Finally, it came time to get back to the office.

As the couple slowly walked back toward the workplace, a joyful thought triggered in Hannah's mind.

"You've got your good news," she said. "Well, I've got some good news, too," Hannah continued with a smile. "You remember Marcius, Pilate's adjutant. He came by the office while you were in Damascus and he told me he had surrendered his life to Christ! I've never seen a Roman soldier so excited!"

"Marcius, a Christian! Now, that *is* really great news!" Jake exclaimed.

"He was so excited!" she continued. "Marcius told me he had been attending Peter and John's Bible studies in John Mark's mother's home! He even recited all the new scripture verses he'd been learning. I just couldn't believe it! It was so neat to hear him declare his faith in Jesus!"

"I am so very happy for Marcius!" Jake stated. "Marcius' personality already causes him to be a good and kind man. With Jesus in his life, I know the Lord's gonna bless him and make him into the best man he can be!"

Hannah smiled at the detective. "Isn't God good," the girl sighed.

"You know, Hannah, there is so much more I want to tell you from these past several weeks," Jake stated. "And through it all I know I've become a stronger Christian. It's really hard to explain. Right in the middle of danger and complex situations, God's grace guided me. His presence was real. I could sense that He was right there with me."

Hannah smiled at her fiancé. "Keep on, honey. I'm enjoying this."

"It was like God's grace strengthened me and helped me, like a sturdy arm holding me up," Jake continued. "There were times when my detective logic failed me but God gave me His wisdom to see the situation from His perspective and make the right decision. I've seen Him lead me in my thoughts. It was like He took me mentally and led me. It's really hard to explain. When it happens, you are just amazed that you are led along to the right place but you're not really quite sure how you got there. I can't explain it!"

Jake looked at the girl. "Am I making any sense at all?" he asked.

"Perfect sense," she smiled. "It was like that for me when I was locked away in prison. My time behind bars could have been a devastating time for me. But instead, Jesus was right there in the cell with me. I felt His presence. It was like a glorious string stretched between His heart and my heart. And his presence was real, so very real, just like you said."

They both laughed out loud. "It is fascinating that we both have experienced the leading of the same Lord Jesus at different times and in different places, but in exactly the same way!" Hannah remarked.

"Sweetheart, there is so much to look forward to in the future," Jake stated. "The Lord Jesus is in full control. I'm confident about that. He is Sovereign over everything. Life may seem to be out of control, but Jesus is fully *in* control of everything. He has shown Himself to be strong in my behalf every step of the way."

Hannah gazed at her fiancé with a new respect. "I can tell you're a different man, now," she stated. "And I kinda like this new guy." As they walked along together, she brushed up against Jake and playfully bumped him, knocking him out of stride.

Jake exaggerated her playful jostle and pretended to stumble momentarily. He glanced over at Hannah from the corner of his eye, then returned her lighthearted bump.

"Oh, I see," she challenged, "that's the way it's going to be."

"Uh huh."

"Okay, mister. You'd better be ready, 'cause you'll never know when the next one is coming."

"Bring it on, sister! I'm ready!"

As the couple approached the office, Jake asked, "How are your parents? I haven't seen them since they were released from prison."

"They're doing fine. I'm so grateful for Governor Pilate intervening and getting them released from jail."

Hannah then focused her pretty eyes on Jake. "I want you to know, my dad wants to talk to you. He told me that just as soon as you got back from Damascus, he wanted to have a serious man-to-man talk with you. He's figured out a way for you to provide a dowry so we can get married."

"R-e-a-l-l-y," Jake said with amazement on his face.

"Really. He knows that sometimes your investigative work gets a little slow, especially now that the Jews are shunning all Christians just for being followers of Christ. So, how does this sound to you? He wants you to come during those times when your investigative work is slow and work in his shop learning the leathercraft trade. He can teach you all you need to know about the trade. He can use the extra help anyway. He is still getting a good bit of trade from the Romans and some of his previous Jewish customers. It would be a great relief to him to have the extra help and not have to shoulder the entire load."

In delight, Jake gazed at Hannah and his eyes flared, as if to say, 'Go on.'

"Now, here is how this arrangement will supply your dowry," she continued. "The extra help you would provide to my father would be enough dowry to take care of our marriage custom. Plus, he would pay you the standard wage for your work. He thinks this arrangement will satisfy all the quibbles regarding our customs. What do you think?"

"I'm in shock," Jake yelped, "I think I'd better go talk to your father right now, before he changes his mind!"

And so, in the midst of swirling harassment of Christians and very unstable times in the church, Jake and Hannah's plans for tying the knot suddenly soared a giant leap forward!

Chapter 21

THE DEMISE OF SAUL OF TARSUS

Three years. So much can happen in three years.
It was a bright and sunny Tuesday morning when Hannah burst through the door of Jake's office in a breathless panic.

"Jake! Someone told me just now over at Caleb's Doughnut Shop that they heard a rumor that Saul ... I mean Paul is here, in Jerusalem!"

"What! Paul is here!" the detective exclaimed. "It has been three long years since I left him in Damascus. Did they say where he might be in the city?"

"Nope, that's all I could get!" she said, catching her breath. "Three years. He might have changed back into his old, mean self again!"

"Nope, sweetheart, not a chance!" Jake exclaimed. "The Paul that I left in Damascus was radically changed. He didn't even think the same way he did the last time you saw him. Remember, Jesus makes the difference in a man's life."

"Well, the person I talked to was really scared of him. I think a lot of people are afraid of him"

"I'll tell you what I'll do," Jake said calmly. "I'll go and see if I can find Paul and bring him back with me. Then you'll see. He ain't so scary, after all ..."

But before the detective could finish his sentence, they both heard the door open from the corridor and someone moving around in Hannah's office. Hannah hurried to find out who had entered her office. She opened the door a crack and peeped out. In a moment, Jake heard a familiar voice.

"Hello, miss, is this the office of detective Jake Jezreel?" the voice asked.

Hannah jumped back into Jake's office, her face pale pink. "It's Paul!" she exclaimed. "I recognize him! He's in my office! What should I do?"

"Shoo him in, silly. He won't bite. He is one of us now."

Hannah warily opened the door wider. "Sir, you may come in," she said in a cautious tone.

"Thank you, ma'am," Paul said to Hannah, as he entered Jake's office.

Jake quickly jumped up and skirted around the end of his desk, ready to greet his friend.

As Paul entered, Jake grabbed the preacher by the hand in a firm handshake.

"Paul! It is so good to see you after all these years!"

"Jake Jezreel, you are a welcome sight!"

"I thought you had dropped off the face of the earth!" Jake laughed. "Nobody has heard any news about you since after the time I left you in Damascus. Please sit down. And Hannah, stay here. I want you to hear all of this."

Then pointing toward Hannah, Jake said, "Paul, this is my secretary. This is Hannah, the very best secretary any boss could ever want to have. She is also a Christian. Hannah, this is Paul, the preacher of the Gospel."

"Pleased to meet you, sir," the girl shyly said.

"And it is a pleasure to meet you, as well, ma'am," Paul said, placing his right hand on his chest and slightly bowing.

"Hannah, I want you to stay here in the office with us," Jake told the girl. "I'd like for you to hear all about what the Lord has been doing." Then pointing to the two armchairs in his office the detective said, "Both of you, please sit down. We have so much to talk about. Tell us all about your adventures of these past three years."

"It's been exciting! I have been on a fantastic journey!" Paul exclaimed. "After I escaped over the wall at Damascus, I slipped out into the Arabian desert. That was the instruction Jesus had given me. There in the wilderness, Jesus met me. He instructed me. I did not confer with flesh and blood. I didn't communicate with any man. I spent much time in seclusion and prayer and meditation on the scriptures. The scriptures are clear in picturing Christ in His coming as the Suffering Servant-Messiah. I thank God for my earlier studies and training in God's Word. I had already memorized much of the scriptures, so the Lord could readily recall from my memory key verses that validated who Messiah would be."

"It sounds exciting!" Jake remarked.

"It was an exciting time! As I said, the Lord Jesus, Himself, instructed me in these truths of His plan of salvation. His Good News is for all people. I now have my message to preach to the world! It's His message of salvation!

"That time in the desert was precious to me, as you might imagine. It has given to me the firm foundation I need for my future ministry for Jesus Christ.

"In many ways, that time in the desert with my Lord was the ultimate demise of Saul of Tarsus! Saul is now gone forever! He no longer exists! That time in the desert was the spiritual emergence of Paul, the servant of the living Savior!"

"What an incredible story!" Jake stated. "The Lord has truly transformed you! And I like what you just said. That part about the 'ultimate demise of Saul of Tarsus.' That is a perfect description of what I watched happen to you in Damascus. It was the demise of Saul and the rise of Paul."

"And I'm glad of it! Saul of Tarsus was a vile, despicable man! Good riddance to him! God killed the old man in me and now God truly has transformed me," Paul proclaimed. "After my desert training, I went back to Damascus for a short time to preach and to fellowship with my many Christian friends. Many of them I owe my life to for helping me escape."

Hannah sat on the edge of her chair, mesmerized. Finally, she found her voice and asked, "Do you know what the Lord has in store for you in the future?"

"No, not at all. I'm just letting Jesus lead me step by step," Paul said confidently. "But I know I'm ready – ready to get to preaching and winning souls for Christ."

Paul edged forward in his chair with a more earnest expression.

"Jake, can you do something for me?" he asked.

"Sure, if I can."

"I know you've got many connections here in Jerusalem," Paul continued. "There is really one thing I would like to accomplish as soon as possible. I really want to set up a meeting with the apostles and all the church leaders here in Jerusalem. The problem is they don't want to meet with me. They are still afraid of me. I need a friend right now."

"Well, you know you've got a friend in me," Jake insisted. "But I won't be able to help you with your problem of meeting with the church leaders. I've already gone to them after I got back from Damascus and tried to convince the church leaders that you have surrendered your life to Christ. But they still were skeptical. They still seemed to have their guard up."

"Well, I'm not giving up."

"And I'm not either," Jake stated. "There is a really great Christian man here in Jerusalem who I think can solve your problem. His name is Barnabas. He has the gift of mercy and he has a gift of being able to bring people together and make peace between folks who are at odds with each other."

"Sounds like the very man I need to talk to," Paul cheerfully said.

"Then I'll introduce you to Barnabas. Come on. Let's go. I'll take you to meet his right now!"

Three years. So much could change in three years. But somehow it all stays the same.

Paul had been in Jerusalem for several weeks. He began preaching with boldness in the capital city. As was Paul's usual custom, he preached Christ in the Jewish synagogues. Paul even decided to preach in the same Greek speaking synagogues where Stephen had preached years before, where he lost his life. Paul counted on the fact his former association with these Greek speaking Jews would give him the common ground, the mutual understanding, he needed for them to trust his message about Christ. At first all went well for him. Paul preached in great power!

Then the trouble started for Paul.

Paul began declaring that Christ had come as the Son of Man, to save all the people groups of the world. He made it clear, just as he had stated in Damascus, that Jesus Christ had come to be the Messiah for all people of all nations of all the world. And very predicably, the same angry resentment billowed up in the Jerusalem Jews as it had in the Damascus synagogue. The Jerusalem Jews' were greatly offended, as their religious pride took a severe hit. They bristled in anger. At Paul's declaration, the mood in the Greek synagogues turned ugly. The Greek speaking Jews confronted Paul in an aggressive debate.

"Messiah has come exclusively for the Jews and our nation!" many of the Jews argued.

"Brothers," Paul declared, "Messiah has come for all nations. I have preached this truth everywhere I go. The believers in Damascus finally have believed it. Remember the original promise to Abraham. God promised him that the Lord's plan from the very start was to bless all nations. And God stated that Abraham's seed would bless all nations. That Seed is Jesus Christ.

"Jesus Christ Himself has made both believing Jews and believing heathens into one spiritual family. Christ has broken down the wall of separation dividing the two groups. Christ has created in Himself a new creation, one new people from the two."

Indignation flared up in many of the Jews. "No! No! We will not intermix the holiness of Judaism and mingle it with godless, vile heathens!" many of the Jews shouted.

Quickly the debate plunged into the sleazy depths of angry character assassination. Hatred against Paul fueled the hysterics of the religious mob. Paul could say nothing right. If he declared God's love was for everyone, the enemy reprimanded him and called him a liar. The Greek speaking Jews could not let go of their resolute belief that Judaism is for Jews only and not for the barbaric nations of the rest of the world.

The lethal die was cast.

The contentious Jerusalem debate rapidly twisted into a poisonous, vicious cauldron of loathing for Paul. Paul had insulted the nationalist and religious pride of these Jews. They could not and would not permit Paul to continue to spread his lies! Suddenly, the debate had become life-and-death! Their only answer to this inflamed argument with Paul was to kill him. Death would silence his "blaspheming tongue" forever!

"We killed Stephen for preaching the same despicable lies!" the Jews fumed among themselves. "This man, Paul, is no different! He is preaching the same repulsive corruption that Stephen preached! We must kill Paul, too! And the quicker we kill him the better!"

The boiling rage of the Jews secretly planned out their plot to kill Paul. All the details of their murderous plan were hastily thrown into motion. Today would be the day. After this day, Paul would be no more! As the trap was about to be sprung, word leaked out about their impending assassination plot.

Pudge the pickpocket caught wind of the plot. His first instinct was to get to Jake's office as fast as his pudgy, little legs could take him.

Hannah opened Jake's office door and said, "Pudge is out here in my office. He says he's got a very urgent message."

"Send him in. When he comes to my office, it must be very urgent."

Pudge burst into Jake's office. "Jake, my man, ya gotta do sum'um quick! Sum'un bad is gonna happin'!"

"Something bad? How so?"

"Ain't you good friends wid Paul da preacher man?" Pudge excitedly asked.

"Yeah, I am. So …?"

"Word on da street is dat the religious crowd is gonna 'bump off' yur buddy sometime today!"

Jake jolted up straight in his chair in surprise. "Kill him? You kiddin' me?"

"I got it straight from da horse's mouth! Dey gonna put da 'big sleep' on him! I stake my repatation on it!"

"Wow! I've got to do something quick! Thanks, Pudge! I owe ya one!"

"It's a pleasure ta work wit ya. Dis way I gets ta play like a detective. Now, hurry! Ya gotta get going!" Pudge insisted. "Yur preacher friend's neck is hangin' in da noose."

Jake quickly went in search of Paul or anybody he could find to give the warning. He searched the streets. Crowds of people were everywhere, but Jake couldn't find any Christians.

"The most likely place where I'll find Christians is at John Mark's mother's house," he told himself.

In short order, Jake arrived at the house and vigorously knocked on the door. Inside the home, Paul sat discussing a theological question amongst a group of Christians, which included Peter and John.

"Paul, I'm glad I found you," Jake stated excitedly. "I've just caught wind of a plot being cooked up by the religious leaders to kill you! And it sounds like it's undeniably planned for today!"

"We have heard some rumors to that effect. But nothing definite," Paul said calmly.

"Well, this is definite! And it's more than a rumor," Jake insisted. "The enemy plans to spring their trap today! I don't know exactly how or when but it will be today! They will not rest until they have killed you before the sun goes down. We can't waste another minute. We've got to get you out of the city, right now!"

Paul thought for a moment. "My hometown is Tarsus. Probably the best plan is for me to go back to Tarsus and wait for Jesus' further instructions for me there."

"Then let's do it!" Peter exclaimed. "Let's get you out of Jerusalem right now. Probably the quickest means of sending you on your way to Tarsus would be to book passage for you on a ship sailing from the seaport at Caesarea."

"We've got the fare if we all combine our money," John stated. "Let's go!"

The plan worked perfectly. Without hesitating, the disciples smuggled Paul out of the city and whisked him away to the seaport of Caesarea. From there, Paul caught a sailing ship headed for his old hometown of Tarsus. So quickly had the Christians hurried Paul out of town, it was reported later that the religious leaders flew into a blind rage, frustrated that their "enemy" had slipped through their fingers. As Jake watched the ship carrying Paul to safety navigate its way out of port and get under full sail, he could sense that bigger things for the Lord Jesus were waiting on the horizon for Paul. Bigger things and, more than likely, many more struggles.

When the ship was nearly out of sight, Jake's imagination quickly kicked into gear and he pictured the church as a sailing ship. The future looked brighter than ever with Jesus at the helm, steering the affairs of His church and all mankind. Jesus had launched Paul out into the world to declare salvation through Christ to vast numbers of folks. Peter and John and all the apostles whom Jesus sent out into the nations, were already declaring Christ's salvation everywhere. The proclamation of Christ's Kingdom was expanding by leaps and bounds out into the far-flung world under full sail with Jesus Christ in command of the helm. There would be confrontations by many who opposed and denied the truth. That was a given fact. But Jesus and His Gospel plied the seas of the world, triumphantly winning the battle! Jake had a good feeling about the future. Nothing could stop his Lord and Savior, Jesus Christ!

With Paul safely out of harm's way and headed for Tarsus, Jake hurried back to his office in Jerusalem. Hannah needed to hear this fantastic tale of Paul's miraculous escape.

"Angel, it turned out to be a very close call," Jake told Hannah, as he explained the excitement surrounding Paul's escape.

"So, if you and the Christians hadn't hurried Paul out of town, he would probably be dead by now," she said, realizing the hard truth.

"It was within a hair's breadth of being a catastrophe. Pudge spilled the beans to me about the plot and I was able to run that info over to Paul and the others. With Pudge's help, we got a head start and got Paul outa town quick."

"So, Pudge was an important factor in getting Paul out of the city," she stated.

"Yeah, he was. You know, Pudge is an odd sort," Jake mused. "He's a gentleman. And yet he's on the wrong side of the law."

"You need to tell him about Jesus," Hannah said tilting her head, emphasizing her point. "You're his friend, you know. He'd listen to you."

"I will go and talk to him about Christ. I'll talk to him about the Lord when we meet up. If Pudge had not made that special effort to find me and tell me about the assassination plot, it might have been too late for Paul."

"I wonder if we'll ever hear from Paul again," the girl said wistfully.

"We may never hear from him, but I'm confident we'll hear about him. The Lord has a great ministry planned for our friend, Paul. Not just a great ministry. But an epic ministry!"

"And to think at one time Paul was our enemy," she said. "I called him a monster. Now he is off winning souls for Christ in some far-off land. God's grace and forgiveness are so wonderful."

"I agree. And now Paul is scattering the seeds of the Gospel out further and further, way out to parts unknown," Jake mused.

Hannah sat quietly for a moment. Then she thought out loud, "You know, you used the exact word to describe it. This is the way it's supposed to be."

"What's supposed to be?"

"You said 'scattering'. The scattering of Christians across the whole face of the earth was always Jesus' plan," she stated with wonder in her eyes. "This whole business of the Great Persecution is what scattered Christians all over the place. Jesus told us to go out to all nations and make disciples. When the church scattered out from Jerusalem, believers have been spreading the Good News of Jesus everywhere they go. It's like the cross of Jesus has been broken up into a million pieces and then scattered out into a million places."

"Hmm. Never thought about it that way," Jake stated. "Jesus had His hand in all of this, for sure. And it's a real mystery the way He worked His plan to spread the message of His salvation to the world. But it's for certain that Jesus did the scattering. No doubt."

The couple sat in silence letting these new thoughts sink in.

"I guess we all had gotten too comfy in our little cloister here in Jerusalem," she mused.

"Yeah, we sorta had it good. We were fat and happy until the persecution came."

"Jesus saw us sitting around and not spreading the Gospel," she said, "so He had to scatter us out to the world."

Jake thought for a moment. "At the time, it was hard to imagine how the Great Persecution could be beneficial," he stated, leaning back in his leather chair. "But now in the bigger picture, it makes more sense. The Lord had to scatter His church. He used the Great Persecution to get us out there in the rest of the world to accomplish His world mission."

"*That* is the mystery of it all!" Hannah exclaimed with a smile. "God scattered His church into a gazillion places so His people can spread the Good News of Jesus' salvation to all the people of the world."

"It is a mystery, an intricate mystery," the detective stated. "You summed it up perfectly, honey. And now the mystery is solved for all to see! The Cross of Jesus is flung out into the world! I think I know how we should label this case file."

"And what is that?"

"We should label this case file *The Mystery of the Scattered Cross*."

Hannah smiled even bigger. "Oooo, I like it! That will look great on a file folder label."

Jake rubbed the back of his neck. "Well, it's all the Lord's doin's," Jake said heaving a sigh. "But this 'scattering cross' stuff sure does keep a body hoppin' around an awful lot. I'm bushed."

"Oh, you sound like you're a pretty tired puppy from serving the Lord!" Hannah laughed.

"Well, I am. I am pretty worn out. First, Pudge blows me out of my chair with plots and conspiracies and assassinations. Then I'm running all over Jerusalem trying to find somebody to help me warn Paul. Then I'm hurrying with Paul and all the Christians to Caesarea to get Paul on a ship and out of the country. And then back home from Caesarea. Do you know how far it is to Caesarea? It ain't no leisurely walk in the park!"

"Poor baby," Hannah smiled in her ever-sweet charm. "Mister detective, it sounds to me like you've had a very big day, full of daring adventures and heroics. What do you say to us closing up shop for the afternoon and going home? I'll cook a yummy supper for you. You can take off your shoes and relax. You've earned it. Serving the Lord can actually be a very tiring business. And ... we might even find some quiet time to do a little snuggling later tonight."

Jake's eyebrows raised in delighted arches. "I like that part about snuggling even more than all that other stuff."

Hannah glanced at Jake with a teasing twinkle in her eye. "I've always known you were a hopeless romantic," she whispered to him.

"But I'm supposed to be a hardhearted detective. How can I be a romantic?" he whimpered.

Hannah just dropped her head a little and gazed at him along the top of her eyes, with a sweet, seductive look. Then she lowered her eyelashes until her eyes were nearly closed and gradually raised them again. A thin, fetching smile appeared on her lips.

"I see," Jake resigned. "That's how it is. You're casting your spell on me. Your alluring enchantment. Well, what are we waiting around this ol' boring office for?" he smiled. "I can't resist your charms any longer. Let's go home."

And at their home that night, they did spend a wonderful evening together.

Actually, a wonderful life together.

Oh! One piece of important information that you need to know. Yes! Jake and Hannah finally did get married! The nuptials occurred somewhere between Jake's Damascus adventure and Paul's return to Jerusalem three years later.

Three years. So much can change in three years. It was a beautiful wedding!

Addendum

<u>I Love You, Lord Jesus</u>

I love you, Lord Jesus.
You are the one who set me free.
I love you, yes, I love you,
'cause you love me.

I was lost, alone, without a friend,
Then you came and saved my soul.
I love you, yes, I love you,
'cause you made me whole.

Chorus:
I can see, your love was meant for me.
All that you are is everything I can be.
I put my faith is you – and be set free.

I praise you, Lord Jesus.
You fill my heart with jubilee.
I Praise you, yes, I praise you,
'cause you love me.

Chorus:
I can see, your love was meant for me.
All that you are is everything I can be.
I put my faith is you – and be set free.

I love you, Lord Jesus.
You are the one who set me free.
I love you, yes, I love you,
'cause you love me … 'cause you love me
… 'cause you love me.

Lyrics written by Donald Craig Miller

About the Author

Donald Craig Miller has been writing Christian papers for local churches and newsletters for more than 50 years. In 2018, he launched his first in a series of Christian books based on a first century detective. His Christian writing is a result of attending a Billy Graham writing school in Minneapolis in 1971. This experience encouraged him to develop his already growing desire to write and redirect his desire toward glorifying the Lord Jesus Christ in his writings. Through the cooperation of pastors, he has been able to write for church newsletters and bulletin inserts for churches in the Dayton, Ohio area, and more recently in the Macon and Warner Robins, Georgia area. Miller also has been a Bible teacher for over 54 years, teaching in Sunday school and church settings, in home Bible studies, and as a lay preacher. He found Christ through The Navigators while stationed at Kadena Air Force Base in Okinawa. Not long after accepting Christ, Miller realized that God had gifted him with the gift of teaching. From then on, his great desire has been to dig scriptural truth from the Bible and pass it on to others.

Milton Keynes UK
Ingram Content Group UK Ltd.
UKHW042039080724
445206UK00009B/57/J